SEOUL
DEMON

SEOUL DEMON

ALI ARCHER

Seoul Demon (Minnie Kim: Vampire Girl #3) © 2019 Ali Archer
Published by Novel Ninjutsu

Cover Design by Kuro Ishi Cover Design
Typography by Mikey Brooks
Editing by Lorie Humpherys

www.aliarcher.com

Dear Minnie:

Enjoy your adventures in Seoul! Be sure to record your experiences; you won't want to forget them. And believe me, once you've lived a hundred years or so, you'll be glad for the little glimpses into your youth.

I also thought you might like to use this journal to get a start on the new and improved guide for young vampires you keep talking about. If anyone can make a difference in the lives of others, it would be you.

Home won't be the same without you. And Manuela will appreciate hearing all your stories over the dinner table when you return.

Much love, David

CHAPTER ONE

PHILO LEANED IN TO GIVE ME A KISS GOODBYE, BUT MY parents were watching. I gave him a wry smile and a handshake. Yeah, that's the way to keep a much more experienced boyfriend interested while you take off for a couple months. I was so not gonna survive this summer vacation.

Philo adjusted smoothly to my redirect and traced his thumb over my pulse, which jumped beneath his touch. Beyond him, Manuela dabbed at her eyes with a red handkerchief—which was a good thing because the last thing my parents needed to see was blood spewing from her eyes. This . . . understanding . . . between my parents and me was relatively new and based mostly on my *normalcy*. My goal was to never let them see me, or my vampire family, doing anything even remotely vamp-like.

I stepped back from Philo and turned. I wish my family would stop saying goodbye and wishing me well and telling me to write and text and call, because they were gonna make me cry if they didn't. You'd think I was gonna be gone forever the way they were carrying on.

"Bye!" I called again as I climbed into the backseat where someone had already put my backpack. "Bye!"

Everyone stood on the porch, waving and calling goodbyes—everyone except for Philo who stood with his hands in his pockets, his eyes lost in the shadow of his dark hair. He looked like a little storm cloud standing there between Fearghus and Siobhan who were waving like maniacs trying to outdo each other. Even Mrs. Hamburg waved a white handkerchief in my direction.

It might have made another girl think Philo didn't care, but not me. I smiled as I kept my gaze glued to his. I knew he saw my eyes, just as clearly as I saw his. I knew he knew I was really saying goodbye just to him.

Eventually though, Dad drove around the circular drive and I had no choice but to look forward toward what was probably the scariest experience of my life: a family vacation with my parents.

I was still a little unclear about just how much "vacation" this was going to be. Other than the fact that it was happening during summer break, and I was traveling to a place I'd never been before, not one thing had been said about anything resembling fun.

Dad had talked about his family and honor and I might have even heard him murmuring about how having a *gangshi* for a daughter ought to be good for something. While Mom had talked about *helping* and being *good* and not making my father regret this. *This* being me, I figured.

Because up until just a few months ago, Dad hadn't accepted that a terrible monster like a vampire—a *gangshi* as he called them—could also be the same little girl he once loved. He'd sat down to dinner with me a few times. He'd had a couple conversations with me. But he hadn't looked me in the eyes even once. He'd never been one for physical affection, but I couldn't remember if he'd even touched me since I'd been reMade. I didn't think he had. He was probably doing his best, but I was getting tired of pretending it didn't hurt.

It might not be much of a vacation, but at least I'd get to see Seoul, where my parents were from. I'd get to meet my extended family and most of all, I'd have three whole months to prove to my dad that being a vampire didn't make me a monster. At least, not figuratively. It didn't mean I was all bad, just because I was undead. He could still love me, if he wanted. Because despite the way he'd been treating me, I still loved him.

I sent Philo, then Stacey, a text before checking my backpack for the essentials. And I'm not talking about headphones and books and lip balm—though I had those, too. No, it was absolutely imperative that I had snacks and that I had the contact number for the local vampire council. I had their number on my phone and David had written it into the new journal he gave me, plus on a separate piece of paper tucked inside my backpack.

I needed all the contingencies I could get because I could not allow myself to get hungry while surrounded by hundreds of people on a plane for the next twenty-three hours. I had enough snacks to get me through, but I'd need to resupply pretty much as soon as we landed. I still hadn't figured out how I was going to manage getting my deliveries without causing my family too much stress. Yes, they knew I was a vampire, but if my uncle and his family were anything like my dad, it wouldn't be good to flaunt my blood supply in their face.

I'd already made arrangements to have a little fridge delivered along with my first supply so no one had to see the blood in the fridge. And I'd brought along a couple large travel mugs that I could sip on without anyone seeing the deep red liquid inside. Still, I had to get from now to then and there was a lot of time, a lot of stress, and a lot of beating hearts between now and then. I took a deep, bracing breath and let it out slowly through my nose. I could do this.

Please, god let me do this!

We drove to the airport in silence. I didn't put my earbuds in just in case my parents wanted to talk, but of course they didn't. I got the feeling they were a little nervous. I was a little nervous, too. For one thing, I'd never been to Korea before. When you looked different from everyone else, people just assumed you were different. But other than having parents who spoke another language, I was as American as they came. Sure, I felt pretty confident that I could hold a conversation in Korean. I mean, I'd be able to make my way around town and order my lunch and stuff. But I didn't know anything about what it was like to be a teenager in Seoul. I had a feeling that the K-dramas I loved to watch would only educate me so far, ya know?

I was nervous my clothes weren't cute enough—that the style I'd adopted and long thought of as cool would look like I was a faker in Seoul. Like I'd get off the plane and all the locals would take one look at me and only see a wannabe. Gah! And I was gonna be there for three whole months! With no Philo and no Stacey to help me feel human. Okay, maybe I was more than nervous. Maybe I was freaking out.

We'd be living with my uncle, aunt and cousin. And my cousin was a nineteen-year-old guy, so I didn't expect I'd see him much. I mean, it's not like we'd have anything in common. What I was gonna do all day, every day, was beyond me.

Nerves pooled in my stomach as we parked in the long-term lot and got out of the car. I'd never flown in an airplane before, let alone on such a long flight. But it wasn't the flight that made me nervous, at least not really. It was the whole customs thing and having to present my *papers* in front of my parents. It was humiliating to have to provide them like I was some livestock or something. I understood why they had to pay special attention to the travel of vampires, but couldn't they just put a little red dot on my passport or something?

Mom and Dad argued for a minute as Dad unloaded the car. He was bugged we'd brought so much but Mom said we'd be gone for three months and did he expect us to run to the laundromat every other day—to which Dad replied we could wash our clothes in the sink like he used to do as a child.

Omo.

We checked our bags at the counter inside the airport and, as expected, the woman printing our boarding passes gave me long, side-long looks but wouldn't hold my gaze when I caught her staring. You'd think I had horns growing out of my head or something. At least no one else in the crowd gave me a second glance—no one would know I was anything other than human unless they looked at my darn papers, which that agent lady had. The next step would be even worse: Security.

And I wasn't wrong. Because jelly-like squares are particularly a no-no in TSA rules, I had to get out my container of blood pudding and the doctor's prescription, and hand them over to the TSA agent for scanning. Not only did all the agents shift into a kind of on-guard posture and eye me warily, I had to stand to the side while my food was examined for explosives. No, my food wouldn't explode, but I might if they didn't let me have it.

It bugged me, but more than that, it embarrassed me. Mom and Dad were already through the line, already had their bags gathered and their shoes back on, waiting. And Dad refused to look at me. The way he stood way off at the very limit of the security area made it seem like we had absolutely nothing to do with one another. Too bad for him we were the only Koreans and I was a minor, so it wasn't hard to figure out, for anyone who might be watching, that I belonged to him. I wondered if he'd ever be proud of me again.

The man inspecting my food finally closed the lid and handed the box back to me, along with an index-sized, laminated card. "Read that, please."

I picked up the card and started to read, *I promise, on my immortal soul, that I will abide by the laws—*

"Out loud." The agent gave me an exasperated glare as if that should have been obvious.

I glanced around. The security checkpoint was packed with people pushing their things down the little belt things, but everyone near me were quiet. They were trying to hear why the little Asian girl was being interrogated by the TSA. And now this guy wanted me to read this . . . this . . . *disclaimer* in front of everybody?

He tapped the end of a pencil on a camera that sat on top of the bomb detecting machine he'd run my food through. "And look into the camera."

What the? "Seriously?" The expression in the man's eyes said seriously. "Fine." I glanced around again, then kind of curled around myself, trying to hide as much of myself from the nosy onlookers as I could. I cleared my throat and stared up at the stupid camera.

"Oh, and say your name and where you're traveling to, first," the man added. It did say that at the top of the index card, but I didn't realize it was part of this whole charade. I held back a dramatic sigh.

"I, Minnie Kim, traveling to Seoul, Korea, promise on my immortal soul, that I will abide by the laws and tenets as outlined by the agreement between the Transportation Security Administration and the Council of Vampires, pursuant to the Rights and Responsibilities Act of the Treaty of London. I state that I have brought along sufficient sustenance for the duration of my journey and should I—" Holy guacamole were they really making me say this? I glanced around furtively, this time finding that a few people were openly staring, their mouths hanging open, while they neglected their luggage.

"Seriously?" I whispered to the agent.

He smirked and nodded. Seriously.

I shook my head. This was ridiculous. Where were *my* rights? Why did they have to treat me like some kind of evil murderer? My voice took on a hard edge as I continued, even though inside *ticked off* faded more to *insecure*.

"I state that I have brought along sufficient sustenance for the duration of my journey and should I attempt to harm any passengers or crew, the Marshal, attendants, or passengers, have the right to restrain me by any means necessary. I will not charm, coerce or force any human onboard to do anything they do not wish to do of their own free will.

"Furthermore, should I fail to arrive at my destination in my current animated state, and am unable to be revived by normal measures, my Maker and family, both living and dead, will not seek restitution for damages. I hereby release the TSA, the airline, and all its agents, from any responsibility regarding my health and wellbeing."

By the time I'd finished speaking, my whole body hummed with rage and my jaw ached. I wanted to let my fangs descend and roar bloody murder at this pompous man and this farce of an agreement between me and everyone here. My hand shook as I handed the crumpled card over to the man. To his credit, he had the good sense to seem afraid as he took it, and he didn't say a word. I wasn't a vamped-out kind of girl. I didn't go around threatening people. But I glared at him, and let my eyes go black as I picked up my plastic container of freaking blood pudding and stuffed it into my bag.

 Talk to the Council about changing the whole TSA debacle!!!!!

★ Maybe give the oath in private?

★ A signed affidavit?

★ Where are MY rights?

CHAPTER TWO

THE FLIGHT TO LA WAS ON A SMALL PLANE AND BLESSEDLY uneventful. I stuck my earbuds in as soon as my butt hit the chair and I stayed that way for the entire flight. I must've dozed off because when I woke up, Mom and Dad were whisper-fighting. I stayed still, trying to hear what they were arguing about.

It soon became clear they were lucky they were Korean on a plane with a bunch of white people because the things they were saying would freak everybody out. Of course it seemed to be about me, but it also seemed to be about my uncle and the family and honor and . . . a *gwishin*? And a whole lot about our ancestors.

Great, I thought. Dad hadn't told my uncle about me and he was afraid I'd offend their ancestors while Mom thought he was stupid for not telling the family before that they had a vampire living with them. I didn't know if that's exactly what they were saying, but that's how it sounded to me. Well, whatever it was, it was just more of the same. I'd really hoped we were over all that. When Mom invited me on this trip, I thought it was going to be like a new beginning for our family. That we could be a family again. Apparently, I was wrong.

I stood in front of my seat and stretched. I was small, so it wasn't hard to do. The man in the row in front of us ushered his wife out in front of him before grabbing down his bag from the overhead bin. While he lowered his arms, his eyes caught mine and I recognized the look in his eyes. He knew what I was and it frightened him.

I did a quick check of myself to make sure I didn't have my fangs out or any blood tears on my cheeks or anything, but when he flicked a glance at my parents before hurrying down the aisle after his wife, I figured it out. He'd heard them speaking and understood everything they'd said. It was unusual to find Americans who spoke Korean, but not unheard of. Mom and Dad should really be more careful.

"You ready?" Mom asked as she waited in the aisle for me. I glanced at her and tried to offer a small smile.

"Yeah." But really I was thinking I wasn't sure I was ready for this at all. We'd never be a normal family again. Because I wasn't normal. I suddenly missed my vampire family—Fearghus and Siobhan, David and Manuela. It was okay to be what I was with them. And they'd tried to warn me—David and Manuela had even sat down and had a talk of sorts with me, where they tried to explain how isolated and alone I might feel while away with my human family, and how and where to get help if I needed it. But I'd barely listened. I was so sure it wouldn't be that way for me.

We had a three-hour layover in LA, so we decided to get something to eat. We found a Chinese place where we could sit on stools and eat while watching all the people walk by on the concourse. It was pretty fascinating, really. There were all kinds of people here. It was almost overwhelming. And not all of them were humans. Most were, but there was the occasional glance my way that gave me that special tingle that said *yes, I know what you are because I am the same as you* feeling.

Truth be told, those vampires scared me. They felt like predators. Like any second they could snap and devour the entire airport full of people.

I shook my head and scolded myself. When I thought like that, I was being no different from the people who made me recite *you can kill me if I look at you the wrong way* declarations before boarding an airplane. My phone buzzed and I fished it out of my hoodie's pocket. I had five texts from Stacey and even the previews of them made me smile.

I set my chopsticks back into my rice bowl and opened the text app.

Stace: 😳 😳 😳 I'm already dying. I can feel myself withering away. By the time you get back there'll be nothing left of me.

Stace: I just killed a spider in my room. A SPIDER. And I didn't feel a thing. Because without you around I'm just a shell of myself.

Stace: The pool called and I got the lifeguarding job. Yippee. There is no sunshine when you're gone.

Stace: Omo. And now my mom says I have to work in the store when I'm not at the pool! What am I gonna do? I really am gonna die.

Stace: You're lucky Mack is here. You're lucky he isn't going anywhere. Cuz without him I really would be dead from sadness and then you'd be sorry. Guess what??? He got a job at the pool, too! He says he'll come hang out with me when I'm working and whistle at me and ogle my body. Sigh. I love him.

I laughed at that last one and felt my cheeks warm. I've never been as carefree or open about my body and stuff as Stacey, but I still felt a twinge of jealousy at the idea of Philo whistling at me and teasing me about how cute and sexy I was. Philo would never do that. Like, never. The closest he ever came was at the dance in February. There'd been this one point when he'd devoured me with this delicious, smoldering gaze, but it was just the one time and it was a long time ago.

Philo and I were doing great. We hung out together all the time and enjoyed each other's company, but I couldn't really think of anything fun we did together. Not like Stacey and Mack, anyway. Maybe it was just a vampire thing. And Philo was way too old to be as silly as Mack. He was classier than that.

"Aren't you hungry?" Mom asked in Korean. They told me when they first invited me on the trip that this would be a Korean only trip. They wanted to fit in there, and they wanted me to be able to speak fluently. After years of trying to get me to speak perfect English, now they wanted me to speak perfect Korean so no one would know I was American. Sheesh.

I smiled at her and bumped her shoulder. She looked so pretty with her new sleek chin-length bob and crisp white blouse and capris. She looked stylish for an older woman. Stacey's texts had done a lot to lift my spirits and here I was with my parents, ready to enjoy a summer-long bonding experience. This was my chance to disprove all those foolish human opinions of vampires. This was my chance to prove I was the same girl they knew and loved.

"I love you, Ma."

She gaped at me a moment before narrowing her eyes at me. She chided me for letting my lunch go cold, then bumped my shoulder with hers and told me she loved me, too.

When we first stepped inside the airplane to Seoul, I stopped short, my mouth hanging open. "Wow." Mom jostled me from behind and I stumbled forward. Dad moved briskly down the aisle ahead of me as if he flew to Seoul every week. I didn't think he'd been back once since they'd moved here and that was before I'd even been born.

There were two aisles in this plane—one branched left and the other right, with three seats in the middle and two on each side against the windows. Everything was blue and white and looked so sleek and fancy. I gaped at the first-class section because *holy wow*—but a man caught me staring and gave me a *mind-your-own-business* glare, so I hustled on.

Dad glared at me too, when I reached him. I swung my little pink plaid suitcase up into the overhead bin and then, after a moment's hesitation, took the seat beside him. He didn't say anything but gave a little nod, which I took as approval. But I noticed he didn't put his arms on the armrest which made me think he wasn't actually comfortable sitting so close to me.

"You wanna sit beside Mom?" I asked him in Korean. Just then Mom sat down on my left.

Dad made a shooing motion to dismiss my concern, I guess, and said, "No."

Well alrighty then. Good talk.

"Look how many Koreans there are," Mom said. "Do you think they all live in California and they're just going home for a visit? Or were they visiting here and are now going home?" She wore a big grin on her face as she looked around. At least she was excited. I kinda leaned up in my chair to look around. There really were a lot of Koreans on that plane.

Dad yanked at my sweatshirt. "Stop making a scene."

"I was just looking at all the Koreans," I said to him. I leaned toward Mom. "I can't tell. They look normal to me."

"Well of course they look normal." Mom stared at me aghast, like I was crazy for looking at them. I laughed and shook my head—she'd been the one staring at them just a second ago. It felt so weird to have so many Asians around me. What the heck was I gonna do in Seoul? I almost felt like I wanted to glom onto the white people on the plane and ask if I could hang out with them.

I pulled my blanket up to my chin, stuffed my little travel kitty pillow behind my head and settled in for an afternoon of reading. Dad glanced at my book, then said to Mom, "You let her read such drivel? What is that

Aristos character teaching her? Is this why she is—" he glanced at me, "what she is?"

I rolled my eyes and flipped the book over. Except that wasn't much better. The front had a pic of a vampire girl with bat wings, but the back had a picture of the same girl kissing a boy. Why didn't I think of this before bringing this book with me? Stacey gave the entire series to me to read, saying it was the best series she'd read all year, but I should've put them on my Kindle or something.

"I'm not a—*what I am*—because of a book I read, Dad. And Stacey gave me this book. She said it's really good."

"It looks like smut," he said.

"It's just a young adult book." I laughed at the constipated expression on his face. "It's about this ancient vampire girl who falls in love with a human boy." I don't know why I told him, because his scowl just deepened.

"Ooh," Mom said, snatching the book from my lap.

"Hey!" I reached for it, but Mom had already opened the book.

Then she realized it was written in English. "Pah," she said as she tossed it back onto my lap. She didn't read English very well.

I started to read, but it wasn't long before the plane revved up and the attendants went to the front of each section to start demonstrating what to do in case of an accident. I paid close attention, watching the demonstration on the little screen in front of me and glancing at the live demo from time to time. I realized that the screen was giving the instructions in Korean while the attendants spoke accented English. And while I listened, my mind played what Dad had said over and over until by the time the demo was finished, I was really mad.

I turned to my dad, ready for a fight. "I didn't choose to be this way. I didn't *want* to die. Don't you get that? Someone killed me, Dad. Someone murdered me." I was shaking by the time I was done and Dad hadn't once glanced my way. His jaw clenched though, so I knew he heard me.

"You need to accept me the way I am, or why am I even coming with you? I thought you'd accepted that I was still your daughter. I thought you still loved me."

After a long beat he slowly turned to face me. It shocked me to see tears brimming in his eyes, but they didn't fall. Somehow, he managed to suck them back into his eyeballs as he stared me down. "I am trying." He bit the words out as if they pained him to say them. When he continued, his voice shook and the tears returned. "I know you did not choose . . . this."

We stared at each other for a minute, both of us made speechless by his surprising admission.

I put my head on his shoulder, pleased when he didn't push me away. "I've missed you, *Appa*."

He patted my head awkwardly.

"I've missed you too, daughter."

We stayed like that for a long while, even though it wasn't the most comfortable for me. When I heard him gently snoring, I carefully leaned back and straightened myself out—only to discover my book was gone. I started to look for it, thinking I'd dropped it, but when I found it in Mom's hands, I had to shake my head at the ridiculousness of it. She had her reading glasses on and was painstakingly reading the book, her lips moving as she sounded out the words.

I sighed and leaned my head back. Finally content and comfortable between my parents, who I loved more than anything in the world, I fell asleep.

THINGS I WANT TO DO
IN KOREA

♥ See an idol!!!!

BOYS:

★ Sehun
★ Jungkook
★ JIN!!!!!!
★ Baekhyun

GIRLS:

★ Seolhyun
★ Somi
★ Sana
★ Jisoo

♥ See a live concert??? (amazing!!!)
♥ Deoksugung for the changing of the guards
♥ The National Museum!
♥ All the idol studios!
♥ Namdaemun market (yummm)
♥ Changdeokgung

CHAPTER
THREE

THE SMELL OF GROUND BEEF AND RICE WOKE ME AND I yawned loudly as Dad dropped my tray table for me just in time for the waitress to set down a tray full of amazing food. I didn't realize how hungry I was until I smelled all the deliciousness and felt the steam rising from the tray.

"How long was I asleep?"

Mom gave me a sidelong glance partnered with a smirk. "Four hours."

"Four hours?" Thank goodness for my vampire body—my neck would have been cricked beyond recovery if I'd been human.

We dove into our food. I couldn't believe how good it all looked. I expected—well, it wasn't this. Everyone told me airline food was terrible, but they obviously hadn't flown on Korean Air! I dumped the rice into the bowl of *bibimbap*, added a squirt of sesame oil and *gochujang* and mixed the whole thing together. It might not have been the prettiest thing ever, but I groaned with pleasure as I took the first bite.

The ground beef, zucchini, and mushrooms mixed with the red pepper sauce and rice and . . . wow. I wolfed it down. I was working on the holy yum spinach soup when Mom said, "Have you told her yet? Because you said you were going to tell her."

I glanced between her and Dad. "Tell me what?" I took another spoonful of soup and watched Dad scowl.

"She was sleeping," he said.

"She wasn't sleeping before that," Mom said smugly.

"We were eating. We were in the airport."

"We had an hour drive to the airport," Mom said.

"Did I tell her on the drive?" Dad was starting to sound ticked off, so I kept quiet and pretended not to be listening while I ate my soup.

This wasn't at all unusual for my parents—to argue about me as if I wasn't even there. It was actually quite handy because I tended to learn a lot about myself and their plans for me when they forgot I was there.

"I don't know," Mom said. "You tell me." Of course, she was just bating him. She'd been in the car, too, and no one said anything about anything.

They fell silent. We all ate our soup. I finished before them and popped a piece of pineapple into my mouth. When I finished chewing, I leaned back and crossed my arms. "Tell me what?"

They ignored me. Which was pretty typical, too.

I ate another piece of pineapple.

"Dad?"

He scowled. "I'm eating." He loudly slurped his soup.

I swiveled in my seat. "Mom?"

She dabbed at her mouth with a napkin, then said primly, "Your father should tell you. It is his family."

"Ugh. Please don't tell me now that something's really wrong with them. Please don't tell me I have to sleep with my cousin or sleep in the bathtub or something." I turned to Dad.

He kept eating and I watched him. I'm pretty sure Mom watched him, too, because I swear, I could feel her eyes glaring over my shoulder. Eventually the weight of our combined attention got to him and he set down his chopsticks. He took his sweet time wiping his mouth, and setting everything back straight on his tray, just so. Then he slowly swiveled in his seat so he could see me. And he looked. Right. At. Me.

I leaned away, suddenly unsure I wanted this talk. This was something a whole lot more serious than just where I was gonna sleep. Dad hadn't looked me in the eye since I was reMade for longer than a split second and now he was . . . well, it was unnerving is what it was.

"What?" I pressed.

Dad wore his stern, *let's get this over with* expression, which is to say, he looked a lot like he always did. But there was something in his body tension that told me he did not like what he was about to say. "My family knows what you are."

I waited a beat.

I wasn't exactly expecting him to have told his brother that I was a vampire, but I figured he must have told him something since they would surely have known that I died, yet here I was coming with them on a family vacation. "Ohhkay," I finally said.

"They—"

"They wanted you to come," Mom broke in.

I focused on her, relieved to be free of Dad's freaky eye-lock. "Well that's good then, right? I mean—if they know about me and they wanted me to come, that's good." I smiled at her, then at Dad. His stern expression hadn't changed.

"They think because you are—" he flicked his eyes downward, but I knew what he meant. Because I was *gangshi.* A vampire. "That you can help them with their, uh, problem."

Okay. Well, I wasn't expecting that, but hey. I was good at solving problems. I didn't have to be a vampire for that, but whatever. "Ohhkay," I said. "What's the problem?"

Dad's scowl turned into a full-on frown. He looked like one of those ventriloquist dolls with the deep grooves on the side of his mouth and chin.

Mom leaned in close to me and whispered, "Their ancestors have returned and they are not happy."

"What?" I turned to her. "Whaddya mean their ancestors have returned? Are they like me?"

Dad made a sound an awful like spitting and I whirled to face him. I felt like I was in the middle of a tennis match going from left to right, right to left. I was gonna end up with whiplash if they kept this up. "Not like you." My heart sank as those words hit me. Whatever it was my ancestors returned as, it wasn't nearly as bad as me. Clearly.

"They are *gwishin*. They will not give them rest. Their power keeps going out, and other things that are interfering with their ability to have peace in their home."

I had to think for a minute before I could figure out what the word *gwishin* meant. I furrowed my brow. Finally, Mom said. "Ghosts, Minnie. Our ancestors are haunting them."

"Huh." I sat back. That was completely unexpected. "And how do they think I can help? How do you think I can help?" I asked Dad. I wanted to make him happy. I wanted him to see that he could still count on me. That I was still a good girl—his girl. I'd do whatever I could to make him see me that way again.

"Well, they're dead," he finally said. "And so are you."

I just kinda stared at him for a long minute. I was too stunned to feel hurt or angry. To feel anything at all, really. I stared into his defiant brown eyes and felt a strange change come over me. I loved my *appa*. But he was wrong. He was dead wrong.

I drew in a long, slow breath and let it out just as slowly. His eyes flicked away briefly and when they returned to mine, I saw a tiny glimmer of fear there—which was not what I wanted at all.

"*Appa*," I began. I had to get this right or I could totally mess everything up. "I'm not . . . dead. Not like that. Not even close. You know that, right?" I risked putting my hand on his arm and sagged a bit in relief when he didn't move away.

He tightened his jaw but didn't respond.

"Tell me you know it."

But his lips remained pressed into a thin line.

Mom leaned in close to me. "They can't keep their electricity on. And Auntie Bora works from home on the computer—she's been trying to work from a local cafe, but it's no good. They can't get a good night's sleep. The *gwishin* are ruining everything for them. You have to try to help, daughter."

When I faced her, her eyes were so full of sincerity and hope. She was also trying to smooth things over between me and Dad and I couldn't fault her for that. "I'll try, Ma. I just—" The hope in her eyes flickered. "I'll try."

She patted my arm and sat back, content that she'd managed to return the peace to our little family. I slipped in my earbuds and covered my eyes with a mask so I could finally be alone—as alone as you can be on a plane with 600 passengers.

So this wasn't going to just be a family vacation, like I thought. The disappointment was as bitter as oxidized metal on my tongue—I should know because I'd tasted it one time in science class. Hey, it was for science.

But this—well, I guess this would be for family. I didn't know anything about ghosts. Even since learning that other supernatural creatures existed, I hadn't heard anyone talk about ghosts and you'd think a bunch of immortals would have a lot of ghosts hanging around them. Were these *gwishin* different from ghosts? How in the world was I expected to reason with them? And even if I could, would they be as offended by me being a vampire as Dad was?

I fought back tears beneath the hot pink silk mask I wore. If I couldn't figure this whole *gwishin* thing out— would Dad give up on me for good?

With the arm rest up and our seats slightly reclined, I actually managed to get a decent night's sleep tucked in close against my mom. Even though I woke up with a kink in my neck, being held by her all night long put me into a good mood right away. And the smell of eggs didn't hurt my mood any, either. We'd be landing in just a few hours and nerves, mingled with excitement, sent zings of electricity through my arms. I wanted to jump up and move around, but aside from standing and stretching in place, there wasn't much I could do. So I read my book, which Mom had finally given up on, discreetly munched on puddings so as not to offend my father, and anxiously awaited our arrival.

When the moment came, I nearly flew out of my seat, only to be restricted by the crush of people also trying to get off the plane. People elbowed and jostled one another trying to get their baggage down and be the first ones out of the plane before it had even finished docking. I quietly mocked them for being so impatient but the second I saw an opening in the line of people I dashed into it and held it for my parents.

We rushed through the beautiful Incheon airport, barely giving me time to marvel at the art or the view of the ocean outside, before Dad ushered us onto a shuttle to take us to baggage claim.

Outside the airport, we got onto a bus packed full of passengers. I gripped the bar while my body swayed with the movement of the bus and marveled at how I'd ended up on the bus so fast. But Mom and Dad seemed to know where they were going and Dad was carefully watching the stops go by, so I tried not to stare too openly at all the Koreans around me. It was so weird to see my kind of face reflected back at me from almost every person there. There were a few people from other countries—mostly Westerners from their appearance—but still. I was used to being in the minority. I wasn't sure I liked seeing so many Korean faces.

We took a couple more transfers before we stood on a street with our suitcases in hand, while Dad peered around us. "Are we almost there?" I asked for the millionth time. But this time Dad didn't answer— he just jutted out his chin and began marching down a side street.

Mom and I hurried to keep up, dragging our luggage behind us. We were surrounded by apartment buildings, many with shops on the ground floor, and I gawked at everything as we passed. My mind struggled to read the shop names—I could read Korean, but at first glance, my mind always tried to see it as English, so it took me a minute to translate it. It was more like I was translating from English into Korean, even though I knew Korean. So frustrating.

Finally Dad took us up the stairs of a four-story building. Of course his brother would live on the top floor. The door was a rusty red color with a peephole and the name Kim spelled out in gold Korean letters just beneath it. Dad knocked loudly and we all stood, waiting breathlessly. Like, literally breathlessly. I was afraid Mom would pass out right then and there. The door swung open and a man who could have been Dad's twin stepped out and wrapped his arms around my dad.

They hugged each other for a long time, patting each other's backs so hard I wondered how they could stand it. I shifted my feet uncomfortably while Mom watched on, a sort of distant smile on her face. Then Dad yanked me forward, making me stumble awkwardly toward him, knocking over suitcases as I did.

"Here is my daughter, Minnie. She will talk to your dead."

Well, alrighty then.

My uncle looked at me expectantly, as if I would perform a magic trick right there in his doorway. I lifted my hand in a wave. "Hiii."

Hey, it was the best I could do in the moment.

First Impressions:

♥ I did not bring enough cute
clothes! All the girls here are
dressed so nice.

♥ Did I even bring any makeup?
Everyone looks so put together.
Even my mom, who never
fancied up at home. Why didn't
she warn me?

♥ O.M.G. The shopping! The lights!
The food! Everything seems kinda
fancy. Back in the residential
maybe not so much, but I will
love checking out the rest of
Jongno-gu - it looks awesome!

♥ I thought our house at home
was small, but the fam's
apartment is SMALL. And Mom,
Dad and I are all sleeping in the
same room (cousin Junu's room).
Good times.

CHAPTER FOUR

I SLEPT LIKE THE DEAD. WELL, I MEAN, I PRETTY MUCH always do that, but I've never done it in front of living people before. I woke to a hastily scrawled note in my mom's handwriting telling me that she tried to wake me but I wouldn't get up (*omo*) and that they'd gone down the street to the porridge shop for dinner. She invited me to join them when I woke up, but as I sat on the narrow cot that had been shoved into my cousin's room for me and my parents to stay in, I realized I wasn't in any hurry to be around people at the moment.

I dug into my suitcase and pulled out a small cooler and, with a container of pudding squares in my hand, wandered around the apartment. I wasn't snooping—I didn't open drawers or anything. But if they were already open a crack, I might have peeked.

It was interesting how much the same and how different my aunt and uncle lived. They had a two-bedroom apartment with a rooftop garden in Jongno-gu, which was a pretty suburb of Seoul. Their furniture was a lot like our living room furniture, except where we had a regular sized kitchen table, they didn't really have a dining area. Not exactly sure where they must eat—at the large coffee table in the living room, I guess.

But the apartment was nicely decorated with Korean art and modern touches. They had a small shrine to their ancestors, which I recognized as similar to the one my parents had at home. Their religion didn't exactly require ancestor worship, but it was more like they paid homage to them out of respect and to keep their memory and wisdoms alive. I'd never really been into it or anything, but I liked the idea of it.

I studied the little candles—all lit—and the incense burners and the little figurines that represented my grandmothers and grandfathers back three or four generations. "Are you guys really haunting this place?" I asked the little statues. Of course they didn't answer.

After a while I wandered outside and climbed the steps to the garden. My aunt and uncle grew squash up there that they sold to local shops for use in their noodles. Apparently whatever kind they grew made for delicious noodles that were popular. It wasn't their fulltime job, just something on the side.

I could smell the green before I saw it. It was like the air was cleaner and brighter. But nothing could have prepared me for what I saw once I reached the top. The entire space was green. Trellises stood row upon row in the small space with big, leafy plants climbing and draping all over them. Hanging down the center of each walkway were snakes. At least, I thought they were snakes. I almost took a step back and tumbled down the stairs before I remembered that it wasn't regular squash my family grew but something called tromboncino. Looked like snake squash to me.

I approached slowly, keeping my eye on the dangling gourds as if they might come alive at any moment. But of course they were just long, twisty, cucumber-looking vegetables. I stood under one of the trellises, surrounded by the odd garden, and had to laugh a little at myself. I could be such a dork sometimes.

At the other end of the roof, there was a small wall which I walked toward so I could look out over the neighborhood and toward the heart of the city in the distance. I could only catch glimpses of the shining skyscrapers in downtown Seoul as it was a cloudy evening, but the lights in Jongno-gu were already bright and welcoming. This was a cool little neighborhood, actually. I would have liked to come here with Philo.

I snapped a picture of my view and sent him a text.

Me: Wish you were here.

Philo responded immediately, as if he'd been waiting for me to text him, which made my heart do a little flutter. Sometimes—okay, pretty much all the time—I wondered what Philo could see in me. I mean, he was this ancient man-boy and I was just me. A sixteen-year-old barely experienced, newbie vampire. But he insisted that I made him feel alive and young again and other stuff that I found hard to believe, but whatever. He treated me so well and made me feel special and cared for, so as long as he wanted to be with me, I was happy to be with him.

Philo: We'll go again someday. Just the two of us.

I held my phone to my chest, then did a little happy dance. Like, I literally squeezed my eyes shut and squealed while my feet danced about. Hey, no one was watching. I don't think. Suddenly I glanced around at the neighboring buildings which I now realized were spaced really close together.

Me: ♥♥♥
Me: I'd like that
Me: Oh! I've gotta show you this crazy garden my aunt and uncle have. Stand by for picture!

I opened the camera app again and spun around to face the garden. I held the phone up to get the best shot, then just as I was about to take the picture I looked up over the edge of my phone.

All I saw was a wide, red mouth with a million sharp, deadly teeth before I screamed, threw my arms into the air and fell backward. I hit my head on something hard and the lights went out.

When I woke, a brief flash of pain told me I'd been injured, but thanks to my superfab vampire body, I was already healing. Only a bit of residual pain lingered.

And then I remembered what had made me fall in the first place.

"What the—" I scrambled back so I was propped against the low wall—which must have been what I hit my head on—and opened my eyes in one motion. I did one of those comedy double-takes as I tried to make sense of what was in front of me. And let me tell you, there was nothing funny about it.

Coiled on my legs with its upper body raised up so it could stare directly into my face—was a snake.

And it was no ordinary snake, either. This thing was massive.

I went to the zoo one time and Stacey dared me to volunteer to help the snake handler. He'd draped a boa constrictor over my shoulders and I nearly collapsed, the thing had been so heavy. And so long it draped on the ground on both sides of me.

This thing—this snake-thing—must have been at least as long that boa. And judging by how numb my legs were, it was definitely as heavy. It was a shimmering green, not quite the same color as the gourds hanging in the garden now that I was up close and personal with it. Its scales were green, but they shimmered with a hint of purple and maybe even black here and there. Its head flared, but not quite like a cobra, more like the purple ruffles along its cheeks and the top of its head made it appear bigger. I don't know. It was kind of hard to look at, and when I did, it was mainly its large golden eyes with shimmering pools of purple deep inside them that caught my attention. That and the wide red mouth with its many scary-looking teeth.

Who are you? a male voice said in my mind. The only other time I'd heard anything like that was from another vampire and that was the last thing I needed right now. I was in no position to greet a new vamp and try to prove to them that I wasn't any kind of threat to them.

I'm Minnie Kim. This is my aunt and uncle's house. I'm from America. I swear, I'm not here to take over your territory or anything. I figured it was better to respond right away because I didn't want the vampire to take offense and try any more intrusive techniques to get me to talk. It was already rude enough that he'd spoken in my mind without invitation.

I am Honja and you are in my garden.

"Wait. What?" I tried to look around, but the snake's head was even closer to mine than before and I didn't dare move in case it bit me. "Please don't bite me."

Promise you will leave this place and I will not bite you.

That was when I went a little crazy inside my head.

"You mean, you're the one who's talking to me inside my head?" I said to the snake.

It is inefficient to speak with one's mouth and tongue and teeth. I have no use for such things.

"Holy crap."

If that means that you are sorry for intruding upon my garden, then I will accept your apology. But you must leave and never return.

"I, uh. What? No, that wasn't an apology, but yes, I am sorry for bugging you. It's just that I didn't know you were even here and—and I can't leave."

Honja reared up and flared the frilly things on the side of his face. It was pretty much terrifying. *What do you mean you will not leave? What is this trickery?*

"It's my aunt and uncle's place and I'm staying with them for the summer. I literally can't leave. Besides, they want me to figure out who's been haunting them and get rid of them, so I'm gonna be moving all around here a lot, I guess."

I narrowed my eyes at the snake. "Wait a minute. Are you the one causing them all this grief? Are you the one haunting my family?"

Somehow, the snake actually managed to look affronted at my accusation. *I cause no troubles to anyone. I only wish to remain here, hidden, until my time has come.*

"Your time? When's that gonna be? Can't you just like . . . move along to someone else's garden?"

No! Honja roared inside my head while he hissed and swung his head all around. *I cannot abandon my prize! I will not!*

"What prize?" I tried to adjust myself, I really couldn't feel my legs anymore, but they were still just as stuck beneath the creature as before.

What do you know of my prize? Who told you?

Okay, this was so not cool. Not only did I have a strange, supremely heavy snake sitting on my lap, but he was flat-out crazy to boot. This was probably the most dangerous situation I'd ever been in, and that's counting the time I sat in the middle of a bunch of power-hungry vampires who wanted to see me dead. Crazy was hard to reason with.

I tried to make my voice smooth and even and channel my inner calm when I replied. "Um, you told me about it. Just now. But I promise I don't want it. You can keep it!" I added the last with a bright smile, but it seemed to be a mistake because Honja narrowed his eyes at me.

You lie. Everyone wants the pearl. They fall so rarely and everyone is so lazy they want to take mine rather than work to get one of their own. And I will not give it up, I tell you. I swear it on my ancestors.

I held up my hands in protest. "Honestly, I respect that you value your, um, pearl thingie, but I don't want it. I swear on *my* ancestors. All I want is to figure out why my ancestors are haunting my family and help them return to their rest or whatever. My dad seems to think that because I'm a vampire I'll be able to talk to them but it doesn't work like that. Does it?" I looked up hopefully at the snake.

I mean no disrespect to your father, but he is an idiot. Just because you once walked in the valley of death does not mean you are, in truth, dead now.

"Yes! Thank you! That's exactly what I told him!"

Honja regarded me silently while I thought about my dad and the ancestors and all my problems.

If you truly do not desire the pearl, perhaps we can be of assistance to one another, he said.

There was the hint of slyness in his tone that should have made me question the next words out of his mouth but I was too desperate and heck, too ignorant, to know any better.

"I could really use the help," I said. This creature seemed to know about vampires so it stood to reason that he'd know about gwishin, too.

It is likely that your ancestors are drawn to the power of the pearl. Help me ascend and become a dragon—

"A dragon?" I rudely interrupted—and immediately regretted having done so at the death-glare Hanjo sent me. After a pause I added meekly, "Carry on."

Once I have ascended to my true form, I can properly secure my pearl and I will leave this place for a more suitable location. He sniffed as he swept his gaze over the garden as if it was already beneath him. *If that alone does not solve the problem of your restless ancestors, I shall help you find the solution. Do we have an accord?*

"Two questions: First, how will leaving here with your pearl do anything to help me with my ancestors? And second—forgive me, but how can a snake become a dragon?"

He blinked at me—that horizontal inner-eye-lid blink thing serpents do and it made me quiver a little with grossness. Then he leaned way down close to me so I could feel the tip of his forked tongue flick against my cheek. I squeezed my eyes shut and held my breath. *Call me a snake again, vampire, and I will bite off your head.*

I felt the intensity of his presence fade a little so I peeked open one eye and then the other. He'd returned to his resting position. "Sorry," I squeaked.

I am an imugi. I was born to be a dragon. But I am not yet a thousand years old and as such, I must either wait until I am old enough to possess a yeouiju—that precious pearl of power—or I, or my proxy, must complete a quest given to me by a man of spirit, one of learning and also of wisdom.

Will you help me find such a man and assist me in my quest?

"I—" I wanted to say yes because I could so use the help with the ancestors, but I didn't know anything about imugis or pearls or whatever. "I-I don't know."

Hanjo abruptly swept himself off my legs and toward the trellis. He paused to peer back at me. *You have twenty-four hours, little vampire. If you do not respond to my offer within that time, it will no longer be yours to choose and you will be on your own with your problem.*

He began to climb up the trellis—it was already hard to spot him among the snake squash. "But what about your problem?" I jumped to my feet, ignoring the burning tingles in my legs. "If I don't help you, you're stuck being an imugi or whatever for however much longer."

Ah, Hanjo said. *But I am perfectly content to wait here. No one knows where my pearl is and no one but you knows I am here. It will remain that way until my one thousandth birthday, which isn't too far away. Only a few hundred years or so. I can wait. Can you?*

Could I?

I stood there, dumbly waiting for some smart come-back to occur to me, but when I realized I was fresh out, and that Hanjo was done talking to me, I shook out my arms and legs with a long breath of air. I spotted my phone on the other side of the garden and jogged over to it, suddenly anxious to talk to Philo and get his take on everything.

But my phone was smashed and cracked to bits. Never mind the fact that the screen was completely filled with cracks, the stupid thing wouldn't even power back on. I crouched there for a long moment, mourning the loss of my phone, before I dragged myself downstairs to the apartment.

What in the world was I gonna do?

★ Met a "baby" dragon today. ★

First of all—dragons are real???
Mind. Blown.

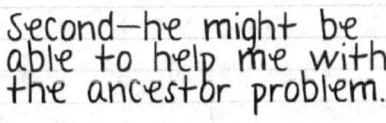

Second—he might be
able to help me with
the ancestor problem.

Third—
dragons are real!!!!

CHAPTER FIVE

I CLOMPED HEAVILY DOWN THE STAIRS, POUTING OVER MY ruined phone and pondering everything Hanjo had said—and everything I'd promised to do. I was so lost in my own thoughts that when I stepped into the living room, I stumbled right into the midst of a super uncomfortable scene.

There were my aunt and uncle, a look of disgust on their faces, and my cousin who I hadn't met yet, and my stony-faced parents—who were in the process of receiving a cooler full of blood from a wickedly handsome vampire. He was in full vamp-mode, too. Totally flaunting his undeadness with a long black trench coat, even though it was sweltering and humid as a greenhouse outside, which emphasized his ashen appearance and—and!—he had his fangs out! The nerve!

He slid me a meaningful glance and I recognized his presence as the vamp I'd briefly felt when I first met Hanjo. He must have intercepted the delivery guy—because there was no way this vamp was a delivery driver. He smoothly swiveled in my direction and super-sped until he stood right in front of me. My family's eyes nearly popped out of their heads. I was gonna kill this guy. He might have just set me all the way back in my efforts to prove to them that vampires were people too. Dang him!

He held the cooler to me, but didn't move his hands, which meant I had no choice but to touch him in order to get my fingers curled around the handles. He grinned wickedly at my unease. He was a beautiful man—Asian, reMade in his early thirties, I think, with black eyes, full lips and glossy black hair that hung over his forehead in one of those carefully messy styles that looked so good on a guy. He wasn't tall, but he exuded power. I couldn't tell if he was ancient or not, a Maker or not, but he sure as heck intimidated me.

I felt nothing but awkward when our fingers touched and I took the cooler from him.

No flash of memory, no insight into who this guy was. I was getting better at controlling my talent, but this was one time when a bit of insight would have been helpful and I totally struck out. He frowned as if he knew what I'd tried to do.

"Uh, thanks," I said, setting the cooler on the floor between us. I did not want this guy getting any closer to me than he already was. "But you didn't have to bring this in yourself. You could have just sent a delivery guy."

He gave a slight shrug, never taking his eyes off me, or that grim frown off his lips. "I wanted to meet you," he said in a warm, cultured voice that held no accent at all that I could detect. "And welcome you to the neighborhood." He lifted his right hand and waved it in the air. He had a suave way about him that did nothing to ease the dangerous feel of him.

"Thanks." I toed the cooler at my feet. "As you can see, I'm not a free-range, uh, diner. I've already set up regular deliveries for the whole time I'll be here, so you don't need to worry about—" I gulped. Technically it was illegal to feed from humans without contracts and stuff, but this guy gave me the feeling he might live a little outside the law. I didn't want to give him any reason to resent me living in his territory for a while.

He leaned toward me, seemingly unperturbed by the cooler between us. "And how long will that be?"

My mind hiccupped. "Um?"

"How long can I expect you to stay?" There was something curious in his expression that gave off mixed vibes. Did he hope I'd be staying a while? Or did he want to take me to the airport right now? I leaned back.

"Just until the end of July. I'm visiting my family!" I said the last super brightly, and waved my hand toward the group of relatives who gawked at us from the other side of the small room.

The vampire somehow leaned even closer. "I am Sang-hyeok." His voice hit me like a warning and I shivered. He held his hand out between us, begging me to take it. "And you are?"

I hesitated. Touching wasn't exactly something vampires did, and I wondered what this guy's talents were and if they had anything to do with touching. Maybe he hoped to get a read on me, like I did him. Reluctantly, I took his hand. Did I really have to tell him my name, though? He squeezed my hand slightly, and I gulped.

"Kim Jung-min." No way was I gonna tell him my nickname. That felt too personal.

He gave me a slight bow. "Until we meet again." And then he was gone. Like, in a flash, super vamp-speed, gone.

The hand he'd held tingled, but otherwise had nothing to tell me. I'd seen absolutely nothing when we touched, but maybe it had to do with the fact I was concentrating really hard on keeping my own mind shut down tight, just in case he was a mind-talker, too. What would be the odds? Pretty slim, if Thor was to be believed. Maybe I'd have to ask him if he knew this guy, Sang-hyeok.

My father cleared his throat and I slowly came back to the present—and found each of my family members staring at me. The only one who didn't look like they were about to kick me out of the house and call the authorities to come and get me, was my cousin. I bent one knee and relaxed my body, then gave a little wave.

"Sorry about that, everyone. That shouldn't have happened. A delivery person—a human delivery guy—was supposed to drop it off. And I expected to be the one here to get it, and, well. Sorry for that. That guy was way out of line and shouldn't have been here at all."

For some reason my cousin looked a little disappointed about that, but my aunt and uncle visibly relaxed. Mom just looked nervous—probably because my dad looked seriously ticked off. Like, if I wasn't a vampire, he might spank my bum with a wooden spoon. It would not be because I was sixteen-and-a-half—my age wouldn't have stopped him. He narrowed his eyes at me and opened his mouth, but Mom jumped between us. Literally.

"Minnie!" she exclaimed. "Come meet your cousin, Jung-woo. He's going to university for computer programming, aren't you, Jung-woo? And he's absolutely brilliant. Just brilliant. Like you! How old are you now? Are you eighteen? Nineteen?" Mom paused to take a breath and I dove past her to shake Jung-woo's hand. The wide grin on his face suggested he was not unfamiliar with a mother's tendency to ramble when she was trying to defuse a bomb in the shape of a father.

Jung-woo pushed my hand aside and wrapped his arms around me, instead. "Call me Junu," he said against my ear. There was laughter in his voice and an ease in his embrace that made all the awkward feelings and worry disappear. I held on a little longer, just to stay in that safe hug for a moment longer before I had to face my father.

The ease and camaraderie between us felt instant and real. Instant BFFs. At least that was one less thing to worry about.

When Junu let me go, Father cleared his throat. He was standing nearby, his arms crossed over his chest, talking with Uncle. He flicked his gaze toward the cooler and gave me a meaningful look. Right. Get the evidence of my evil undeadness out of sight. Right. Now.

"Be right back," I said to Junu, to Mom, or to myself. I dashed to the cooler, picked it up easily, and took it to the room I shared with my parents. The small fridge I'd ordered was wedged at the head of the cot I was using. Mom had been so concerned about my "supplies" until I told her about the fridge. Sheesh. It wasn't like I wanted to guzzle blood in front of them and watch their faces pucker in disgust. The only thing that sucked was that I'd have to drink cold blood all summer. Gag. It wasn't the worst thing, but it would be nice to get home and enjoy a nice warm cup when the vacation was over.

I'd stuffed all the blood bags and about a quarter of the puddings I'd ordered into the fridge before the lights went out. In the absence of electricity, the apartment became eerily quiet.

The elders murmured in the other room, and I tuned in my hearing to catch their words.

"—this is what it's like!" Auntie exclaimed. "All hours of the night and day. On and off, on and off. But this isn't even the worst of it. Sometimes there's—"

I heard it then: whispers layered upon whispers. I couldn't understand them and it wasn't because they were speaking Korean, it was because there were so many voices that they ran over and under and around each other to the point that none of it made sense. I sat back on my heels and dragged in a deep breath as the air around me grew thick with . . . with . . . presences.

As in, ghosts.

My aunt and uncle had been right. There were ghosts haunting their house. And from the press and feel of them, there were a lot.

I shoved the last of my supplies into the little fridge, rearranging some things to make it all fit. Man, I hoped the power never stayed out for long or I'd have a mess on my hands. I returned to the living room where my family sat on two couches facing each other. Junu lay half-reclined on a couple pillows like a Roman emperor or something. I picked up a big pillow and dropped it on the floor next to his head, then sat on it.

"So. Ghosts," I said.

Junu glanced up at me in surprise, then a mischievous grin split his face. He held up his fist and I bumped it with my own. He made an explosion with his fingers and I laughed.

"This is no laughing matter, daughter," Father said, and I immediately sobered. That was his no-nonsense voice. I knew better than to mess around with Dad when he brought out the Voice.

"Sorry, *Appa*. Sorry Auntie and Uncle." I looked at each of their faces and was surprised to find mixed emotions on both my aunt and uncle's faces. It seemed like they hadn't made up their minds about me. Like, they weren't sure if they should be wary of me because I was a *gangshi*, like my father believed, or if I was something kinda cool and interesting and no less their niece than I'd been before. I smiled warmly at them. I just wanted them to love and accept me, so that bit of hope I found in their faces warmed my heart.

Auntie leaned forward, her hands clasped together. She was an attractive woman—more refined and elegant than my mom, but not necessarily prettier. Mom just didn't do herself up. She was like a soccer mom—a comfy clothes, easy-to-fix hairdo and no make-up kinda woman. Auntie Bora was more what I pictured when I imagined a Tiger Mom. Everything perfect and put together. Her hair was so full of product that even when she leaned forward as she did then, not a strand fell out of place.

"You felt them, then? The ancestors?" Her words sounded anxious and hopeful. Maybe even childish in the way they seemed full of wonder. It was a weird contrast to her I'm-the-boss persona.

I nodded, and she, my uncle and Junu all sighed with relief. That's when I realized they hadn't been positive all this time. Or maybe they'd been sure, but they'd all feared they were going crazy. I could imagine a little what that must have been like. It still kinda freaked me out that they thought I could do anything at all about it, though.

"Well, that's wonderful," Auntie said, sitting back and clapping her hands. "Just wonderful." I understood her relief to discover that someone else knew for a fact they had a ghost infestation, but just because I knew they were there didn't mean I knew how to send them away.

I thought of Hanjo and his suggestion that the ancestors were gathered here because of his power pearl or whatever it was. Could that really be true? Could it be that simple?

How hard was it to help a baby dragon level up, anyway?

I had no idea about any of this stuff and the not-knowing was just about the worst thing ever to a girl who liked things that had explanations and meanings and reasons and purposes. This—this was folklore. Myth.

Then again, wasn't I?

Gah!

"Minnie?" Mom's voice cut through my thoughts and I struggled to bring my attention back to the family gathered around the cluster of flickering candles on the coffee table. "Answer your uncle."

"Oh," I said, facing my uncle. I searched my brain, but I'd been totally lost in thought—I had no idea what he'd said. I gave him a sheepish smile. "I'm sorry, Uncle. Could you please repeat the question?" Junu snickered beside me, but I ignored him.

"I said," Uncle said with a touch of the irritation Dad often sported. "Can you put our ancestors to rest?"

And that was the million-dollar question, wasn't it?

I studied my uncle for a moment. He was taller than my dad, and bigger, too. I think he was just a few years older than him, but he seemed younger. There were smile lines around his eyes and mouth—not the frown lines Dad wore. Otherwise, there was no denying they were related. Same angled face, same warm-brown eyes. Same cowlick at their hairline that made their hair lift and stand up. Uncle Jung-ho smiled encouragingly, the irritation I'd glimpsed before, gone now.

Why couldn't Dad be more like Uncle?

"Well," I hedged. "I have an idea of how I might be able to help."

My dad leaned back and expelled a breath of air while everyone else spoke at once—mostly words of relief and hope. Even some comments about how glad they were that I'd come. I didn't pay attention to them, though. I watched my dad. Waited for him to say something. After a moment, he flicked his gaze around the room, his attention landing on his brother and sister-in-law.

The lights popped back on, and a steady hum of electronics filled the air. Still, I watched Dad. Waited. Hoped.

After Mom patted his shoulder and got up, Dad's gaze finally settled on me. We were the only ones who hadn't gotten up yet. He gave me a brief nod. Then said something to Uncle and stood up.

I thought about that nod and what it might mean. I guess it was the best I was gonna get. For now.

I wonder if I'll ever earn my dad's approval. When he looks at me, it just hurts so much. I don't see the appa I used to know. He's always been stern and strict. He's always wanted the best for me. But he also used to be proud of me. He used to love me. Mom says he still does, but...I don't know. I don't see it. Not like I used to. I'm standing right in front of him, and all I feel is alone.

CHAPTER
SIX

THAT EVENING, UNCLE JUNG-HO SHOWED ME THEIR shrine to our ancestors and talked about all they'd done to honor them. There was cash, ticket stubs from recent trips out to the country where our ancestors had lived, candy, dried fish, and gold jewelry all in little dishes spread across the small table. There were also photographs. Lots of photographs.

I picked up one that I'd never seen before. It showed an ancient woman in traditional garb with a small boy on her lap. The boy was handsome and dressed very nicely in a tiny little suit. There was something familiar about him, so I peered more closely. Maybe it was my dad.

"That is your brother, Jung-jae. And your father's mother. Your grandmother." My mother's voice was soft, almost a whisper, and her breath ruffled the hair by my ear. She put her arm around my waist, something she didn't often do, and we both gazed down on the photograph.

"How come I haven't seen this picture before? Why don't you have any pictures of Jung-jae at home?" We had a shrine to our ancestors too, but I never even knew I had an older brother until a couple months ago. I peered at the photo more closely. Now that I knew he was my brother, I could see myself in him. See how we both had our mom's eyes, and our dad's cowlick at our forehead. "He was so cute," I said in a whisper. Tears welled in my eyes as I thought of what it would have been like to grow up with an older brother who I imagined like Junu. I missed him, which was weird since I'd never known him.

Mom squeezed me and rested her chin on my shoulder. "I have a picture I keep in my nightstand. I look at it sometimes, but I could not bear to have it out, to see it every day. And I suppose I was afraid that if I put out photos of him, he would see how much I love you, and what a beautiful life you were living in America, and he would curse you, and take you away from me."

"Oh, *Eomma*," I said, using the Korean word for Mommy which I hardly ever used. I set the photo down and turned to pull my mom into a tight hug. We weren't a very demonstrative family, but Stacey's family was all about the hugs and kisses so I was a bit more familiar with the custom than my mom. But sometimes you just need to hold someone. Especially if that someone's your mom.

She was stiff for a moment, but then she gave in and I felt her soften. She rubbed my back a moment before letting go. It was a brief hug—no need to go crazy or anything.

We both turned back to the shrine and Uncle Jung-ho resumed his storytelling as if nothing strange had just happened. My family was excellent at ignoring elephants in the room. Like the photo of my big brother who had mysteriously died as a little boy. Or the fact that I was a vampire. No one had even commented on that strange visit from Sang-hyeok, or the cooler I took to my room. I wondered if Sang-hyeok had managed to compel them to forget the details of his visit. Aside from being thrilled I'd agreed to help them with their *gwishin* problem, not another word had been said.

Auntie Bora and Mom brought out sticky rice, noodles, fish and kimchi and we all gathered at the coffee table/kitchen table to eat. We sat on our knees at the low table just like real Koreans. It was neat—for like five minutes. I wasn't used to sitting on my knees, which embarrassed my mom and dad. I got the impression they didn't want their family to know that we sat at a regular American kitchen table and not on the floor at a low table like Koreans did. But Junu slipped me a pillow to put between my heels and bum, and that helped. He winked and a rush of love for him filled me. This trip was worth it for the chance to meet him.

Junu was a character. He was a lot like me in that he was nothing, and I mean nothing, like his parents. He looked like a Korean pop star and I wondered what a good-looking guy like him was doing hanging out with his family. Koreans had a world-famous nightlife, so what was he doing here? Maybe he was required to be here since it was our first real night with them.

"So, what will you do to put our ancestors to rest?" Uncle Jung-ho asked. He was friendlier in general than my dad, but he was also pretty no-nonsense and the expression on his face said *let's talk business.*

I gulped down the ball of rice I'd just shoved in my mouth and it stuck in my throat. Junu pounded, unhelpfully, on my back until I could take a drink of tea. "Um," I said with my usual grace and charm.

Well, first thing, I thought, *is I need to figure out how to help a weirdo dragon baby thing level up so I can get him out of your vegetable garden.*

But what I said was, "I think I need to do a bit of research." True. "I mean, I've never done anything like this before." Also true. I glanced at my dad. I wanted to say that talking to ghosts wasn't exactly something

63

vampires could do, but I didn't want to offend him. I decided to stay quiet about that.

Uncle nodded thoughtfully as if what I'd said made perfect sense. Whew. I breathed a sigh of relief.

"Jung-woo," Auntie said loudly. "You will help Jung-min with whatever she needs, you hear?"

"Yes, *Eomma*," Junu said without hesitation. "I've got an audition tomorrow, but other than that—"

"Pfft!" Auntie scoffed. She even rolled her eyes. "Forget about the audition. Your family's honor is more important. You know you don't have what it takes, anyway."

Junu kind of shrunk a little and I frowned. My mom and dad never talked to me like that. They always believed in me and believed I could do whatever I wanted.

"What kind of audition do you have? I'd love to come watch, if that's okay," I said to Junu.

He brightened, and his cheeks turned a little pink. Man, he was a good-looking guy. Full lips, big dark eyes that twinkled with mischief and gorgeous long, dark lashes. He could totally be in a boy band or starring in some K-drama, he was that good-looking. "Well," he hedged.

"He wants to be a pop star," Uncle said. "Which would be great, but no one ever wants to hire him, so it's time for him to get serious about his life and do something useful for a change."

I barely kept my mouth shut while Uncle talked. *A pop star!* "You wanna be an idol?" I gushed as soon as Uncle was done. "That's so cool! I'd love to be a pop star! Now you really gotta let me come to your audition!" Yes I was talking in exclamation points, but I was really, really excited. Maybe I could get discovered, too! How cool would that be?

Junu's blush was back and he sat a little taller. "You can totally come," he said. "I'd love to have you with me. Maybe you can be my good luck charm."

"Totally!" I said. And I meant it. "Can you dance? Can you sing?"

"Yes." Junu gave me one of those cool sexy looks that dared me to question him.

I laughed. "Oh, yeah. I can totally see you in one of my K-dramas!"

He bumped me with his shoulder. "Thanks."

This whole summer thing was looking up and up.

"Then it's settled," Auntie said. "Jung-min—"

"Minnie, please, Auntie. No one ever calls me Jung-min."

She gave me an indulgent smile, but at least she accepted my request. "Minnie will go with you to your audition, and you will show her the library, our

65

ancestors' burial place and anything else she needs to help her do her work."

Her work. Ha! I nearly snorted but covered it with a cough at the last second.

"Okay." Junu grinned, a lot more into the whole idea than he had been earlier.

I, on the other hand, felt my heart sink. How was I gonna figure out how to help Hanjo with Junu hanging around me all the time? I didn't need to know anything about the ancestors—I needed to know about *imugis* or whatever Hanjo had said he was.

I watched Junu out of the corner of my eye. He was sitting beside me and didn't seem at all disturbed by the fact I was a vampire. He did know, right? Because none of my family seemed concerned. I narrowed my eyes at Dad and wondered. Because if Junu knew about me, and was okay with it—and heck, they were being haunted by their ancestors, so it wasn't like he was a stranger to supernatural things, right? —then maybe I could tell him about Hanjo and everything would be cool. On the other hand, well. What if he totally freaked out and I ruined everything by telling him?

Because there was no way this was gonna work if I had to keep him in the dark the whole time. I just wasn't that good at lies and misdirection.

A knock sounded at the door and everyone turned to look at it. It was after 10 pm. Kinda late for someone to drop by. After glancing around, Junu hopped up and answered the door. I couldn't see who was at the door because Junu stepped out onto the walkway and I could only hear murmuring.

"Who is it?" Auntie hollered. Well, that was one way to get your questions answered.

Junu leaned back into the apartment. "Delivery."

"Delivery! Who delivers this time of night?"

Junu stepped inside holding a white bubble envelope. He closed the door and walked toward us. "It's for Minnie."

Auntie pursed her lips. That's right. Vampires deliver at this time of night. At least that's what I imagined she was thinking.

"For me?" I asked dumbly as Junu handed me the envelope. There was something hard and sorta heavy in it that filled up one corner of the package. I glanced up at Junu. "It wasn't . . . you know?" I weirdly pantomimed Sang-hyeok. *Scary vampire.*

Junu grinned and shook his head. He dropped to the ground. "Nope. Just some regular delivery guy." He nudged my shoulder like he'd done a couple times before. It must be his thing. "So, what is it?"

I wanted to take it to my room and open it. Who knew what could be inside? Maybe it really was a vampire thing and I was about to expose my poor family to the unseemly side of my life? Not that I had any reason I'd get something unseemly. It just made me nervous. But it was obvious from the focus of every gaze in that room on me, there'd be no getting out of this.

Reluctantly, I tore at the perforated edge and dipped my hand inside to retrieve the box. Huh. "It's an iPhone."

"Who'd send you an iPhone?" Mom demanded.

"Is it your—that leader of yours?" Dad asked with a bitterness in his tone I hadn't heard from him before.

I quirked my brow and looked at him. "You mean Mr. Aristos?" I could understand him being a little jealous of David, my vampire *father*, for lack of a better way of describing him—I mean, I did live with David and the rest of my vampire family in a gorgeous mansion and he provided pretty much everything I'd ever want. But he wasn't my actual father. He wasn't my *appa*.

"Look," Junu said. Thank goodness for his interruption. "There's a card."

I took the tiny notecard from him. It was one of those flower shop type cards you put with flowers or balloons.

I had a feeling you might need this. Call me.
Love, Philo

My heart flopped over in my chest. Oh. What a sweet thing! He couldn't have known—well, maybe he did, actually, I had been texting with him when I fell and the phone smashed.

I flashed the card at Dad. "It wasn't from Mr. Aristos, Dad. It's from Philo."

But that only made him narrow his eyes even more. "Why would he send you a phone? Why is a boy sending you a phone?"

I didn't bother to correct him that Philo was in fact two thousand years old, because doing so would just point out that my boyfriend was a vampire. A vampire who was way older than him—another source of contention—and who could whoop his butt if he wanted. It was much better to just stick with the whole *boyfriend who buys me things* vibe than all the other reasons Dad had to disapprove. Not to mention he didn't believe in me dating until after I graduated with my doctorate, anyway. Silly Dad. Like I'd do that.

"Because I broke my phone." Oops. I didn't actually mean to tell them that.

Dad frowned. "How did you break your phone?" I don't know how he managed to put so much suspicion into those few words, but he did.

I shrugged. "I, um." What the heck do I say? How do I get around this? "I went up to Uncle's garden to check it out and I, um, dropped my phone over the wall."

"And why would you do that?"

"Well I didn't do it on purpose!"

"Hmm." Dad seemed to think that's exactly what I'd done.

"Why would I do that?" Like only an idiot would on purpose throw their perfectly good phone to the street from three stories above.

"So you could get a new one."

I gasped. "I'm not that shallow. Is that what you think of me?"

Dad stood, towering over me. "No child of mine will use that tone of voice with me."

Mom stood too, but Dad wasn't having any of her soothing or calming words. He shook her hand off his arm. "You are not too old to be punished, daughter. And I am not too proud to punish you in front of my brother and his family. You dishonor us with your insolence."

Now everyone, including me, was on their feet. Me, mortified, and everyone else just trying to defuse the situation.

Eventually Uncle managed to convince Dad to go play a game of chess with him and Mom skillfully directed me to our bedroom so Dad and I didn't have to see one another.

"I'll just take that. We wouldn't want to upset your father any further."

Then she took my new phone and switched off the light, leaving me alone in the dark.

CHAPTER
SEVEN

WHILE I RESENTED BEING SENT TO MY ROOM LIKE A little girl, it did give me time to think. Time I desperately needed since it had been one thing after another since the whole garden incident.

First of all—dragons were real? Like, what the heck? Sure, I only had the word of this *imugi* creature to go on, but still. Since he was real, and talked to me in my mind in Korean, I didn't have any reason to suspect he was lying about the dragon thing.

It was one thing for fairies to be real, since they were tiny and could be invisible and stuff, but how did the whole world not know about *dragons*? Could they go invisible too, like the faeries did? They had to—there just wasn't any way they wouldn't have been spotted on radar or by airplanes. Unless they were super small like Hanjo. Maybe my idea of a dragon—giant flying serpents as big as a house—wasn't the reality. Maybe all Hanjo needed to become a dragon was to grow thumbs so he could hold onto his power ball thingie.

Ha. That made me laugh. Made me think of a Pokémon ball.

What if that is what the pearl of power was? I sort of gasped to myself and had to lie there pondering the possibility that Pokémon were based on real-life creatures. Holy. Guaca. Mole.

Next, there was this business with Sang-hyeok. Unless the rules were different here in Korea, which I didn't really think they were, vampires weren't supposed to go around being all vampy in front of humans. It just wasn't good public relations. Yet here was this guy playing up the whole Dracula thing and scaring my family. And me.

Hopefully he got an eyeful and now knew that I wasn't anyone he should be afraid of—I mean, not that he'd be afraid of me. More like, I wasn't about to encroach on his territory. He knew I'd had a blood delivery, so it wasn't like I'd be hunting here. And ew. Was that guy hunting humans? I swear I hadn't heard anything about that being okay when the family talked to me about this trip. The vampire council made the rules and the rules were the same for everyone everywhere. I was positive. Maybe I'd have to ask about Sang-hyeok when I went to the local council office. Maybe he was a rogue or something. Which was pretty darn terrifying, especially since I had family living right here in his territory.

I closed my eyes and willed myself to think calm thoughts. There wasn't anything I could do about it tonight. But tomorrow—tomorrow I had to report to the local office so they knew I was in town and I could reassure them that I knew the rules and had made arrangements for blood delivery. The council already had my travel plans logged with them, and my blood orders on file—since I had to order through them—but apparently I was still required to check in personally within 72 hours of arriving in a new place.

Which would be fine if I wasn't spending the day with Junu.

On the one hand, I was grateful I wouldn't have to be alone. I'd looked at the map and metro stops, trying to plot out a route to downtown where the office was, but making my way around town by myself was super intimidating.

And Junu seemed to be pretty cool with the whole vampire thing. But how would he handle the news he had an *imugi* living in his garden? And that the key to putting our ancestors back to rest was helping this *imugi* become a full-grown dragon?

Should I tell him? How could I tell him? Just, "Hey, Junu. You know how I'm a vampire, right? Well, vamps aren't the only supernatural creatures out there. There's fairies and unicorns and oh yeah, dragons, too. Wanna help me level one up?"

Yup. Probably just like that. And I knew me—knew I'd have to tell him. I just hoped he'd take the news okay. One thing I knew for sure was that I'd definitely wait until after his audition. No way did I want to risk ruining it for him by freaking him out beforehand.

I couldn't believe Junu was auditioning for an agency. That was so cool! I wish I could audition, too, but while I'd always fantasized about being a K-pop star, I knew it wasn't really me. Especially not now that I was a vampire. Then again, what better way to show the world that vampires were the same as people than on the public stage like that?

I let my mind drift along with that fantasy for a bit and was just in the middle of me being interviewed on a popular talk show and telling the host how even though a person might now be basically immortal and drink blood to sustain their health, didn't mean their hopes and dreams changed—when my bed started rocking. It was subtle at first and even though I noticed it, I didn't worry about it. But in about twenty seconds it had morphed into a full-on, *shake you out of bed* kind of tremor.

Omo! Were we having an earthquake?

I bolted out of bed and rushed into the living room where I found Auntie and Uncle and Mom and Dad holding onto each other, and Junu standing under the archway between the hall and living room with his hands over his head.

"What's going on?" I asked him as I assumed his same position. We got earthquakes in Utah, but never anything like this, and I completely forgot everything I knew about what to do when one struck. "Do you get a lot of earthquakes?" I tried not to sound scared. But come on, we were in an apartment. Didn't apartments collapse during earthquakes?

Junu gave me a quizzical look. "This isn't an earthquake. It's our ancestors."

I snorted. "No way."

"Way."

"Seriously?" Holy smokes. Was this what they were living with? Was this what I was dealing with? I thought the ancestors were just pulling pranks, like turning off the lights—not full on shaking the whole building. That was outright scary.

Junu showed me his serious face for the first time since I'd met him. "Seriously."

Wow. "Has this happened before?"

He raised one eyebrow. He really was super handsome. I hoped he did awesome on his audition tomorrow.

"It has happened before?"

"Try every night?"

"Wait. What?"

"Yup. Every. Single. Night."

I gaped at him. Like, with my mouth hanging open and the whole bit. "*Omo.*"

His face lit up with a bright smile and the shaking suddenly stopped. He patted me on the head. "You're funny, *yeodonsaeng.*"

"Hey! Did you just call me your little sister?"

Junu just smiled and winked at me before striding over to give his mom a hug. Which was sweet. And made me feel like I should do the same.

I approached my own parents cautiously, and when they turned toward me, I stopped. What I saw in their eyes—what I saw in my dad's eyes—brought on stupid tears which was a very bad thing since vampires cry blood. I whirled around and dashed into the tiny bathroom, grabbed like ten tissues, swiped away the blood, flushed away the evidence, then grabbed a few more tissues for good measure before going back out to my parents.

Their expressions were full of compassion—they probably thought I'd just been sick or something, which was fine by me—and love.

Dad pulled me into his arms and hugged me tight. I squeezed my eyes closed and drank in the smell and feel of him. My daddy. My *appa*.

"Can you help us, Minnie? I don't think I can live like this any longer." Auntie Bora's nasally voice cut into my moment with my dad and ended it. I resented her for it for half a second, then sighed and pulled away from Dad.

There were so many things I didn't know. Like, was Hanjo telling the truth? Would he, could he, actually help put my ancestors to rest once he became a dragon? Was that even possible? What if we did everything we could do only to discover that moving the pearl away from here wasn't the solution? What if we couldn't level him up, at all?

But I had to try, didn't I? And since I at least knew the supernatural world was real, whether vampires had anything to do with ghosts or not, it made a sort of sense that if anyone could figure out how to put an end to my ancestors' unrest it would be me.

I took a deep breath. *You can do this*, I coached myself. I really hoped Junu would be up to helping me because that would make everything so much easier, but even if he didn't, I could do this. *Heck, I will do this!* I mentally cheered myself on. *Rah rah siss boom bah!*

"Yes, Auntie." My voice was strong and confident, my posture straight and sure. "I'll do everything I can to make things right."

I glanced at my dad and caught the look of gratitude and something else in his eyes. I think that look was pride. For the first time since before my death and reMaking, my dad was proud of me.

I'm going to watch an idol
audition tomorrow!

★AT SM ★ENTERTAINMENT!!

Think I'll die of happiness.
Oh yeah! I'm already dead.
I crack myself up sometimes.

Go JUNU!!!

CHAPTER EIGHT

I WOKE UP AT NINE THE NEXT MORNING AND DISCOVERED no one was home but Junu. He was in the living room, playing League of Legends. He looked like he'd just rolled out of bed, with his hair all mussed and wearing a pair of basketball shorts and a Team Liquid T-shirt. He still managed to look like a million bucks. I scowled. Morning was not my best look.

"Where'd everybody go?" I asked around a yawn. I sluffed into the kitchen and took a mug from where it hung from a hook under one of the cabinets.

"Gone sight-seeing," he said.

Oh, right. I'd wanted to go sightseeing too, but I guess I had other things I needed to do first. Still, it would have been nice if my parents had asked me. Or told me. Or said goodbye. Sigh. I was expecting too much from them. Things weren't what they used to be between us. I didn't even live at home anymore and I guess, in a lot of ways, I wasn't their little girl anymore. I still felt like their little girl, though.

I was just about to open the fridge when I realized my blood wasn't in that fridge, it was in the tiny one in my room. And I'd have to drink it cold. I stared at the mug in my hand. A warm cup of blood would be so good right now.

I glanced at Junu. He wasn't paying any attention to me. He was totally focused on his game. I bet he wouldn't even notice if I filled my mug and nuked it in the microwave. I quietly moved into my room with the mug and filled it up, sucking down the leftover in the bag from the tube built into it. That was one negative thing about blood bags—it was a *use it or lose it* situation. I suppose you could pour the leftover into a bottle or something but I didn't have that luxury here. Someone needed to come up with a better blood delivery system.

I took my mug back into the kitchen and popped it into the microwave. I knew it wouldn't be good for me once it came out, knew it wouldn't hold all the proteins and nutrients I really needed, but I just wanted that feel of warm blood, like comfort food you know isn't good for you but you *feel good* eating, anyway. Plus, it reminded me of Philo taking care of me when I'd first turned and went to live with the Aristos family.

I curled onto the couch behind Junu, who sat on the floor in front of their widescreen TV, and sipped on the yum in my cup. Junu didn't even glance my way. Score.

"So when's your audition?" I asked.

"Noon." His laptop sat open on the table, but he was casting it to the big screen.

"How long will it take? 'Cause I have to go somewhere today, like an appointment. I have to get there before they close or—" *Else*, I was gonna say. I didn't know exactly what would happen to me if I didn't report within 72 hours, but no way did I want to take that chance.

"No prob."

Okay. *Just chill, Minnie.* Junu knew his way around and I didn't. I'd just have to trust that he knew what he was talking about.

"What time do we have to leave at?"

He twisted his body as if he was physically being threatened by the magic wielding wizard on the screen as he stabbed his keyboard in rapid fire movements. "Like, 10:45. If you need a shower, better take it now 'cause I'm gonna need the bathroom for like an hour before we leave."

I snorted and nearly spilled some of my blood on the couch. Instead, I only got a drop on my hello kitty pajama shorts. Dangit. "What level are you?"

I waited while he finished his battle, which seemed to be winding down. Mack, Stacey's boyfriend, played LoL and Stace and I'd spent our fair share of Saturday afternoons watching him. Stacey played now too, but we hadn't been hanging out as much since . . . since Minnie 2.0, I guess. Maybe I should play. Looked kinda fun.

Junu pulled his headphones off and turned to face me. "I'm Diamond Three." I didn't exactly know all the levels, but by the look on his face he thought he was pretty hot stuff.

"Could you go professional?" Next to being an idol, being a professional gamer was pretty much every young Korean's dream job. And League of Legends was huge here.

Junu grinned. "Maybe. I'd need to level up a bunch more to be grandmaster ranked, which is where you need to be if you even stand a chance. Challenger's better. And it's incredibly hard to level up when you're already this awesome." He waggled his eyebrows and I laughed. He had this endearing, adorable way about him that even though he'd just totally bragged about himself, didn't make him seem conceited.

"Um," Junu said. He threw a meaningful glance toward my mouth. "Looks like you got a little something—" He pointed at the corner of his mouth.

I quickly swiped at my mouth with the back of my hand and saw a smear of blood across it. "Omo!" I shot to my feet—careful not to spill any more blood—and went into the kitchen for a paper towel. "Oh my gosh. I'm so sorry. I won't do that again, I promise."

Junu strolled across the room behind me. "Do what?"

I dumped out the rest of my blood, washed the mug, washed my hand, my mouth, all in super speed.

"Drink blood?" Junu asked.

I dried the mug with a dish towel but didn't turn around to face him. I was so mortified.

"It's okay, Min." He moved to the counter and leaned his hip against it. He pushed a little on my shoulder. "I get it. Think I want you to go hungry in my own house? Think I want you to have to eat in your room like a cat locked in her room?"

I laughed at that. "Like cats have their own rooms."

"Mrs. Lee next door has a two-bedroom apartment and lives alone. With two cats. They get their own room."

"No way," I said, full on laughing now.

"Way." Junu's expression softened and his eyes held a seriousness that hadn't been there before. "Seriously. Don't hide away in your room."

"What about Auntie and Uncle?" I was pretty sure my own parents would not be pleased if I poured myself a tall glass of blood and snacked on blood puddings in front of them.

Junu shrugged with one shoulder. "Maybe not so much around them. But with me? Just be yourself. Deal?" He held out his fist and I bumped it.

"Deal."

Then he knocked his knuckles on my head. "Now get going, 'cause I need all the time I can get making myself gorgeous." He turned me by my shoulders and gently pushed me toward the bathroom.

Since I didn't have to impress anybody, I didn't spend much time fussing. Thanks to my vampirism, my hair, eyelashes and lips were lush and lovely, so I didn't usually wear makeup and didn't do anything with my hair. I'd probably regret that later since my weather app promised another hot and humid day. I had a hair elastic around my wrist just in case. Otherwise, I threw on a pair of short-shorts that made my relatively short legs look longer, and a white T-shirt that said, "Never mind, find someone like you," in red lettering. I thought it was funny. Sneakers and a pair of socks with red ruffles finished me off. Done.

Took me like, forty-five minutes, tops. It was now 11:00 and I was still waiting on Junu.

"If we don't go now, you're gonna be late!" I called out. "The last thing you want is to rush in there all sweaty and out of breath." I'd said something similar at least two times already, but Junu hadn't replied. At least it gave me time to set up my new phone and answer the million texts I'd received that ranged from mildly frustrated that I wasn't texting back to full on threats to call in the council, the Red Cross or the Army if I didn't respond by . . . pretty much now.

I'd already sent texts to Philo, apologizing, explaining and thanking him for the phone, and was in the middle of texting with Stacey when the bathroom door flew open and banged against the opposite wall.

I looked up. And literally did a double take.

What the—?

"O.M.G.," I said with awe and admiration. "You are HOT!"

He stood posed in the bathroom doorway, one hand braced against the doorjamb while the other was slipped into his front pants pocket. He wore a dark gray suit, very well-tailored, and a white silky shirt—with most of its buttons undone. His chest was well-shaped and—had he oiled his skin? If he did, I had no complaints, because he looked good.

He might have applied just a little eyeliner to make his lashes look extra dark and full, and wore his hair expertly tousled like some lusty woman had just run her hands all through it.

"You really do look amazing. Like the real deal. Sheesh." I was gushing. I knew I was gushing. But my own cousin was making me weak in the knees. "Can you sing? Can you dance? Can you act?"

Junu strutted toward me, a smoldering look in his eyes. "I've got it all, baby."

Holy crap. Why in the world was this guy not on the big screen?

"I think you do!" And I didn't even feel the tiniest bit of shame for thinking that about my cousin. It wasn't like I wanted him, but I could respect a beautiful specimen and appreciate his eligibility for his career choice. "There's no way they can say no to you."

He threw me a quick glance that belied all the strut and swagger of a moment ago. This look said he was afraid and wasn't nearly as confident about his abilities as I was. Hmm. I'd have to see what there was to see about that.

"Come on, we gotta hurry."

"No guff," I said as I snuck out past him and into the hall so he could lock the door behind us.

We had to run to the bus stop, but once there, Junu seemed to think we'd be just fine. I took a seat while he held onto the handle hanging from the ceiling of the bus. He gazed out the window, while every woman in the bus, young and old, gazed at him. A few even snapped pics of him, and shot me dirty looks, which I thought was hysterical. I wasn't his girlfriend. For one thing, Junu wasn't a famous idol yet, and we were cousins. Cousins!

For his part, Junu seemed oblivious to the girls' attention, which struck me as weird. I would think their reaction was exactly what he was going for and he'd soak it up. Instead, he ignored them in favor of the view outside. Occasionally he'd glance at a really nice-looking guy about my age sitting at the back of the bus. I'd noticed him too, because he was really cute in a B-boy kinda way, but he hadn't once looked up from his phone since we got on. Maybe Junu knew him.

Junu nudged my knee with his. "This is us." The bus came to a stop and Junu reached down to pull me to my feet which I thought was super sweet. But when the B-boy came up behind him, he dropped my hand like a hot potato. Which was fine because I didn't want to hold Junu's hand or anything, it was just another checkmark in the weird column.

Junu out in public was nothing like Junu at home. He still looked hot and had a casual ease and grace to his movements, but he seemed . . . insecure, maybe? Shy around the girls, and insecure around the guys. As far as I could tell, Junu had nothing to be insecure about. Maybe I could help him with that. It was nice to think about doing some regular human things over the summer instead of all paranormal all the time. It would be fun to take advantage of some of the awesome night-life with Junu.

He ushered me off the bus along with the crowd— and holy smokes, it was a crowd—and down some steps to what I presumed was the subway. There were

English signs, but there were so many people, and Junu was moving me along too quickly, to catch much more than that.

It was so weird to be surrounded by so many Koreans. There were white people here and there, but it was a tsunami of Asian faces. I'd never been around so many people with my kind of face that it was super off-putting. Here's the weird thing: I felt like a white person. I still felt like a minority, even though all the faces around me were like mine. I thought it would be cool for once to be in the majority, but I didn't speak Korean—or understand it—as fast as these people spoke it; I felt like my style seemed faked or . . . I don't know. It just wasn't quite what I expected, and it made me feel kinda lonely.

While we waited for our train, I texted Stacey.

Me: Miss you :(

Stace: Miss you more!! 😦 😦 😦

Stace: Whatcha doin?

Me: Going to an agency audition with Junu

Stace: 😲 😆 😲 😆 😲 😆

Stace: OMO! That's amazing! Is he any good? Do you think he'll get accepted?"

I angled my phone toward Junu who was standing beside me and snapped a pic. He glanced at me just as the picture took, which gave him a smoldering, *come hither* appearance. I sent it to Stacey.

Stace: O.M.Geeeeee! He's gorgeous! Why didn't you ever tell me your cousin was so HOT? Why aren't I with you????

Me: First, you've got Mack. Down girl.

Me: Second, I hardly even knew about him at all until my parents told me about this trip. He's really cool.

Me: Third, I think he's the total package, but he says he's auditioned before and hasn't gotten in, so??? Kinda curious to see his audition.

Me: Scratch that. SUPER curious

Stace: I bet! I so wish I could be there with you! Maybe you'll get discovered or something!

Holy crap. I'd thought of that, but then I'd dismissed it like it would never ever happen. But Stacey saying it made me think maybe it really was possible! I patted self-consciously at my hair and glanced down at my cute but not idol-cute outfit, and sighed.

Me: I hope not today cuz I look like crap.

Stace: I highly doubt that. You couldn't look like crap if you tried.

Me: 😗 😗 😗 😗

"We're here," Junu said in a rush, and started pushing me toward the door. The subway hadn't even started slowing yet and people were already pressing toward the exit.

"This is nuts!" I said with a nervous laugh. I'd never been around this many people at one time in my life. Like, everrrrrr.

The train slowed, stopped, the doors opened, and I, along with a thousand other people, burst through the doors and onto the platform. And it didn't stop there. With his fingers wrapped around my backpack strap, Junu moved me speedily across the platform, up the escalator and out onto a very crowded city street. I stumbled to a stop.

"*Omo*," I breathed.

"No one says that anymore." Junu took my hand and pulled me through the crowd. "Come on!"

I glanced at my phone and saw that it was 11:52. "Holy crap! We're gonna be late!"

"No, we're not." Junu's grip on my hand was fierce and his words sounded like a commandment or something. Like he should've followed them up with something like, "Over my dead body." It might be over *my* dead body because at this rate I was bound to either get trampled to death, run over by a crazy, curb-hopping car, or drop dead of a heart attack.

Never mind that I'm a vampire and can't have heart attacks. I'd have something if we didn't slow down soon.

At the light, Junu dropped my hand and swiped his palms down his thighs.

"Nervous?" I asked. He shook his whole body, like he was getting ready to run a race.

He ignored me and pointed to a building across the street, right on the corner. "That's where we're going." I looked up at the giant glass and concrete structure and gasped. It had two massive screens on it, showing clips from dramas and music videos, interviews with stars and then SM ENTERTAINMENT splashed across the screen.

"*Omo*! You're auditioning *there*?!" I thought I might pass out right then and there. "We're going in there?" What if I saw Lay? Or Baekhyun? I'd die. I'd die and go to heaven, that's what.

Next thing I knew, Junu had his fingers wrapped around my wrist and he was dragging me across the street along with half of Korea. He pushed me through the doors and suddenly . . . we were inside.

I, Minnie Kim, stood among the stars. Banners featuring my beloved singers and actors hung from high above, gently swaying in the breeze. This really was heaven.

CHAPTER NINE

WHILE I STOOD GAWKING AT THE SCENERY—I WAS IN THE heart of all things Korean entertainment! Ahhh!—Junu spoke to the security guard and got us both passes for the auditions. He grabbed my elbow and dragged me toward the back of the large foyer and down a hallway. He held up a finger in front of his mouth in the universal *shh* gesture, then pulled open an inconspicuous door with Stage C written on it.

We moved inside as quietly as possible and I was super glad for my vampire reflexes because the old Minnie would have totally klutzed her way through this whole venture. As it was, I was able to stop the door from banging shut, navigate my way over the lip of the carpet, which was raised a little bit, and slip into the top row of seats.

We were suddenly in a theater, sitting high above a stage which was something, but also nothing, like all the other stages I'd seen in my life. I gaped at the camera crews—plural—large screens to allow everyone to have a clear view, and green screen backdrop. I half-stood and peered down at the director's table where two men sat with laptops in front of both of them. How could he judge the talent if he was watching a monitor?

On the stage was a young man with white-blond hair with black tips and a pale complexion that reminded me of Baekhyun from the group EXO. A couple girls were busily touching up his makeup and wardrobe.

"He's beautiful," Junu breathed.

"What?"

But the director called, "From the top!" and distracted me from Junu's reply. Which I vaguely noted he did not give.

Even though there was just a green screen on the stage, the screens showed him standing on a tropical beach. Awesome. He slung his pale gray suit jacket over his shoulder and swaggered to front center. He looked down and at his feet, adjusted his stance, then looked up, giving a brief nod off to the side. The music started, and a fan gently blew on his face while the palm trees on the monitors swayed. Then he began to sing.

I didn't know who to watch—the singer, who was mesmerizing and awesome, and gorgeous and so talented, or the director who occasionally watched the action on the stage but who mostly watched the monitor on his desk, or the screens. Because what I saw on the screens was the fantasy. It was everything I'd come to expect from my favorite Korean bands. Moody, sensual, beautiful . . .

Junu nudged me with his elbow. "You're drooling."

"Am not!" But I swiped at my mouth, anyway. The last notes of the song drifted away, and I hadn't even noticed it was over. I'd just been lost in those dreamy eyes on the big screen. Junu snorted.

"Next!" A male's voice called. Down at the director's table, a young man stood facing the dark theater with a clipboard and a little light attached to it. "Kim Jung-woo?"

I gasped. "That's you! *Omo*! You're gonna be awesome!" I pushed at Junu as he climbed over me and out into the aisle. "Knock 'em dead!" I called out, a little too loudly, in English. A few voices from the dark theater snickered and I looked around, but I really couldn't see anyone. All I could see of Junu was a dark shadow moving down the steps.

"Coming!" he called.

I moved to the edge of my seat as Junu jogged down the steps toward the stage. "Break a leg!" I whisper-yelled a little late. I had no idea if Junu really was any good but I hoped he was! How embarrassing would it be if he was terrible? But how cool would it be to have a cousin who was an idol? And, ya know, maybe I could get discovered, too. When I looked a lot better than today, that is.

"Name?" the man down front asked as Junu swaggered onto the stage.

"Kim Jung-woo. But everyone calls me Junu." Man, he just oozed sex appeal. I was seriously impressed. The camera focused on him, and his image came to life on the screens. He looked pretty great to me, with his slightly crooked smile and this devil-may-care glint in his eyes.

A couple rows ahead of me a group of girls loudly whispered about how hot he was, and I smiled. Junu totally had this in the bag. But of course, I hadn't seen him sing or dance, yet.

"All right, Junu," the man said. "What have you prepared for us today? Let's start with the monologue."

Junu grinned wickedly. "You bet. I chose the, 'Why don't you like me?' scene from *Boys Over Flowers*."

"Whenever you're ready." The man's voice sounded bored, and I wondered how many auditions they'd had already today.

Junu took a moment to center himself, which I, and the girls in front of me, found to be adorable, then he looked up into the camera, an expression of confused vulnerability on his face. His emotions were so clear that I felt a stab to my heart that made me want to soothe away his worry. It didn't take me longer than four or five words before I had the scene pegged—it was the moment Gu Jun-pyo asked Geum Jan-di why she didn't like him. It was a big scene in the show because up until that point, Jun-pyo hadn't shown any feelings at all. You knew he had them, but he was so arrogant, so used to getting his own way that he'd never had to ask someone why they didn't like him. Because people always liked him— mainly because he was rich and powerful and they wanted stuff from him. But Jan-di wasn't like that, and it drove Jun-pyo crazy.

And Junu? He rocked it.

I felt like I was watching Lee Min Ho himself performing the role. No, it was even better than that—I felt like I was watching the real live Gu Jun-pyo.

The monologue was short, but supremely amazing, and I laughed a little when the audience girls sighed. I laughed because it had almost been me before I remembered Junu was my cousin. My freakin' cousin. But hey, I was allowed to be impressed by his skill and talent, right?

"And, it looks like you put down here that you'll do *Butterfly*?" the director asked.

"Yes, sir," Junu said. His grin widened in response to the tittering filtering through the auditorium from the unseen onlookers. The girls in front of me certainly liked the choice. He winked and the girls in front of me went all gaga.

Girls patted his face with powder and added eyeliner and whatever, instructed him to take his jacket off and then he was ready. He stood in front of the green screen, but on the monitors we saw a pink background with butterflies flitting around.

"And, go." The music began and Junu moved his body in the dance BTS did in their video. And man, he had moves! *Butterfly* was a slow song, very sensual, and so far, Junu looked like he could have actually been one of the BTS boys. The other guy had just stood and sung, he hadn't danced at all. I wondered if Junu was already doing better than him.

And then he started to sing.

Okay, I'll admit that I totally expected to not like his singing. I mean, he said he'd auditioned before, and he was so far great at everything so he had to be bad at something, right? But . . . he wasn't. He was totally awesome! He sang and danced that song like he was part of the group already.

When he finished his performance, the director had him pose for photographs. Did that mean they liked him? It didn't take long before the director thanked him and sent him on his way, saying they'd be in touch if they felt they could use him.

Junu swaggered up the steps toward me, occasionally waving at girls that whispered to him as he passed. The director called a break and the house lights came up slowly, letting our eyes adjust. The girls in front of me jumped to their feet and rushed Junu in the aisle, so I leaned on the seat in front of me and took in the sights.

My attention snagged on the director's table down front and I watched him and his assistant with curiosity. How cool would it be if he turned around and saw me— and asked me to star in his next show?

And then the director stood. He stretched his back and slowly turned around—looked directly at me.

My jaw fell open.

The director in charge of my cousin's future was Sang-hyeok, our not-so-friendly neighborhood vampire.

His mouth grew into a slow and sinister smile as he began to move toward the aisle, his eyes never leaving mine. *Omo*. He was coming to talk to me! Or kill me! Or something. I had to get out of there. I grabbed my bag and jumped into the aisle, reaching for Junu as I moved.

"Come on!" I cried as I grabbed his wrist. "We gotta go. *Now*."

"Easy," Junu said as if I was one of his fan girls. "No need to get pushy."

Over his shoulder, I saw Sang-hyeok getting nearer, that smile still stuck on his face and his eyes still glued to me. What was with this guy? Why didn't he just leave me alone?

I tugged on Junu's arm, but it was too late. The girls had noticed him and gone even more twitterpated at having the director approach them. Junu bowed slightly and mumbled something about it being an honor, but it was clear to everyone that Sang-hyeok was fixated on me as he ignored all of them and moved toward me.

He reached his hand out to me and with everyone staring on with rapt attention I had no choice but to let him clasp my hand in his. He turned my hand slightly and lightly stroked his thumb over the pulse at my wrist. He definitely had some gift that had to do with touching. There wasn't anything sexual in his touch, rather it felt demanding, as if he'd *take* something from me. My mind roiled with ways to get out of his little meet and greet without ruining Junu's chances of being selected for SM's academy. Gah! How did I find myself in these situations?

"Hello, little flower," Sang-hyeok said. "What is your name?"

Ah, so we were playing it like that, eh? I suppose it made sense. "Uh, hi," I stammered with my usual class. "I'm Kim Jung-Min." Again. Did he not believe me?

He quirked his head a little. "You're American." It wasn't a question, either, but for some reason it made his smile grow wider. I nodded dumbly. "Tell me how it is we have the remarkable gift of your presence in our fair country?" I resisted the urge to roll my eyes. Seriously?

I narrowed my eyes at him. So what if he was a big-time director. "I'm visiting my family for the summer." *You already know all about it,* I sent into his mind. His left eyebrow quirked upward and he tightened his grip on my hand.

I struggled to pull it from his grasp, but he resisted letting go—and then he did, lifting his rejected hand to run through his hair as if we hadn't just had a battle of the wills.

I gripped Junu's arm with both my hands. "This is my cousin, Junu. He just auditioned for you." Ugh. Of course he already knew that.

Sang-hyeok glanced at Junu, but didn't seem to care about him at first. He took a step toward me, then a strange look crossed his face, like something had just occurred to him. He turned to face Junu fully and grasped his hand. I watched as he shook it firmly, giving Junu a penetrating gaze. Junu blushed a little, which surprised me. He hadn't shown an inch of insecurity up until this moment.

"Junu," Sang-hyeok said. "It is a pleasure to meet you personally."

Junu bowed a little. "Thank you, sir. It is an honor to meet you."

Sang-hyeok inclined his head and slowly released Junu's hand. "You did well today."

"Thank you!" Junu beamed and the girls, who had multiplied in number, all laughed as if they were all Junu's best friends and his success was theirs as well.

"I expect we'll be meeting again, soon." Sang-hyeok said the words to Junu, but the way his gaze flicked to me as he turned away, I was positive he really meant them for me. And the promise definitely did not make me feel all warm and fuzzy like it did Junu. "Excuse me." Sang-hyeok walked through the crowd and out the doors just above us.

Everyone started jumping up and down and squealing their congratulations to Junu, but I hung back, partly because Junu seemed to be enjoying his moment of glory as every girl wanted a chance to hug him and take a selfie with him, and partly because—what the heck had just happened?

I didn't know what Sang-hyeok had planned but there was no way it was gonna be good.

Dear Philo,

How are you? I'm okay. Things are weird with my dad. Still. I thought things were going to be different, but they're not. If anything, it feels worse. I like Junu, and my aunt and uncle seem cool. Cooler than my parents, anyway. But I feel trapped here with Mom and Dad. I feel like they expect me to perform in some way and if I don't, I'll be fired from being their daughter.

I'm sorry. I didn't want to just complain.

So...What's going on with you? I know we're texting, but you wanted me to write, so here I am! Except I have no idea what to write. Do I have to? I don't think I'm any good at this.

Gah. I think I'll just text you instead.

CHAPTER TEN

"I CAN'T BELIEVE IT!" JUNU SAID FOR LIKE THE hundredth time. "Did you hear Mr. Lee? He liked me! I think he really liked me!"

"Totally." I'd already responded with all the happy things you'd expect and was getting pretty bored with the whole refrain. Not that I wasn't totally excited for him, but while Junu was replaying his moment with the *director*, I was replaying my moment with the *vampire*. Sang-hyeok had only talked to Junu because I made him, but I couldn't very well tell Junu that.

I stumbled to a stop as I peered at the number above the door on a narrow building. The sign in the window said, "Happy Fun Time Tours," but I was pretty sure this was the address of the vampire headquarters.

"Is this it?" I asked Junu, holding out the black card David had given me with the address printed on it in embossed silver.

Junu looked at the card, then up at the number, then up and down the street. "Yup!" His cheeks were still a ruddy pink from all his excitement and his eyes had an almost feverish gleam to them. I'd asked Junu if he'd ever met him before, but he said he hadn't. He didn't seem to recognize him at all. In fact, he only seemed to have a vague recollection of someone delivering a box to me, but none at all of how a scary vampire had practically threatened our family. Had Sang-hyeok compelled them to forget, or something?

Some vampires had the power to do that—but only the old ones. And of course, his gift wouldn't work on me, even if he'd tried. I supposed a gift like that would come in handy in the entertainment industry.

It took some effort, but I pushed thoughts of my evil nemesis to the back of my mind as I squared my shoulders and pushed open the door to Happy Fun Time Tours.

"Hello!" called a cheery, ancient woman from deeper inside the office. She rose from behind the desk and shuffled over to us, and I felt so bad because she was tiny and bent nearly in half with age. "Next tour not start for another hour. You wait?" she asked in broken English.

And then I shook her hand. This ancient old lady was a vampire. Her eyes were steely black as they focused on me and her formerly welcoming smile grew tight and a little predatory.

"Hi," I said as I forcefully pulled my hand from hers. What was with these Korean vampires and their handholding? "My name's Minnie Kim and I'm here on vacation. I was told this was where I needed to come and, um, register? I looked around at the posters on the wall depicting double-decker busses filled with smiling people, and beautiful scenic places around Korea. There wasn't a single thing in sight that would suggest this was the Korean council office. "I submitted my travel papers a month ago." The woman still hadn't moved or reacted to anything I'd said. "You should have it on record." I gestured lamely toward her desk.

I glanced at Junu, but he just shrugged. Not much help there. Maybe I was in the wrong place. After a too long minute of waiting for some kind of reaction from the little old lady, I opened my mouth. "I'm sorry, we must—"

"Come, sit down," the old lady barked. She turned swiftly on her heel and moved back to her desk with a lot less stoop and shuffle than she had when we first arrived.

I shot a glance at Junu who was soaking every little thing up with wide eyes all while he tried, and failed, to pretend to be reading a brochure. I wondered what he thought of this whole thing—not the fact that the vampire council was run out of a tour company, but about the whole vampire *thing*. He acted so cool and nonchalant about it, but was he really?

As I followed the old lady to her desk, I decided to treat this experience like a job interview, or an interview for college admissions. I'd be confident and intelligent and prove to this old vampire that I was an asset to their organization. I'd done it before as a human, why should now be any different?

I sat in one of the metal folding chairs facing her desk, conscious to sit all the way back, to show I was relaxed, but straight to show I was confident. I smiled at her dour expression. I reached into my backpack and pulled out my travel papers, along with a letter of recommendation from David, and my passport. No one had said she'd need to see my passport, but I'd brought it along just in case. I'd rather be overprepared than under, any day.

The lady took what I offered without a word. She hadn't told me her name, so I glanced around for a name plate or something but couldn't find one. I didn't like talking to people when I didn't know what to call them.

She abruptly tossed my passport back to me and nearly thwacked me in the face with it. "I no need that."

"I can speak Korean." I tried really hard to keep the annoyance out of my voice, I really did. But come on.

Throwing stuff at my face? Please. If she thought she was going to intimidate me that way, she was wrong. Tick me off, yes—intimidate me, no. I'd faced down Hashiki and her evil Maker Ying Yue—this little old lady didn't scare me. Much.

She gave me such a dubious glare that I wondered if she was doubting that I actually could speak Korean, or if she'd read my mind and believed she did scare me.

"Why you here?" she asked, still speaking in English.

The answer was right there on the travel papers, but whatever. "My family is visiting for the summer." I waved over my shoulder at Junu. "That's my cousin."

The lady narrowed her eyes at him. "Your sire's family?"

I frowned. She had to be able to tell that Junu was human—why was she talking about vampires in front of him? That didn't seem to be a very good idea. What if he didn't know? "No," I said simply.

She quirked her left eyebrow and I wondered what she meant by that. Gah! I felt my confidence slipping.

"You have made arrangements for your needs?" Again, with the questions that were already answered on the papers directly in front of her. Even upside down I could read the answers from where I sat.

"Yes."

"Who you contract with?"

I couldn't resist—I leaned forward and pointed to the answer written right there in Korean on her page. "I actually contracted with your preferred delivery service. I arrived the night before last and received my first delivery last night."

She frowned at the page—whether at the words written there or my finger, I didn't know. I withdrew my hand. She turned to her computer screen and began punching onto the keyboard with two gnarly index fingers, her frown deepening all the while.

"We sent delivery yesterday. You no sign for it." She looked at me as if I were lying. "You must always sign."

"Oh, well. My, uh—" *delivery driver*, I was gonna say, but there was no way SM's casting director was moonlighting as a delivery boy. "I didn't get an invoice."

She glared at me. "Always sign. We no tolerate hunting here." She put so much venom in her voice, as if I was trying to get out of taking deliveries just so I had an excuse to let the blood hunger drive me into a killing frenzy.

"Ew," I said. "I promise I won't do that. I've never even drunk from a human before. You can ask my Maker." My Maker wouldn't have a clue what I had or hadn't done, but for ease of communication I always just referred to David as my Maker.

"What about the delivery guy? He should know that he delivered to you. Maybe he just forgot to have you sign." Junu asked from behind me.

111

I threw him a glare—I did not want him getting in trouble from this nasty old lady—but then I realized he was right. I just didn't want him to hear what I said next. I leaned across the desk and lowered my voice to a point where human ears couldn't hear. "The man who brought me my delivery was Lee Sang-hyeok. He's the director or something over at SM Entertainment. He could vouch for me."

Her eyes grew wide but I couldn't tell if she was surprised that an important man like Sang-hyeok had delivered my order to me, or if she was surprised because I really had received a delivery like I said I had. Either way, once she got over her initial shock, she turned and began pecking at her keyboard again.

Finally, she turned slowly to face me. There was death in her expression and despite myself, I shrank back in my seat. "That not possible," she said loudly.

I didn't quite know what to say about that because it actually was possible because it really did happen. Grr!

"Why isn't it possible?" Junu stood right behind my shoulder now. I wondered if he knew the lady was a vampire, and if he'd speak to her with such confidence if he did know.

The lady didn't spare him a glance, but she answered his question. Eyes fixed on me the entire time. "Because he no member of the council."

Well, alrighty then. That was unexpected. "Aren't all vampires required to be members of the council?" The wizened old lady nodded slowly. I gulped. "What happens if they aren't?"

She stared at me so long and so hard that I began to squirm in my seat before she finally said, "They are hunted down and killed."

I swear I heard Junu's heart stop beating for a second there and the ghost of a smile flitted across the old lady's face.

"But it's *Lee Sang-hyeok*—important business man?"

I heard voices at the door a second before it swung open and a group of American women piled in, all talking at once. The old lady stood and smiled broadly at me before leaning over her desk and reaching out to shake my hand. "Enjoy your stay in Korea!" she exclaimed brightly. "Please come again, soon."

Then she came around her desk and sort of shooed me and Junu out of her way as she approached the gaggle of chatty women. Too stunned to ask or do anything but follow her lead, I nodded and smiled and allowed myself to get shuffled out the door.

Junu and I stood on the bright, noisy street, the humidity immediately making my lightweight T-shirt cling to me uncomfortably. "Well, that was . . ."

"Weird," Junu finished.

I flashed him a glance.

"What?" he asked.

"Is it? Weird, I mean?" I faced him more fully. "I mean, isn't all of it weird—not just . . ." I waved to indicate Happy Fun Time Tours behind me. "That?

"You're a human, and as far as I know you don't know any other vampires." Wait. Maybe he did. "Or do you?" I stepped closer. "'Cause you've taken to all of this pretty darn well, considering."

Junu grinned like the Cheshire cat but I frowned until he dropped the smile and took a step closer. "Look. It is weird. Vampires are real and living among us? Yeah, I'll admit I was as freaked as everyone else when they first came out. But—I've seen a lot of weird things. And ya know? It's more than just that, even."

He looked at the building behind us, then nodded his head in a *come-on* gesture and started walking. "I was in high school when the vampires in London came out and outed basically your whole race or whatever. Suddenly everyone was looking at the kids who were different or strange, and accusing them of being vampires. It was bad. Someone I knew even committed suicide."

"I guess they knew he wasn't a vampire, then."

Junu snorted. "Yeah. He wasn't a vampire—he was only gay."

"Oh." I could just picture it. As much as America had come a long way in accepting people with different sexual preferences and stuff, Korea totally had not. They were such an America-loving people, but they were definitely socially conservative.

"That's when I realized that it doesn't matter what you are—vampire, gay, straight, leprechaun—" We both laughed at that. "What matters is who you are. What you do with yourself. Are you a good person? Are you kind to people? That's what matters."

I danced around until I was walking backwards in front of him so I could grin at him. "That's exactly what I believe, too! It drives me crazy that people are always judging other people for stuff that's not even in their control. I mean, I didn't ask to be a vampire, but I am. It doesn't change *who* I am. I'm still me. And yet my parents, especially my dad, just can't get over it."

Junu offered me a fleeting smile, then glanced away. He had a secret, but he wasn't sure he should tell me—I could see it on his face. I thought about how easy it would be to just dip into his mind and find out for myself, but then I thought about how invaded I'd felt when Thor had violated my mind—no way did I want to do that to another person if I could help it. This was only my first day with Junu. We had all summer to get to know each other.

"I'm sorry about your dad," he said with a bump of his shoulder against mine. "If it's any consolation, my dad isn't too thrilled with what I am, either."

I laughed. "What you are? How could he be disappointed? You're handsome, totally talented—and you're going to school for computer programming, right? So, you must be smart, too."

He shrugged half-heartedly and didn't say anything. I knew I must be getting too close to whatever his secret was, so I let it go.

"So what are you gonna do about the ancestors? You said you needed to go to the library?" He'd stopped at the street corner, scanning the signs as if trying to decide which direction to go next.

"Well, about that," I started. I wasn't very good at keeping secrets and honestly, with what Junu had said and how cool he seemed to be about everything, I didn't see any point in keeping things from him. Plus, I could really use his help. I grinned up at him. "Is there a place we can get a drink or something? I've got something to tell you that's totally gonna blow your mind."

Things I think people should know
about vampires:

★ Making us hide and keep secrets
makes us feel like we need to
keep secrets

★ I think we should do a really
great documentary, showing the
life of a normal vampire. Not one
of those stupid mockumentaries
that have been going around.
Those just make things worse. The
council should make one.

★ Humans can be a lot more
accepting of us than we give
them credit for.

CHAPTER
ELEVEN

"SLOW MY MIND? THAT'S A BIG PROMISE," JUNU SAID. HE gestured toward the crosswalk and we started across along with what felt like half the population. My feeling of being an outsider was almost erased by my feeling of being a nobody since there were just so many people of all different nationalities that it felt like I could slip away and no one would notice.

Except for Junu, who was such a gentleman and kept a finger looped through mine as he plowed through the crowd. I didn't even bother answering him until we made it across the street.

"I'm pretty sure it's a promise I can deliver on." I grinned and enjoyed the look of pure curiosity on his face. "Where we going?"

"The perfect place," he said. "Come on. It's a bit of a hike."

I could tell the tourists around me thought I was a Korean citizen because they threw me curious glances and smiles and when I bumped into them, and said, "*Mianhaeyo*" in broken English. Even when I said "sorry" back to them in English, they didn't get the hint. I'm surprised all my gawking up at the tall, tall buildings didn't give me away as a tourist just like them. Or the way I stared at the Korean girls moving by me in chittery groups.

Junu grabbed my hand. "Come on, slow poke. I'm starving all of a sudden." I jogged to catch up to him, then followed him for a couple blocks as he led me away from downtown where the buildings got older and smaller. The air felt cleaner here and I took in a deep breath, relishing the fresh air. He took me into a neighborhood with small, crowded streets and little shops all crammed next to one another. When he drew me to an old glass door that just said *café* on it in peeling green paint, I threw him a dubious glance. We'd already passed a lot nicer looking places to eat.

"Seriously?"

"Trust me." He pushed through the door and suddenly the smell of noodles and herbs filled my nose— and the sound of birds. Hung from hooks all over the ceiling were a dozen bird cages, and no one seemed to mind the seeds that fell to the floor. At least none of the cages were suspended over the tables. "I know it looks a little shady, but this is who we sell our gourds to and they make the best noodles in the city. Promise."

I peered at the hand-painted menu on the plain white plaster wall and struggled to make sense of it. I'd kinda thought Junu would take me to a Starbucks or something—I'd never heard of Korean dishes like the ones listed here. And everyone was drinking bubble tea, which I'd heard of, but never tasted.

Junu glanced over his shoulder at me and frowned as he took in my expression. "Trust me to order for you?"

I nodded, a little shell-shocked. There weren't a ton of people in the café, but I felt more out of place in that moment than I had yet. And that was saying something. At least the noodles would be a good lead-in to tell Junu about the imugi living in his garden, so there was that.

In just a few minutes, Junu had a tray full of food while I carried two cups of bubble tea and followed him. I assumed we'd sit at one of the small tables in the room, but instead he used his back to push through the back door.

"Are we allowed to go out here?" There weren't any signs or anything saying there was additional seating, and it felt like we were going into someone's backyard or the back alley or something.

Junu just grinned that crooked grin I'd come to associate with his *trust me*. And once again, he did not disappoint. Behind the restaurant was a narrow piece of concrete with a concrete wall boxing the area in. But the owners had bamboo fencing laced with climbing vines in front of the wall, placed large potted pots of bamboo around the corners with statuary, and had even installed a large waterfall that cut out the sounds of the city. A handful of small round tables filled the space, but no one else was out here. It was still warm, but the café wasn't much cooler and near the fountain it felt really nice.

"This okay?" Junu asked as he placed our tray on the table in the far corner, closest to the fountain and near the wall.

"Are you kidding? This is amazing." I breathed deeply and felt all the tension I'd been holding the past few days drain out of me. "Wow." I sank into the wooden chair at the table. "This is how I imagined Korea to be."

"It's like this out in the country. And there's a few little sanctuaries like this scattered around the city, too."

"I wanna see them all!"

"You mean you don't want to see all the world-famous architecture? The shopping? The food district? You'd be happy just to visit little mom and pop shops like this?"

"I mean, I'd love to see all that stuff, but this feels . . . authentic to me, somehow. It speaks to my soul." I felt my cheeks warm and took a sip of my drink before I realized it was something I'd never tasted before. "Hey. This is surprisingly good!"

Junu rolled his eyes. "There's a reason they're so popular and it's not just because they have cute little balls in them." He set the plates out on the table and began to load food onto two empty plates. "And I get what you mean—I like it here too, for the same reason."

We shared a smile, then Junu handed me a plate. "And while we're being all authentic, I got you *onmyeon*. They have the best noodles and broth here. Dig in!"

I tasted the noodles first, since my family had sort of contributed to them. "Hey. These are good!"

Junu laughed and shook his head. "You say that a lot, you know. Like it's surprising that Koreans like to eat good-tasting things."

"Sorry. Mom cooks traditional Korean food, but mostly rice and veggies and fish. If we have noodles, they're ramen. When you said these were made from those weird snake-like gourds you guys grow, I wasn't at all sure they'd taste good. When I'm not at home, I eat American food. Or Chinese. American Chinese food. I'm pretty sure it's nothing like the real thing. Just like I'm realizing that Mom's Korean cooking isn't maybe so authentic anymore, either."

Junu grinned around a mouthful of food. "I'm just giving you a hard time. So what's this big mind-blowing thing you need to research at the library?" he asked. "The wait's killing me."

Too late to second-guess my decision to tell him everything. Except I wasn't sure where to start.

"Just spit it out. It'll get easier once you start talking about it." Junu stuffed another battered shrimp into his mouth and focused his attention on his food, which helped. I liked it better than having to watch his face as it morphed into disbelief once I told him what was going on.

"Okay." I took a breath and let it out slowly. "So . . . The other day I went up to your garden, just to check it out, ya know? And, um, this *imugi* attacked me and then made me promise to help him level up or whatever so he can move his pearl of power. He thinks that once we do that, the ancestors will no longer be drawn to the power and they'll be able to go back to rest." I pulled up a big clump of noodles and shoved them into my mouth.

Junu, meanwhile, had stopped chewing and was no longer looking at his food but staring at my face. Finally, he swallowed hard. It looked like it hurt. His eyebrows had risen practically to his hairline and he blinked several times before he spoke. "Well," he said. "That's one way to do it. Just . . ." he waved his hand in the air, "spitting it out like that."

"Well, you said—"

"Oh, I know what I said. But I didn't expect you were going to tell me I had a mythological *dragon*—"

"It's not a dragon—"

"—living in my rooftop garden."

"It's an *imugi*. But it wants to be a dragon."

"Uh-huh."

I sagged a little. "You don't believe me." I'd really convinced myself that he would get it and even though I'd dreaded telling him, I thought it would go better than this.

"Oh, I believe you. I'm just trying to wrap my head around the whole *imugi in my garden* thing." He continued to stare at me, chopsticks dangling from his fingers, his mouth hanging open. "And you say it's just living among the vines?" He wrinkled his forehead in thought. "There's not that much room up there. How can it be hiding a full-on *imugi*?"

"Well, he's not that big," I offered.

"He? It's a *he*? And, like, how big is it, exactly?"

I thought about it for a second, picturing Hanjo as he sat on my legs. "Um. I guess he's kinda like a boa constrictor. And," I held my hands up to the side of my face, "these ruffley things at the side and top of its head. He's kinda scary and not scary at the same time."

"Well if I met a giant snake, I'd probably think it was pretty scary," Junu said.

"Exactly!"

"Huh. And how come it revealed itself to you, but it's never, um, shown itself to me or my parents? You're the stranger—so why you?" There wasn't anything mean in his voice, no jealousy—just honest curiosity.

"I wondered that, too, but I think it has everything to do with me being a, um, vampire. He seemed to think I was after his pearl. So maybe only supernatural creatures want the pearls or something?"

"Wait. How do you know about this pearl thing? And how do you know what the *imugi* wants?"

"He told me."

Junu froze with his chopsticks in midair. His shrimp fell into his soup. "And how did he do that?" he asked in a low tone.

I fiddled with my cup, swirling it around so the tapioca pearls bounced around. "He talked to me in my mind."

Junu gulped. I really didn't want to tell him about my gift. *Please don't make me tell him about my gift!*

"Seriously?" he asked.

I nodded.

He took a long swig of his tea and shoveled more food into his mouth. Chewed, swallowed. "That's cool."

"That's it?" I nearly shouted. "Just 'that's cool'?"

He glanced up at me and shrugged. "I figure if I'm gonna believe you met an *imugi* on my rooftop, then I might as well believe all of it. Why quibble over the little things?"

"And mind reading is a little thing?"

He shrugged again, then set his chopsticks down and faced me. "I'm sitting with my cousin who recently became a vampire. The little old lady at Happy Fun Time Tours is a vampire. I live in an ancient land with myths and stories and the vampire is barely a blip in our mythological radar. I know firsthand our ancestors are haunting us because one night I saw our great-grandmother singing in the kitchen. If *gangshi* are real, and vampires are real—who am I to doubt that other creatures could be real, too. And their magical powers, or whatever."

Huh. When I found out that other supernatural creatures existed besides just vampires, it kinda blew my mind. Yet here was Junu, taking it all in stride. "You're amazing, ya know that?"

"So I've been told." He grinned wolfishly and finished off his food. "We had a super short section on mythology one year and they talked about the *imugi*."

I heaved an inward sigh of relief that he didn't push the mind-talking thing. "Maybe we don't need to go to the library, after all."

Junu shook his head. "Like I said, it was short. According to the stories, they don't all become dragons. Most die before they are a thousand years old. But I'm not sure the library's going to be your best resource."

"Hanjo told me he'd picked me to do some quests to help him level up since he's not a thousand years old yet. I thought I'd see if I can figure out what quests he needs to do."

Even while I was speaking, Junu was shaking his head. "If that's what you need to find out, you're definitely not going to find it in the library."

"I'm not?" My stomach dropped. "How am I gonna figure out how to help him, then?"

Junu started gathering up our empty dishes and putting them onto the tray. "I have an idea. Something better than a library. Hanjo, eh?"

I picked up our trash and put it in the can by the door, then followed him back into the café where he deposited our tray on the counter. "Yup. And better than a library?" Except for a really great internet search, nothing was better than a library. And I was pretty sure Google wouldn't have much to say on the topic of imugi quests.

"Yes. We don't need a library. We need a monk."

List of Supernatural Creatures
I've Seen or Know About

- ✔ Unicorns
- ✔ Faeries
- ✔ Tuath de danann
- ✔ Werewolves—haven't met one of those yet! (Or have I???)
- ✔ Imugis!!

CHAPTER
TWELVE

"CAN WE GO SEE THIS MONK NOW?"

Junu laughed and shook his head. "Nah. Master Yi belongs to the Saguksa temple in Eunpyeong-gu. We'll have to borrow Dad's car. It'll be a day trip—it's too late today to do it."

"Oh." It's not like I was expecting a quick fix to my problems, but I guess I was hoping for one.

Junu messed his palm over the top of my head, making me squeal and pull away from him. "I'll show you around, okay?"

I glared at him while I tried to fix my hair, but happily followed along.

We took the subway to Gangnam-gu, where Junu took me to the most extravagant and amazing mall I'd ever seen in my life. We could have spent all day there—they even had an aquarium! —but we finally made our way back home just as our parents were finishing their dinner.

"Where have you been?" Dad asked me with a frown.

Without second guessing myself, I squeezed him in a big hug. "We went to Junu's audition, then he took me to the COEX mall." I turned to my mom. "Oh my gosh Ma, it's amazing! You would love it. It was so, so cool! We definitely have to go there together sometime." Notice how I left out the part about going to the vampire council offices? Yeah, I didn't think my parents would appreciate that little detail. "Oh, and we went to this little café where Auntie and Uncle sell their squash and I had squash noodles! And they were actually really good!"

Auntie gave me an exasperated look. "Of course they were good. We grow the best tromboncino squash in the city." I wondered if Hanjo's precious pearl of power had anything to do with that. I sure hoped not because I didn't want their crop to suffer once we got Hanjo situated away from here.

Auntie and Uncle began talking about all that they did that day—it all sounded like pretty boring stuff with trips to various farms for some reason or another. I pulled out my phone to take a picture of them, because even though I thought their day sounded boring, all four of them seemed thrilled with their adventures and it was neat to see them happy and talking animatedly.

But when I woke up my phone, I realized I'd missed a text from Philo and I was immediately distracted. I hadn't heard the text come in at all and I was sad to have missed it.

Philo: I miss you.

My stomach dissolved into a bushel of butterflies or whatever a bunch of butterflies is. Philo wasn't exactly outgoing with his affections. Even though I no longer doubted that he cared for me, and we were *for sure* boyfriend/girlfriend, and had been for the past few months, it was like courting in the 18th century. Oh, there were some mighty delicious kisses, to be sure, and he held my hand and tenderly stroked my wrist as often as he could— but I could tell he was using a lot of restraint and care to not go too fast. Which I appreciated—but it drove me crazy at the same time.

So for him to say he missed me, just out of the blue— well, it felt like a major declaration of love. Not that I was saying Philo *loved* me or anything.

Me: I miss you too! Feel like taking an afternoon nap?

I added a wink and several sleeping emojis. It'd be early afternoon for Philo by the time I went to bed and that would be my earliest chance to connect with him. But Philo wasn't the kind of guy who usually took naps in the middle of the afternoon. I waited for what seemed like a long time for him to respond.

"Are you ready to set the ancestors to rest?" Dad asked, just as a text came in on my phone.

I couldn't take my eyes from Dad's serious face, but I so wanted to look at my phone. Plus, I didn't have anything to tell Dad today.

"You mean to tell me you played around all day and gave no thought to this serious matter?" Dad said. I frowned at him. *He* played around all day—why was this just my problem?

I opened my mouth to say something—I don't know what, but it probably wouldn't have earned me any points with Dad—when Junu jumped in.

"We learned of someone who could help Minnie and we have an appointment to go see him tomorrow." Junu grinned and snuck a piece of fish from his mom's plate, probably trying to offer up a distraction, but of course it didn't work. My dad was like a dog with a bone—he would not let up on this one bit until he got the answers he wanted.

"Who is this person and how can he help you?" Dad asked. And when I say *asked*, I really mean demanded— he could make a drill sergeant cry.

Junu blanched and this time it was my turn to do the saving. "It's a monk, Dad. He . . . has special knowledge about restless ancestors. I'm sure he'll be able to help us."

Dad frowned a little but he didn't say anything.

"Where is this monk?" Uncle asked.

"We have visited many temples and nothing they have offered has helped," Auntie added.

"Have you been to the Saguksa temple?" Junu asked, stuffing one of his dad's battered shrimp into his mouth.

"Saguksa!" Auntie said. "No one goes there anymore. Are you sure there's even a monk there? Maybe they just have groundskeepers now."

"There's a monk. His name is Master Yi. He's of the Jogye Order."

"Jogye," Auntie said with a nod. "Well that's all right, then."

"But you tell him that we have already tried everything—you know all we have done." From the way Uncle cast a furtive glance toward my dad, I wondered if he was always this stern or if he was putting it on for Dad's benefit.

The lights went out and Uncle and Auntie sighed.

"I know," Junu said. He turned his phone onto flashlight mode then lit the candle in the center of the table. As I took a book of matches from the table and helped Junu light the other candles, all four of our parents prostrated themselves on the floor.

"We honor you, blessed ancestors," Dad said. "We have brought our daughter from the dead to speak with you and offer you peace."

Wait. What?

The lights came on and the fire on my match burned down and stung me. I hissed from the pain and shook the match even though the flame was already out. Dad sat back, his hands on his thighs and regarded us with satisfaction. "This pleases them." Then to me he said, "You will go see this monk tomorrow and you will do all that he says."

Again, with the fate of everything on my shoulders. What was up with that? "Well, Junu's gonna help me."

Dad's steady gaze never left my face. Right. He expected me to do as he said, no matter what.

"Yes, Father." I began blowing out the candles.

"We're gonna need to borrow your car, Dad," Junu said with a lot more self-assurance than I felt.

I glanced over my shoulder at Uncle Jung-ho, who folded his arms over his chest.

"Saguksa's in Eunpyeong-gu. We need a car."

Uncle shook his head sharply. "That won't work. You can take your scooter. The both of you will fit."

Junu blanched. "My scooter! With the two of us on it, it'll barely go the speed limit. It'll take us forever."

Uncle's left eyebrow rose as if to say, 'so?' "And you expect us to stay home and do nothing all day? We need the car."

Junu glanced between the adults then finally sighed. "Fine. Can you at least please pay for gas? We're gonna go through a lot of it."

Dad reached into his back pocket and pulled out his bill fold. "I will pay. Here." He handed Junu a handful of won. "You keep my daughter safe."

"Yes, sir," Junu said. "Thank you, sir." He gave Dad a little bow and I smiled. Aw. Junu was so cute when he was being respectful.

Finally, I snuck a glance at my phone.

Philo: 10:00 your time?

Those butterflies floated up in my belly again, restless with excitement at the idea of seeing Philo tonight. Well, not exactly *seeing*, seeing, but pretty close. We'd practiced my mind-walking several times over the past couple months and I'd gotten pretty good at it. The hardest part was feeling relaxed enough to let my mind drift, but tonight, with my parents snoring on the bed beside me, I was gonna do it. I needed to see him. To feel his strong arms around me. To feel his hand stroking down my hair. I sighed.

"What's wrong with you?" Mom asked. "Are you sick? You are flushed. Come here, let me check you."

Oh. My. Gosh. Could this be any more embarrassing? "I'm fine, Mom. Seriously."

"Come here," she insisted.

So I slipped my phone in my pocket and shuffled over to her. I dutifully leaned down so she could place the back of her hand against my forehead, then listened to her tell me I was fine, that I should quit worrying and that I should have a rest. What I needed was some food. And not the human kind.

"Maybe I will take a little rest," I told her. I gave a little wave to everyone and slipped into Junu's room that I shared with Mom and Dad. I lay down on the cot and opened my text app.

Me: Sorry, was talking with family and it was hard to get away. 10 - I'll be there!

Philo: With bells on?

Me: huh?

Philo: Isn't that how the saying goes? Be there with bells on?

Me: Oh! LOL Yeah, that's how it goes. Idk I wasn't planning on any bells, but I could wear them if you want me to.

Oh my gosh. *Where is the undo button????*

Philo: Bells are too distracting. Just bring you.

I felt a hot burn inside my chest like I sometimes did when Philo looked at me in that certain way that I was positive meant he wanted to devour me—and not in a vampire kind of way. Since the dance, he'd been extra careful not to get too flirty with me, but every now and then there were these innuendos I was sure meant more than I thought they did.

I clutched the phone to my chest and thought about him and how much fun it would be to have him here with me. Well, not with my family necessarily, but to be on an adventure like this with him. I couldn't wait to tell him all about Hanjo and the monk—and about Sang-hyeok and all that weirdness.

I must have dozed off because the next thing I knew, Mom and Dad were talking quietly as they got ready for bed.

"It's okay. You don't have to worry about making noise. I'm awake."

"Shh," Mom said to me. "Go back to sleep."

"Sorry I missed everything." I couldn't imagine that I missed anything particularly interesting, but it seemed like the right thing to say.

Mom leaned over and brushed her fingertips against my forehead. "You needed rest. No need to worry. Go on and sleep now."

"Okay." I didn't bother getting up, just shucked off my shorts and bra and climbed under the covers. "Night, Mama. Night, Daddy."

"Goodnight, Minnie," Dad said. Did I imagine the love in those words?

Under the cover of my blanket I checked the time—10:15. Ah! I needed to hurry and get to Philo before he thought I'd forgotten him. Sometimes it took me a while to get the feel of the mind-walking right off the bat and I'd never tried to do it over anything close to this great a distance. But I settled down into my bed and closed my eyes, ready to give it my best shot.

Grateful I'd already had some sleep and wouldn't risk falling asleep, I settled into a light doze—the state of mind I'd discovered was the best for me to mind-walk. Not exactly sleep, just kinda in that lovely space between sleep and wakefulness where you're totally relaxed and you can let your mind wander, except you're still in control of where it's going.

I imagined myself at the big rock on the Aristos property back home. It was at the turning point of our morning jogging route and had somehow become my and Philo's "spot." We sometimes wandered into the meadow where Philo had first kissed me, but we always met here. Everything always started here.

Philo wasn't a mind-walker, so I was surprised when I heard someone walking down the path toward me. I always had to pull Philo in from his dreams. But he had been practicing his mind skills in an effort to see if he could expand them, so maybe he'd figured it out and wanted to surprise me.

I turned, excited to see my beautiful boyfriend striding toward me with his sexy swagger and secretive smile on his lush lips—and stumbled back instead.

"What are you doing here?" I folded my arms and glared at Thorstein Stringer.

He stalked toward me with none of his usual flirtatiousness. He marched right up to me and shocked me when he grabbed both my arms in his hands. Was he gonna kiss me? Murder me? Either way—*help!*

"You're in danger, Minnie. Ying Yue knows where you are and she's staked a claim on you."

Things I love about Philo:

- ♥ He lets me see a side of him he doesn't show anyone else

- ♥ He treats me as if I'm as smart as he is

- ♥ He respects me

- ♥ He treats me with respect

- ♥ He's a realllly good kisser

- ♥ He's kind

- ♥ He knows everything.

- ♥ He believes in me

CHAPTER
THIRTEEN

"WHAT?" I JERKED OUT OF THOR'S GRASP AND TOOK A step back from him. I bumped into the rock and nearly fell on my butt, but I did not take my eyes off Thor.

I didn't distrust him anymore. I mean yes, he'd pretty much proven whose side he was on when he saved me after Ying Yue's council sentenced me to death; but when he promised that he would be better for me than Philo ever could be, he'd made it clear he would not let me go easily. And yeah, Thor was hot and we had a lot in common, but seriously. No thank you. He felt like a player and I just didn't ever feel like I could 100% trust him. Plus, I had no interest in leaving Philo for anyone.

What Philo and I had together might not seem obvious to everyone else, but it was real. Maybe it wasn't perfect, but I could see myself being with Philo forever. Thor? Not even close.

Thor reached out a hand to steady me but I jumped out of his way, heedless of how stupid it made me look. I was pretty much used to looking like an idiot in front of all these immortals, anyway. Maybe by the time I was their age I'd have the smooth and graceful thing down, but until then, I was me and I wasn't about to start apologizing for that.

He smirked and stuck his hands into his pockets as he watched me stumble around. "It's nice to see you haven't changed." I glared at him. "Really, I enjoy your innocence and . . . humanity. It still clings to you as it did when I first met you. It's refreshing."

I rolled my eyes. Whatever. This was what Thor really saw in me that attracted him to me. He'd told me as much. *It's not you, Minnie, not you and your beauty and intelligence and wit. Oh no. It's your youth. Your newness. Your humanity.* To him, I was almost as good as having a human who also couldn't die and could indulge in his blood games. Ick.

"My offer still stands, you know." He took a step closer.

"Seriously? Don't you ever give up?"

He grinned wolfishly. "Now why would I want to do that?" Another step closer and this time I was trapped with the boulder at my back. "When you've lived as long as I have you develop wonderful patience. You also grow to be very clear on what you want. This isn't a passing thing for me, Minnie. When you tire of Philomon—and you will—let me know."

I rolled my eyes, but his confidence that I could ever tire of Philo made me uncomfortable. "Say what you came here to say, Thor. I'm busy."

He grew serious then and ran a hand through his thick, wavy blond hair. "Since she disappeared in February, I've kept my eye out for Ying Yue—for you, and for myself. We both have our reasons to stay off that creature's radar, yes?"

"Totally. And you found her? Have you reported her?" Whatever I thought of Thor's constant pushing me to pick him over Philo, we'd been through a lot together and I trusted that he wanted Ying Yue captured as much as I did.

"Until now, my intel was insubstantial—but what I learned today is too coincidental to be a coincidence. I believe she will finally be found this time."

"What is it?" I dreaded the answer. Felt it sink like a caustic stone in my gut making me nauseous.

"She is in South Korea. And so are you."

"Right," I croaked. "And—and what did you mean about the claim thing? What does that mean?"

"This I'm less sure of, but it fits—and with her turning up in Korea, well, it confirms it, I believe."

I threw up my hands. "Confirms what? Spill, Thorstein. You're driving me crazy."

He quirked me one of his sideways smiles that I'm sure worked on alllll the girls, then he grew serious again so quickly that it really drove home how serious he was. "I heard through some of my underground sources that Ying Yue has put a sort of bounty on your head. A place at her side to the vampire who brings you to her—alive."

"But the Master's named her an outlaw. What's the point of earning a place by her side if he's just going to kill her anyway?"

He stroked a gentle hand down my bare arm, seeming to notice my T-shirt for the first time. He smiled at the *never mind, find someone like you,* and lifted one brow as if to say, *oh but I think I have.* "Don't you think the Master would have found her and dealt with her by now if he really wanted to?"

"But—"

"He is our Maker. *The Maker.* And Ying Yue is an ancient, one of only a very few—do you really think he wants to kill her?"

"I—" I shook my head. "I don't—"

His eyes grew wide. "You don't know about this? About your own David?"

I frowned. "David. What does he have to do with this?" Belatedly I shrugged off his hand which he hadn't moved.

"What has Aristos been teaching you over there? Do you know nothing of your vampire heritage?" Thor seemed larger all of a sudden. Older. He was younger than Philo by a millennium but where Philo had found humility in his life, Thor still radiated Big and Powerful like it was his suit size.

"It was the end of the semester and there was a lot to do. I didn't have time to study anything other than school stuff." Why was I defending myself? I didn't owe Thor any explanations.

He shook his head and his expression said he did not approve of my life choices. "Your schooling isn't important anymore. You will have an eternity to learn everything you could ever want to know and more—if you survive. Your *survival* is what needs to be valued at this point. I can't believe he even let you go to another country without his protection. What was he thinking? Why didn't Philo go with you at least?"

"Hey. I wanted to be with my family, okay? I needed to be with them. David understood that. And Philo's got some work to do for the council this summer—it's not like he couldn't go do that, right? So, what do you know? You don't know anything about me or my clan."

Something flitted over his face then. Something sincere and vulnerable that was immediately replaced with something darker and more dangerous. "I know enough. I know you are young and naive and terribly inexperienced. I know one of the world's most powerful vampires has a claim on you and there are plenty of vampires who would be honored to stand at her side. I know *family* doesn't live forever but you could. I would never have let you out of my sight with you so unprotected and with such dangers at your door."

He'd invaded my space again and I'd let him as he caught me up in his proclamation of doom and gloom. He had a way of making me doubt things I thought I already knew. Surely David knew about the bounty on me? How come he hadn't been tracking Ying Yue? Why did he allow me to go to Korea without any protection or help from him? Did Philo know all of this, too? Did Thor really care about my safety more than he did?

While I stood there, my eyes locked on Thor's and trying desperately to work through all the information and doubts, he leaned in to kiss me.

That shook me out of my reverie.

I hauled back and slapped him so hard, welts showed almost immediately where each of my fingers had met his skin. "Don't. You. Dare," I ground out between clenched teeth. "I want you to leave. Get out of here. I didn't invite you!" I shoved at his chest and he took a step back, his eyes wide with surprise. "Get out!" I screamed. "Get out!"

And then he was gone.

I slumped onto the ground and cried my freaking eyes out.

A large, warm hand rested on my back and I knew immediately that Philo had come. I whirled around and leapt into his arms, burying my face into the crook of his neck. He held me against him, rocking slightly as he stroked my hair down my back. He didn't tell me to stop crying or that everything would be okay, and I loved that about him. He gave me time to feel and he trusted me to tell him what was wrong when I was ready.

After a moment he sat on the big rock and cradled me on his lap. He swiped at the tears on my cheeks with his thumb, and when I looked into his perfectly blue eyes, I saw so much compassion and love in them, I burst into tears all over again. He kissed my cheeks and rested his forehead against mine.

"What can I do?" he asked in a voice rough with emotion. I shook my head and swiped at my tears. I had to pull it together.

"I'm sorry." I pressed my fingers against my eyes, having caught a glimpse of the horror show my tears had created. "I keep forgetting about the friggin' tears."

Philo chuckled softly. "I purchased a few extra shirts and sweaters since meeting you."

"Because I keep crying all over you?"

He shrugged slightly and I buried my face against his chest, embarrassed but grateful for this kind man who cared enough for me to never complain when I ruined his clothes with my bloody tears.

"Will you tell me why you're crying?"

His words reminded me in a flash that this wasn't real life, but only a kind of dream—and Philo wasn't a mind-walker like me and Thor. "Wait. How are you here?"

Philo plucked at some hairs that had stuck to my wet cheeks, then swept my hair over my shoulder. I loved it when he did that. "I felt you near and assumed you would come get me, but when I felt your emotions, your anguish, I—well, I'm not sure how I did it, but suddenly I was here." I stared up into his eyes. Was it possible his feelings for me were strong enough that his gifts were magnified?

"I think my need to reach you was so great that it overcame the limitations of my ability." He smiled softly. I wanted to remember that smile forever.

"I've missed you." I ran my fingers through the hair that curled over his ear and felt myself melt a little more into his arms. His arms tightened around me and his eyes darkened with a smoldering expression I'd only seen a few other times. It made my stomach do a somersault and my heart beat faster. His eyes dropped to my lips and I licked them self-consciously.

Slowly, he lowered his head until his mouth was a breath away from mine. He looked deep into my eyes. "I've missed you, too, my Minnie Kim." And when he kissed me, I sighed into him. It felt like I'd found the other half of me and we were finally one.

Philo pulled back, and rubbed the side of his nose against mine, our foreheads touching. "What has you so sad?" he asked softly.

I took in a long, shaky breath and leaned back. "Ying Yue knows where I am and apparently, she's here in Seoul."

Philo searched my eyes for a moment. "And it was Thorstein who came here to tell you?"

I knew he must have seen the surprise that flickered over my face, but then I remembered that he'd claimed to smell or feel Thor's presence before when we had mind-walked together.

A muscle jumped in his jaw, and his eyes darkened— but it was not desire that shone in his eyes, but death. "Did he hurt you?" He trembled with controlled rage.

I placed my hand against his cheek. Pushing the memory of Thor's kiss far into the darkest recesses of my mind, I tried to reassure him. "No. Just scared me." That was true.

His arms tightened around me. "You believe him? About Ying Yue?"

My eyebrow ticked downward as I considered the question. I hadn't even thought to question whether Thor was telling me the truth. "I-I guess so. Do you think he's lying?"

Philo wove my hair through his fingers. "Not necessarily. Something's going on, because the Master has summoned me to Italy, and I believe it has to do with Hashiki. But David hasn't received any intel on Ying Yue's whereabouts, so I question how it is that Thorstein knows."

"So you have been searching for her? Tracking her?"

Philo seemed surprised at my reaction and I felt a little stab of regret for letting Thor make me doubt him or my family. "Of course. We haven't stopped looking for her since she disappeared. We will protect you." He held my face in his hands, his eyes imploring me to believe him. To trust him.

"But you're all there and I'm here." It was moments like this that I hated being a teenage girl. I heard the whine in my voice but felt powerless to stop it.

Philo smiled one of his delicious slow smiles and I couldn't help but smile back. "David may be selective about who he adds to our family, but his network is vast. From the moment you told him of the trip he has been making arrangements for your safety. You have to know that you are his and he will do everything in his power to protect you. As will I."

My heart thrilled at his words, but it still didn't stop me from saying, "But you're going to Italy." *Instead of coming here,* I added in my mind.

Philo sighed. "I cannot deny a command from the Master. I know you haven't yet had the experience, and

I hope you never will, of a summons from him, but there is no denying him. Truly. It's like a hook in my chest, tugging me toward him, and the longer I resist, the harder he pulls.

"But my hope is that since I am told Hashiki is lucid and she refuses to speak to anyone but me, that she will tell me something of Ying Yue's plans and I will be able to protect you in that way."

He kissed me softly on my lips. "I promise you that I will come to Korea just as soon as the Master releases me."

I kissed him back, then sighed. "Okay. Thank you."

His smile grew wide until the dimple on the left side of his cheek popped out. Oh, how I loved that smile. "I'll come as quickly as I can. I can't wait to see you."

"It's only been a few days." I glanced down at the buttons on his shirt and began fiddling with them, suddenly embarrassed to let him see my pleasure at his words.

He lifted my chin with his finger and his eyes twinkled at me. "It's already been too long. Besides, it's not so much the time apart as the distance. I don't like it."

"Me neither." I curled against him and sighed with happiness as he wrapped his arms around me. "When do you go?"

"In the morning. I hope I'll be done there within the week, and then I can come to Korea and see you."

I smiled against his chest. "I'd like that."

"I'm not sure what kind of cell service I will have there, but plan to hear from me no later than one week, okay? I'll find a way to reach you, regardless."

With his hands cupped warmly around my face, he kissed me. I put my hands on his chest, not to push him away, but to feel his heart beat beneath my palm. When I got home from Korea, or maybe even when he came to visit me, I'd tell him how I felt about him. How I *really* felt. I didn't want to freak him out or anything, but my feelings were real, and we promised we would always be honest and communicate with each other.

When he pulled back and rubbed his nose against mine, I sighed.

"One week," he said. Then he gave me a brilliant smile that filled me with love to my core, and he was gone.

Things I want to tell Philo when
      I see him again

♥ I love you

♥ I've never loved anyone before,
  and I know teenagers are
  famous for getting it wrong—
  but I don't think I'm wrong.
  I love you for all the right
  reasons.

♥ You're beautiful.

♥ I love your smile.

♥ I love you

CHAPTER FOURTEEN

THE NEXT DAY, I WOKE FEELING REFRESHED AND READY to kick some butt. So what if Ying Yue was looking for me? We always knew she would—that she'd surfaced was a good thing. It meant she'd be easier to track and easier to catch. Philo said David had people on it, and I trust him to protect me.

Which left me to take care of the business at hand—leveling up this *imugi* and relocating him and his pearl so my ancestors could go back to resting peacefully. Then, I could spend the rest of the summer with my parents and maybe Dad would love me again.

That was a little melodramatic, but it was what it was. I knew Dad loved me and I think he wanted to have me wholly back in his life, he just needed proof or something. Proof I wasn't a bad person, an evil *gangshi* or whatever. And he'd have his proof just as soon as we took care of the ancestor problem.

Which was a very real problem, I was reminded, when the shower went sub-arctic cold, immediately followed by center-of-the-sun hot. I leapt out of the shower, grateful I'd managed to rinse out my hair before the onslaught.

"Ancestors!" Junu called from outside the bathroom. "Guess they're anxious for us to put them to rest, too."

I hurried to dress and threw my soaking hair up into a bun. Apparently, we had a long drive ahead to get to Saguksa Temple, and Junu wanted to meet Hanjo first.

We climbed up the stairs and onto the balcony, the long green gourds gently swinging in the breeze. Junu was examining each one as if the *imugi* might jump out at him, but I had a feeling he'd stay hidden since he'd never shown himself to anyone before me. So far as I knew.

"Hanjo?" I called as I meandered around the balcony. "This is my cousin, Junu. He's gonna help me, uh, help you. But he'd like to meet you, if that's okay." I stopped and sat on the half-wall that wound around the rooftop and Junu came to sit beside me.

"How long do you think it'll take?" he asked.

"I have no idea. Maybe he won't even come out at all." But as soon as I'd said the words, I felt a presence in my mind.

Is it safe? Hanjo asked. *Will he truly help?*

It's totally safe, I promised. *I can't do this without Junu's help because I don't know my way around Korea.*

You must help me in order to help yourself.

I know that. And I will. The sooner you can show yourself, the quicker we can get on the road and see what we can do to help.

Junu was staring at me. "What?" I asked.

"You had this faraway look on your face. Is he talking to you?"

I opened my mouth to respond, when over Junu's shoulder I saw Hanjo's sinewy green body slithering down the framework of the garden trellis. I nodded toward the creature and Junu slowly turned to follow my gaze.

"Holy—"

"Guacamole," I hurried to fill in. It was a game Stacey and I played sometimes, replacing swear words with silly ones, but I suddenly felt like a goof for doing it with Junu. Maybe he wouldn't appreciate it. And maybe he didn't even notice, since a mythical dragon baby was crawling toward him.

Hanjo came right up to Junu, and rose up on his tail. With his long purple frills hanging from his head and chin it made him look like an old professor or something.

Is this him? he asked.

"Yup, this is Junu. Junu, this is Hanjo."

Junu whipped his head to me, then back to Hanjo. "Is he talking to you right now?"

"Sure is. Say hello, Junu."

"Uh, hello, Master Hanjo. It's, uh, a pleasure to meet you."

Hanjo snickered in my mind. *He doesn't seem very smart. Are you sure it is wise for him to assist you?*

He's totally smart! I answered through our mental link. *He's just never met a mythical creature before.*

Hanjo swung his gaze to me. *He's met you.*

"Ha!" I barked out. "Touché."

"What's going on?" Junu asked.

"Nothing. Just, um, supernatural humor. So, Hanjo. Is there anything you can tell us that will help you level up—I mean, become a full-on dragon? We're going to see a monk, but if you have any other advice, we're all ears."

Hanjo swayed side to side and I wondered if he was looking at our heads to see how many ears we had. *A human must complete the quests,* Hanjo supplied helpfully.

"A human has to do the quests," I repeated for Junu's benefit. "Do you know what the quests are?" I asked Hanjo.

The monk knows.

"Like, any monk will know the quests?" Wow, that would be weird, but I'd welcome the easy answer.

Hanjo swung his head from side to side.

"What'd he say?" Junu asked.

I frowned. "I dunno. He seems to think any monk would know, but I'm not so sure. So I guess going to see your monk is as good a place to start as any." I stood up and wiped off the back of my shorts. "Okey dokey, then. Might as well go see what there is to see!"

I wish you great success, brave warriors.

I turned back to stare at Hanjo. "Brave warriors? Are we gonna have to fight someone on this quest? Because Junu's just human."

"Hey," Junu objected.

But Hanjo was already slithering back to the shady garden and didn't answer me. Perfect.

We stopped in the apartment to pick up our backpacks and helmets. "That. Was. Crazy!" Junu exclaimed, dancing around and shaking me by the shoulders. "I can't believe I just met a freaking *imugi*!"

"I don't know if you should tell anyone," I said. "I mean sure, vampires are out of the closet, but do you really think the world is ready to find out that other supernatural creatures are real?"

Junu stopped stuffing a hoodie into his backpack and looked over his shoulder at me. "Other supernatural creatures are real?"

Shoot. I rolled my eyes. "Well *imugis* obviously are!" There. That was a good save, wasn't it? "Don't you think if they wanted the world to know about them, they'd make their presence known, rather than keeping themselves secret?"

A shadow of something like sadness or loneliness passed over Junu's face and again I wondered what was going on with him. Maybe we'd become good enough friends that he'd be able to trust me with it— whatever it was.

"Yeah, I get that." He finished with his bag and swung it onto his shoulder. He handed me my helmet, a bright yellow number with an emoji sticking its tongue out on the back. "Ready?"

I took the helmet and raised it like a toast. "Ready as I'll ever be!" And I thought it was a good thing I was pretty much immortal because the idea of riding on the back of Junu's scooter across Korea didn't fill me with a whole lot of confidence.

Far too long later I climbed off Junu's little blue scooter and stood on wobbly legs, trying desperately not to fall flat on my butt. And it already hurt too much for me to fall on it! My life had flashed before my eyes numerous times along the ride and even being a vampire didn't make me any less grateful to be standing on my own two feet. Just the thought of riding that thing back home made me nauseous.

"Woo!" Junu took off his helmet and shook out his hair. He looked gorgeous and exhilarated while I felt like something you'd scrape off the pavement. He set his helmet on the seat. "Come on!"

I took a deep breath as I carefully set my helmet down, and trudged after him. This first quest better be an easy one because I'm not sure I had it in me to do anything but lie down after that awful ride.

We'd parked at the end of a dead-end residential street with the largest single-dwelling homes I'd seen in Korea. We were kind of out in the country, but still I wondered what kind of people could live in houses like these, tucked behind their high gates. We followed the steps at the end of the street that led up into a beautiful green park with aged trees and long grass. It smelled so clean in the park compared to the air where Junu and his family lived. I took in a long, appreciative breath.

Junu gave me a funny look. "What?" I asked.

"Well, you're dead, right? I mean—didn't you have to die in order to become a vampire?"

His question didn't offend me. In fact, I was surprised he hadn't asked me about vampirism before. One day, I was going to help the world understand the truth about vampires so we didn't have to keep living under all this suspicion and bad information.

"I guess I died—but only for a second, like what might happen if you got zapped by a jolt of electricity, or you drown in a pool and are revived. I didn't see the light or go down a tunnel or anything. I didn't know I had died, at all. I just thought I was really, crazy sick."

"Did you hunger for blood right away? And how is it you can eat regular people food? I thought vamps couldn't." He threw me an apologetic glance, but I smiled brightly in return.

"I like that you're asking me questions. I wish more people would just come out and ask what they want to know instead of guessing or believing in the old horror movies or whatever. I mean, obviously I don't sparkle like Edward in the sunlight, so there's at least one vampire story that's got it all wrong." We laughed together and it felt so good. Junu was easy to talk to. He was just really great. I had no idea why his parents were so hard on him, because he was the total package. And why he didn't have a dozen girls swooning over him was beyond me.

"Anyway, our bodies still function and do all the same things that human bodies do, except our internal processes move a lot more slowly. Which is why you won't see me eat a ton of food—I don't need it, and my body would have a hard time dealing with it. But my heart still beats and blood still moves through my veins."

"But you have to drink blood to stay alive, right?"

"Yeah." I shrugged. "But it's all pretty well managed in this day and age. It's really no different than being on a special diet like Nutrisystem or something. I order what I want online, it comes delivered to my door, I eat or drink it. I can have cheat days, or I can eat a little regular food, but my main diet, if I want to be healthy and strong," I said with a cheesy flex of my puny bicep, "is blood."

He was quiet for a bit too long for my comfort. "Does that weird you out?"

He shook his head. "No. It's not that. I was thinking about Mr. Po Sang-hyeok. He's a vampire, isn't he?" I drew up short. He hadn't mentioned anything about it before, so I thought he hadn't realized Sang-hyeok's identity. I slowly nodded. "You guys seemed to have something going on—was that a vamp thing?"

I chewed on my bottom lip as I considered how to answer. I was pretty sure Sang-hyeok was a rogue, which was a weird thing considering he held a position of relative prominence in Seoul society, I guessed. And how he'd behaved—like some ninja warrior evil vampire one day, and suave, elegant human the next—kinda freaked me out. I had no idea which was the real Sang-hyeok, and that worried me. I didn't know what to expect from him, and that worried me, too.

"Min?" Junu pressed.

Ahead, I glimpsed something glimmering in the sunlight. "What's that?"

Junu followed my pointing finger. "The golden temple!" He picked up his pace and I followed, glad for the pause in our conversation.

A clearing opened with a path made of white crushed shells which led to a small, but brilliantly beautiful Buddhist temple, all dressed in gold. "Wow."

"Totally," Junu said.

"Welcome to Saguksa Temple."

Junu and I jumped and whirled around—and came face to face with a real honest-to-goodness Buddhist monk. "Can I help you?"

"Master Yi," Junu said, bowing low before the monk. I followed his actions; having never met a monk before I had no idea what else to do. "Do you remember me?"

Master Yi gripped Junu's shoulder and gave it a squeeze. "Young Junu. How could I forget?" The twinkle in his eye and sly smile suggested he'd helped Junu out of more than one jam in the past.

"This is my cousin, Jung-min." Junu reached back to pull me up beside him. "She's visiting for the summer from America."

"Ah, it's very nice to meet you, Jung-min," Master Yi said with another bow.

"It's nice to you meet you, too. Please, call me Minnie."

He grinned at my nickname. "Of course." He looked between me and Junu. "Let me show you the temple. I'm glad you brought her here, Junu. Not many tourists find their way here and it is truly one of Korea's treasures."

"Oh, um. I'm sure Minnie would love to see the temple, but, uh. We actually came to see you."

The monk had passed us and was walking toward the temple when he turned and faced us again. "Me? What can I help you with?"

Junu stepped forward and ran a hand through his hair. "We, um. Kinda need your help."

"You're not in any trouble, are you?"

"No, no. Nothing like that. It's just, you see . . . Our ancestors are restless and Minnie's dad thought maybe she could help and so they came here from America and—and we grow tromboncino squash on our rooftop—I might have told you about that before and—"

I put a hand on Junu's arm to save him the brain implosion that was about to happen if he kept talking.

"Master Yi, do you believe in the supernatural?"

He smiled knowingly. "To me it is not the supernatural, but the real world. The ancients have long accepted this, but the young world has forgotten."

I smiled at that. "You're probably right. Well, that makes this easier." I smiled brightly at Master Yi. He had that wonderful ageless quality many Asian men have, but I guessed he was well over fifty. "The other night, I met an *imugi* in Junu's garden and he asked that we help him level up to become a dragon. He thinks that once he can move his pearl away from Junu's place, the ancestors will finally rest in peace."

Master Yi stared at the ground for a long moment while Junu and I held our breath.

"Master Yi?" I pressed. Maybe I should have eased him into it more.

He looked up at me, then at Junu, his eyes shadowed and unreadable. He turned away from us and, after taking a few steps down the path said, "Come with me."

Check this out! So I was born in the year of the snake, and I just thought how weird it is that I was the one who met Hanjo—living among the snake gourds! Maybe it's nothing, but I just had this epiphany and I thought it was so weird and funny.

Also, snakes are considered to be really great mediators and good at doing business—so that should help me with the quests and my dad, right?

Let's hope...

CHAPTER
FIFTEEN

WE FOLLOWED MASTER YI AROUND THE TEMPLE AND behind it, where a beautiful Zen garden surrounded by potted flowers, small trees and stone benches made the outdoors feel as sacred as the temple itself.

"Come, sit." The monk, in his crimson and saffron robes, indicated two benches facing one another. Junu and I took the one on the right and Master Yi sat across from us. He smiled in a way that suggested he had things to say but didn't know where to start. As for me and Junu, we had no idea what to say next so we kept our mouths shut.

Master Yi put both hands on his knees and braced himself as he collected his thoughts. "Have both of you met this *imugi* of yours?" He looked questioningly at each of us and we nodded our heads. "Has he spoken to both of you?"

Junu shook his head.

"He speaks to me in my, um, mind," I said. I kind of cringed, thinking he'd definitely think I was crazy now, but he only nodded briefly.

"Because you are a vampire. That makes sense."

I think I might have blacked out a little. In an anime, they would have drawn me with x's over my eyes. "Yo-you know what I am?" I stuttered.

"Of course," he said, and he actually seemed a little affronted. Like how stupid did I think he was?

"And you're not afraid of me?"

"Should I be? You seem like a nice girl. A good girl. And I'm usually a good judge of character. Also, an *imugi* would never trust his quests to just anyone—they are extremely good judges of character. Much better than even me." He smiled at his own joke.

I snorted. "I'm pretty sure Hanjo's just using me. I don't think he thought too much of me."

"I wouldn't be so sure about that," Master Yi said with a knowing smile. "*Imugi* are notoriously cranky, so I wouldn't take his behavior personally. That he told you he had a *yeouiju* and gave you his name, speaks volumes. Trust me. If he had reason to doubt you in any way, you either would not have survived—physically or mentally—your encounter with him, or he simply would never have revealed himself to you."

"Huh." Maybe I'd misjudged the little dragon. Also—that he could have ruined me mentally? Yikes.

"Now. Tell me what is going on with your ancestors, and everything the *imugi* told you."

Junu picked up the story with the ancestors, telling how, for the past eight months or so, they'd become more and more restless. Shutting off electricity, messing with the cold and hot water, moaning and crying, shaking the building, affecting the temperature of the apartment, and stealing small objects.

Master Yi didn't interrupt, only nodded, and when Junu was finished, he simply turned his attention to me. So I told of how I'd met Hanjo, and how he suspected the ancestors were drawn from their rest by his pearl—the *yeouiju*.

When I finished, Master Yi stared out at the Zen garden for a moment before speaking. "I think your Hanjo—" he smiled at the word, as if it was a term of endearment, "may be right. At any rate, you do not want an item of such rare value so close to your home—it will only attract the wrong kind of attention and it could become dangerous, if not deadly, for your family and the others living in the building. So it is imperative we help Hanjo ascend. Failing that, we will have to relocate him, which he may not be willing to do. Once an *imugi* has secured his hiding spot—and it sounds as if he has remained well hidden for quite a long time—they are not easily persuaded to leave it."

I hadn't even considered failing, so his words were sobering. Junu and I shared a look that told me he felt the same. What did we know about leveling up dragons? Junu was the gamer in the group, I suppose he might know something, but still. We were pretty much noobs here.

"It has been many years since the monks have been asked to provide such a service, so I must meditate on this." He narrowed his eyes at us. "But you have come a long way, and I understand the urgency—perhaps more than you yourselves do."

Well that wasn't creepy at all.

"Did you bring a lunch? Perhaps you can enjoy a picnic on the grounds for an hour or two, and we can meet back here later? We shall see then, what I am able to do for you." He stood and Junu and I followed.

"That sounds good, thanks," Junu said, placing his palms together and bowing.

"Thank you so much," I added enthusiastically as I did my best to copy Junu. I was so relieved we didn't have to go back home empty handed. At the very least, we hadn't been laughed at or put off.

Master Yi must have read the relief in my expression because he smiled wide and patted me on my back. "You are still young—young in this human life and especially young in your eternal one. But you will come to learn, as you are beginning to see already, that the world is far larger than what mere humans perceive.

"Don't misunderstand, I myself am no more than a human. But knowledge of the ancestors has been passed down to me and shared among my brethren. We are no strangers to the truth of the world. It is a happy thing to meet such a one as you who has retained all the best parts of your humanity. That will serve you well in the long years ahead. Remember that, Minnie Kim."

This man filled me with all kinds of warm fuzzies and I wished I could hug him—but Korean men weren't really into that, and I had no idea what was appropriate with a monk, so I just smiled my thanks and hoped he understood just how much his words meant to me.

Junu and I spread out a small blanket he'd brought for just this very thing, and we laid out the lunch we had packed. There was everything from noodles to fish to snacks and chips—I'd even packed a couple blood puddings, though I stuffed them into my mouth while Junu had his back turned so he never knew they'd been there.

"I thought I heard you crying last night. Is everything okay?" Junu didn't look at me, and his statement and question left me speechless.

"Um."

"It's okay if you don't want to talk about it. I just wanted to let you know I was here, if you needed to talk."

Gosh. Now I felt like I had to say something so he'd know I appreciated his kindness. "I—"

His phone rang and he glanced at it, then widened his eyes. I heard his heartbeat accelerate so I leaned over to look at the caller ID. It was SM Entertainment.

"Answer it, you goof." I smacked him on the shoulder and he leaned away as he put the phone to his ear.

The conversation was brief but involved Junu making plans to return to the studio. "Well?" I asked, bouncing on my knees like a fangirl.

He smiled, still shell-shocked. "That was Sanghyeok himself. He asked me to return next week to film an audition for admittance to the academy."

"That's amazing! Wow!" I'm pretty sure I said a whole bunch of other exclamatory things—I mean, my cousin was gonna be a pop star!

"Isn't that what you already did at the audition yesterday?"

He shrugged. "That was just a screening. This will be for the admittance committee."

"Wow. You are amazing, you know that?"

Junu flopped back onto the ground and pillowed his head with his arms. "You'll come with me, right?" he asked after a minute or two.

I nudged his leg with my foot. "Of course!" But then I thought that maybe I was cramping his social life or something. "But if you want to take a friend, I'd totally understand. It's not like you have to babysit me all the time."

Junu was silent for so long this time that I began to wonder if he actually did resent me hanging around so much. What if he was just too nice a guy to tell me?

"It's not that," he finally said, but there was definitely a *but* coming. "But—"

My heart sank.

"See, the thing is, I don't have a lot of friends."

"Oh! That's no big deal. I don't have a lot of friends, either." I was so relieved he didn't hate hanging out with me. "Except I find it hard to believe you don't have a lot of friends. You're so cool and have everything going for you. I thought you'd be Mr. Popular."

He turned his head to look at me and grinned. "You think so?"

"Totally! You're the total package. I bet girls are throwing themselves at you all the time. Like the girls at the audition yesterday." Something about my words bugged him, because he put an arm over his eyes and didn't respond. "Right?" I prompted. Because I'd never been very good at leaving things well enough alone.

"It's true the girls used to come on to me a lot."

Ohhkay. "Used to? So did that bug the other guys or something? Is that why you don't have guy friends? Or did you have a bad breakup, or something?" *Shut up, Minnie. Shut. Up.* But it was like I couldn't help myself. I was digging that hole and by golly I was gonna dig it all the way to China, apparently.

Junu sighed. "I'm gay."

Oh. "Oh!" I furrowed my brow, trying to understand how that translated into *no friends*. "Is that it?"

He peered at me from beneath his arm. "Is that it?" The tone in his voice implied I was a stupid idiot and had just said the worst possible thing. "It's not easy to be gay, you know."

"I get it!" I flopped onto my back beside him, staring up at the large, fluffy clouds. "Honestly. It's not that big a deal. And I totally get what it's like to be different, that's for sure."

Junu shook his head. "Maybe it's okay to be gay in America, but it's not okay in Korea. I tried dating girls, but I just wanted to be their friend. I wanted to girl-talk with them, not sex them up."

I snorted. "Sex them up? Seriously?"

"You know what I mean."

I wasn't sure I did, but whatever.

"I had a friend in high school. I'd known him since elementary school and we'd always been friends. I liked him. I liked him a lot. I always believed he was like me—

I was *positive*. In my senior year of high school, I finally got up the nerve to ask him on a date—and he freaked out. Made sure the whole school knew I was gay. Told me I was messed up and abnormal and how could I have ever believed *he* was gay? That he was nothing like me."

The hurt in Junu's voice killed me. I fought back the tears that threatened to come because I didn't want to scare him, but if I could have, I would have cried with him. "I'm so sorry," I finally said, even though it felt lame and useless and too little in the face of such pain.

"Maybe he did like you, but hadn't admitted that he was gay, even to himself," I said. "Sometimes people get really angry when they're afraid." I sure knew a lot about that.

"I thought of that," Junu said. "Not at first. At first I was just so hurt, then angry, then sad and so so lonely. No one wanted to hang with me after that. Not the girls or the guys. I know there have to be other homosexuals out there, but in Korea—we're not out of the closet like you guys are. It's not safe to admit what you are."

"Do your parents know?"

Junu made a scoffing sound in the back of his throat. "No. They don't have a clue. Thankfully, they don't care too much about dating, so they don't push me. They push me to study hard. They want me to get all the best scores at school and get the best job and make the best money and then find the best wife." He laughed without humor.

"Won't they be surprised when the whole wife and family thing doesn't happen."

"Maybe you should move to the States. The distance might ease some of those demands, and they wouldn't be right there to judge your life choices."

Junu rolled onto his side with his head propped up so he could look at me. "I've thought of that. I can't imagine what it would be like to just . . . *be*. To be able to meet guys and be open about what I am. Except I love it here. I can't really picture myself living in America. I want to live here, to be close to my parents so I can take care of them when they need me. I just also want to be free to be me, ya know?"

I wanted to tell him how much I understood. How becoming a vampire wasn't something I chose but totally affected the way I lived and would live my life. I wanted to tell him I understood what it was like to be different from everyone else around you, to lose friends, and to be afraid to be yourself with your parents. I wanted to say all the words—but I didn't. I figured that I was the only other person besides that boy who Junu had ever told his secret to, and I didn't want him to think his feelings weren't special.

I rolled to face him. "I'm sorry, Junu."

He smiled and I felt a new connection between us. He seemed happier somehow, despite the sad topic, and I realized it probably felt so good to have someone in your life who you could be completely open with. I certainly couldn't imagine what it would have been like at school when I first became a vampire, if Stacey hadn't stayed by my side. Or if Philo hadn't come to school so I wouldn't be the only vamp there. Even now, things weren't a walk in the park.

"So you never said why you were crying."

I shrugged. "I just miss my boyfriend." It wasn't a lie, even if it wasn't the whole truth. Ying Yue and Thor were my problems, not Junu's. David's people would protect us, so the last thing I wanted to do was scare him for no good reason.

I just found out Junu is gay. I'm just...Just wow. So I had to have a minute to adjust to that. I think he should come to the States. I bet David would let him stay with us. I mean, maybe not for long. Not sure how that'd work out with a human in a houseful of vampires. Might not be the best situation. :/

OMG Junu's almost done his degree in something computers. Maybe he could work for David at one of his companies?? I'll have to find out more and see what I can do!

CHAPTER SIXTEEN

WE EVENTUALLY PACKED UP OUR THINGS AND WENT IN search of Master Yi. Junu said we should try to get back on the road before the after-work traffic kicked up and, considering the traffic "hadn't been bad" according to him on our way here, I definitely didn't want to see what kind of traffic concerned him.

But we couldn't find Master Yi anywhere. We waited around by the Zen garden for at least half an hour, and were about to head out to the scooter, when Master Yi came strolling out of the temple. Which we'd looked in at least five times.

"Forgive me. I was Skyping with several of my brethren and there were many opinions to be heard."

"You use Skype?" I asked before I could check myself.

"There is a reason why we monks have been around longer than most any other religious clergy. We remember the old ways while embracing the new." He seemed inordinately pleased with himself and I decided Master Yi was my favorite person ever.

"Let us sit."

We sat back down on the benches and I jiggled my leg as I waited rather impatiently for Master Yi to tell me what I needed to do for Hanjo.

"After some meditation and prayer, and a lively discussion with a few of the more knowledgeable members of my sect, I believe I know what you must do. Listen carefully, as I may only tell you this one time. There will be three quests. It is not a matter of whether you perceive the quests to be difficult or easy; it is only a matter of whether they represent the virtues a dragon must possess. Your *imugi*—Hanjo—has chosen you, Minnie, to be his representative, and so you must possess these virtues in order for Hanjo to ascend. Do you understand?"

"So, it's like I'm his proxy?"

Master Yi smiled. "Exactly. How you perform directly impacts Hanjo's success. Moreover, his quest for ascension can only be undertaken one time. If he has chosen his representative unwisely, and you fail, then he may not seek ascension again. Only until he has lived a thousand years may he become a dragon and properly possess the *yeouiju*.

180

"In truth, it is rather remarkable that he is in possession of one now. It's only a matter of time until a dragon comes to steal it from him—or some other creature. They are highly prized and incredibly rare." He shook his head as he contemplated just how surprising it was that Hanjo had one of these treasures.

"You will perform three quests. I will give you one quest today, and you will have twenty-four hours to complete it. Before your time has elapsed, you will return to me and, providing you have completed the quest, I will give you your next quest. Three days, three quests. Can you commit to this?"

I looked at Junu and he nodded. "We can do it."

Master Yi nodded, his gaze flicking between me and Junu. "Hanjo has entrusted his future to you, Minnie Kim. It is permissible for you to have a helper, an assistant if you will, but make no mistake—these quests are yours. *You* must be the one to do the lion share of the work. *You* must report when the quest is completed. Do you understand?"

Junu and I both nodded, but I added, "Yes. Thank you, Master Yi."

He grinned wide. "I am excited for you. You are about to embark on an adventure!"

Hope flared within me at the monk's enthusiasm. This was only my first week of vacation—if I could help

Hanjo, and removing the pearl would actually put my ancestors at ease, then I could have my father back in my life and a whole happy summer here to look forward to.

"Let's hear it!" I said excitedly. This was going to be awesome.

"Your first quest," Master Yi began, "is to climb Mount Jirisan and pluck a blooming *sansuyu* flower. Return, and bring the blossom to me."

I glanced at Junu. "Well that sounds easy enough! Mount Jirisan has roads and hiking trails and stuff, right? I saw it listed in one of our tourist brochures." So why did Junu have a pained expression on his face.

"But, the blooming season for the *sansuyu* has past," he said.

Oh.

Crap.

Master Yi only smiled as he stood. "Indeed." He turned and began walking toward the temple. "See you this time tomorrow afternoon, my young heroes."

After watching Master Yi's receding back for a few seconds, I whirled on Junu, bouncing on my toes with excitement. "Should we go now? I'm totally in if you are."

Junu looked to the left, up at the mountain rising above the park. He frowned. "No. It's—we need supplies. We need to be better prepared. We need a map and to plan where to go. We don't have enough time to make mistakes."

"But if we wait until tomorrow, we'll only have until like, mid-afternoon to report back to Master Yi."

"Come on," Junu said. "Let's get home so we can make a plan. We'll leave early in the morning. It'll be okay. I swear."

"You sure? I mean, I know you know more about . . . well, everything here. I just wanna make sure we can get it done."

"Getting to Mount Jirisan won't be hard. That's not the part I'm worried about. It's the whole flower business."

"Why? It's just a wildflower, isn't it? I saw there's a huge festival celebrating them earlier in the spring." I shoved the bright yellow helmet onto my head.

"Not a wildflower—it's the dogwood blossom, but they've already leafed out. The festival is in the spring. In case you hadn't noticed, it's summertime." Junu put the helmet on his head, muffling the last words.

"The festival only ended a month ago or something, right?" I swung my leg over the bike's seat behind him. He didn't answer, just turned on the bike. I had been feeling super hyped that our first quest seemed so easy, but as we drove back to our apartment, Junu's sour mood seeped into me and I realized flowers don't bloom past their season. That was against the laws of nature. Junu might not have said it in so many words but . . . we were totally screwed.

사랑해
💜

The next morning, while it was still practically dark outside, Junu dragged me out of the apartment and out to his bike. We'd packed food and water last night, and we didn't bother to shower before we left in the morning. It was just up and out in under five minutes. I think it was a record for me.

Junu said it would take about four hours to get to Mount Jirisan, which should give us a few hours in the park to search for a dogwood tree that still had some blossoms on it. I had a plastic container in my bag that should hold the flower without damaging any of its petals—if I could find one. Junu didn't think we would, but I had no choice but to hold out hope. I couldn't imagine Master Yi giving us a quest we couldn't complete. What would be the point in that?

"I'm just saying, if it were that easy to level up an *imugi*, the world would be full of dragons, right? Have you ever seen a dragon?" Junu said when we stopped to stretch our legs. They were his first words when he took off his helmet, as if no time at all had passed between our conversation last night and now.

"Let's not argue anymore." I hooked my arm through his and walked with him into the little house that doubled as a gas station and noodle house. Things were so different here in Korea. It was like living in the Wild West while also living in Utopia. Such a dichotomy of the old and new. "All we can do is try our best, right? Let's just go in with a positive attitude, with the expectation that we'll find what we're looking for—and maybe it'll come true."

"Aren't American's all into that? What do they call it? Manifesting?"

I laughed. "Yeah, I guess it's a popular belief. But there is scientific proof that suggests that if you expect something to be true, it's more likely to be true. Like, did you know that if you were playing on a game show where you had to choose between say, doors 1, 2, and 3—that if you always went with your first instinct, you're far more likely to win, than if you second-guess yourself? I can't remember the exact statistic, but it's significant."

Junu ordered us each a couple bowls of noodles and two cups of tea, then he rolled his eyes at me. "That can't be true."

"It is. I swear. You can look it up if you want to. Anyway, my point is, there's no harm in us trying. And expecting a bad outcome is only going to make us have a bad day. I'd rather have a great day and fail, than have a bad day and fail. That would be like adding insult to injury. Wouldn't you?"

The lady brought our food to one of two tiny tables in front of the windows and Junu and I sat down. He sighed. "I guess you're right."

I scooped up soup onto my spoon and slurped noisily—that was one Asian custom I wholeheartedly embraced. The joy of slurping. "Is there something else bugging you? You seem a lot more upset than just being discouraged about the likelihood of us finding a blooming dogwood tree."

Junu used his chopsticks to pull up some noodles and slurped them into his mouth. His chin glistened with broth, but I tried not to be grossed out by it. In Korea, that was totally normal. All part of the slurping. Which I embraced. When he finished chewing, he set down his chopsticks beside his bowl. "I don't know. I guess just after our talk yesterday I've been feeling sorry for myself."

"You mean about the—"

He flicked some broth at me. "Don't say it out loud." He glared at me. "Yes, that. You said you miss your boyfriend, well I miss having one. I've never had one. I'm a romantic, I want a relationship, ya know?"

I nodded. I wasn't much of a romantic, but Stacey sure was. I was happy being alone and being on my own—but having Mack had really helped her feel more complete.

"Maybe I should consider going to America." He sighed again and lifted his bowl to his mouth to drink some broth. He set the bowl down and wiped his mouth and chin with a paper napkin. "But it's more than that, too. I'm worried that Sang-hyeok will find out that I'm . . . you know . . . and he won't admit me to the Academy. There haven't been any, um—"

"Redheads," I said.

"What?"

"You were about to say that there hadn't been any redheads who became idols, right?" I looked at him meaningfully.

A quick grin flashed over his features. "Right! No redheads. There's this one guy who's gotten a lot of attention on You Tube, but the studios didn't like him because he was, um, a redhead." His cheeks flushed pink and it was the cutest thing ever.

"Why would he find out?" I asked, referring to his worry about Sang-hyeok. "Does he have to find out?"

"Well, I'd have to spend a lot of time with girls. I'd have to get a girlfriend and show myself to be desirable and all that. You know? And I'm just not sure I can do it anymore. Live a lie like that. I am who I am, ya know?"

I leaned forward onto my elbows. "That's exactly how I feel about being a redhead."

Junu's mouth fell open. "Wait. You're ga—a redhead? But I thought you had a boyfriend?"

I rolled my eyes. "No, you dork. Not *that* kind of redhead." I tapped my teeth with my fingernail and his eyes grew round with understanding.

"Oh," he breathed. "Sorry. For a minute there I was completely confused. But what do you mean that you feel the same way as me?"

I swirled the noodles around in my soup with my chopsticks. I wasn't really used to having soup for breakfast and my stomach was rebelling. "One day I was one thing—me, normal—and life was good. Life was normal. Then the next day I was a . . . a redhead. And everyone freaked out. Even my best friend's mom, who's practically been a second mom to me, forbid her from hanging out with me—at least at first.

"I hadn't changed. I was still the same inside, ya know? It was just my-my *hair color* that had changed. So I was a redhead now. It's not like I stopped being me. I've managed to keep a lot of things the same in my life, but I had to work hard to make it happen. But there are a few things," *like drama class*, I thought with regret, "that are gone, and it makes me really sad. And even at the end of the school year I was still getting picked on by some people. Kids can be so mean."

Junu hadn't taken his eyes off me the entire time I talked. "I'm sorry," he said. "I didn't realize. I guess I didn't think of it that way. That we'd have that in common."

"Oh, I'm not trying to say I understand—"

Junu knocked his knuckles against my forehead. "I think you do. More than I realized. It helps hearing about your story. Because you're exactly right. *I'm* still the same me. The things that girls and guys liked about me before I, um, dyed my hair—" I snorted and Junu laughed with me. "You know, they're the same. People could still like those same things. The only thing that's changed is that now they *know* I'm a redhead."

We were laughing now, and he'd barely been able to finish talking without cracking up. It was a serious thing, but man it felt good to talk—and to laugh!—about it.

"Come on, Red." I stood up and started piling our items onto the little tray they'd been brought out on. "Let's go a-questin'."

Junu hooked his arm around my neck and we were both smiling as we walked out to his tiny little scooter. The sun peeked out from behind the fog that seemed to hang over the country every morning and I soaked it in as if it were a blessing from above. We were gonna find that darn *sansuyu* flower, by golly.

3 ♥ Quests to complete
♥ Days to get 'er done
♥ Days I've been here

∞ ♥ Ways my life has changed
♥ Mysteries in this world!

CHAPTER SEVENTEEN

AT THE JIRISAN NATIONAL PARK VISITORS CENTER, THE road and parking area were packed with buses coming and going. And tourists everywhere. Like, ev-er-y-where.

"Good thing we've got a bike," Junu said after he'd parked the scooter in a narrow space that may or may not have been intended for parking. It certainly wasn't big enough for anything larger than the scooter.

"No kidding. Is it always this busy?"

Junu shrugged. "It's the largest mountain in South Korea, so yeah. It's popular." He reached out for my helmet, and this time slid a bike lock through both our helmets and locked them to the bike. "Ready?"

"Sure!"

An information board had a picture of the *sansuyu* flower so I stopped to look at it. It didn't tell me anything

I didn't know, though. The Korean dogwood tree produced various colored blossoms, but those on Mount Jirisan only bloomed yellow. The *sansuyu* flower festival was in the spring when all the trees were in bloom. Blah blah blah. I looked around at all the dogwood trees—and not a blossom among them.

Of course I didn't say anything. It was far too early to admit defeat and Junu would probably jump at a chance to go back into his Dougy Downer routine. Plus, we knew our best chance at finding a blossom was at a higher elevation where the climate might be a little cooler.

We hiked for an hour before the crowds started to thin and I finally felt like I had some elbow room. "Should we go off the trail? Would that help, do you think?" I asked Junu. "We've only got like another hour before we have to turn around if we're gonna make it to the temple in time."

"I don't know if it'll help, and we might get lost. Let's just keep climbing as quickly as we can. I think we've got time for a little more before we turn around. We'll make faster progress going down, anyway."

If I used my vampire speed, I could run ahead, cover twice the distance, but I also wasn't sure if I'd be able to see any blossoms if I went that fast. This quest was starting to feel hopeless.

"Do you think Master Yi knows for sure there is a blossom here somewhere? Or did he just come up with a quest from thin air? What if there aren't any flowers anywhere and the quest is literally impossible?"

Junu didn't stop scanning the trees while we walked. "If it was anyone other than Master Yi, I'd wonder about it, but I do trust him. I have no idea how he'd know if there were any flowers out here, though. Then again, Master Yi just knows things sometimes. I don't know how—I've never questioned him about it. But when I visited him before, he said some things there's no way he could have known. Besides," he looked over his shoulder toward me, "do we have any choice?"

I shook my head. "Nope. Do you think he has magic of some kind?"

"I think he talks to the ancestors, for sure. And maybe Zen masters have access to even more than that. The universe. Ya know? We should turn around at the falls. That'll be about the right time to start back."

I sighed and sharpened my eye on all the branches around me, seeking out anything that flashed yellow. Nothing.

Eventually, a rushing sound filled my ears and I noticed several of the tourists pick up their pace as they chatted excitedly together. After a long up and down, up and down path, the trail suddenly began to decline rather steeply, but as soon as we rounded the bend, I felt the cool air wafting up to me. from the waterfall below. Before me spread a vista of green, rock and glimpses of white, foaming water.

I stopped dead in my tracks, just taking it all in.

"Pretty, isn't it?" Junu asked as he stopped beside me.

"It really is." And it was. But there was something else, too. I didn't mention it because I couldn't quite put my finger on it. I just felt . . . a feeling of destiny. Of rightness. Something inside me whispered, *here*. Such a weird feeling.

"You okay?" Junu nudged me with his elbow.

"Yeah." I made a point of looking around, as if searching for a blossom—which I was, but it was more a cover for the weird feeling that grew stronger every moment we stood there.

"Come on." Junu started down the trail.

I followed behind him at a distance, trying to figure out the feeling, to see if it would guide me, but it didn't seem to do anything helpful. I caught up to Junu at the top of the waterfall where he leaned against the guardrail. It was significantly cooler here by the falls, but I still didn't see any blossoms. My heart sank as I realized this was our best chance and we still hadn't found anything.

"What's that down there?" I pointed toward the bottom of the falls where a pile of rocks seemed to shape a crude little house.

"A hermitage—like a little hideout. A monk from a long time ago lived there seeking enlightenment. The falls are named after him."

"Inner enlightenment, eh?" I could sure use some of that right then. I wandered away from Junu, peering at the trees and trying to reconcile the feeling inside that told me we were in the right place to find what we needed. *But where?* I stopped at the guardrail a short distance from Junu and closed my eyes. Who cared what I looked like? I was out of time and I needed to finish this quest. I pressed my palms together and sought inner quiet.

It took a long time.

After I finally quieted the voices that told me I'd failed, I pondered Thor's warning, followed by a few calculations of the probability of finding a dogwood tree still in bloom. Once I'd concluded the chances were pretty much slim to none, my mind finally went quiet.

And there, highlighted in my mind's eye, was a single blossom clinging to the end of a delicate branch.

I opened my eyes, still in that Zen-like state of peace, and cast my eyes about for the blossom I now knew, with absolute confidence, existed somewhere nearby.

At first I didn't see it. Tree branches bounced and swayed in the breeze, confusing the view and making it hard to examine every branch within my sight. Sunlight cut through the cloud cover and a beam cut through the trees and lit up over the falls—and highlighted a single blossom at the end of a long, slender branch.

I whooped loudly and shouted for Junu—making the tourists around me scatter as if I'd just announced I had a gun.

"What? What is it?" Junu jogged toward me, his eyes flicking from side to side as if he'd save me from some advancing foe.

I slugged him on the shoulder. "I'm the redhead here, remember. I don't need you to save me, goof." I took him by the shoulders and manually turned him in the direction of the magical, miraculous bloom. Grabbing his hand, I folded his fingers so his index finger was extended and, peeking over his shoulder, aimed it at the last, solitary flower.

"We did it? We did it!" Junu whipped around and high-fived me, and we followed it up with a bizarre happy dance that made my heart swell and scared more tourists. People just didn't know how to have fun anymore.

We rushed over to the guardrail to get a better look at the flower and how we could get it—when reality landed like a bomb on our happy little party.

"Min, there's no way we can get to that freaking flower."

The tree must have been an old one. It had a twisted, curved trunk and it seemed to barely hang on to the rocks as it leaned out over the rushing waterfall. How did it even survive with so many of its roots exposed as they climbed over the boulders and rocks? All its branches reached out over the water as if trying to grab the other side, and on one slender branch that reached the furthest, a tiny golden flower sat.

Junu was right. The flower was unreachable. Not only was it clinging to a branch extended far out over the rushing water, but the branch was narrow and weak. Flimsy. No way would it hold my weight if I tried to climb on it.

We leaned against the guardrail, staring at the flower, thinking about what we were going to do now that our quest was a total fail. After a while, Junu looked at his phone, then tucked it back into his pocket.

"We've gotta go, Min."

"Why does it matter? We're gonna be going back empty handed, anyway."

Junu put his arm around my shoulders and tugged me to his side. "Maybe when we tell him what happened, he'll give us another quest. He only said he wouldn't repeat the quests, not that we couldn't get another one if we failed one."

I leaned back to look up at him. "Now who's being the optimistic one?" He grinned, but I saw the truth in his eyes. He didn't believe what he said. And neither did I.

Master Yi wouldn't be giving me another quest. If we failed this one, there wouldn't be any more. The whole thing would be over. Hanjo wouldn't be leveling up, the ancestors wouldn't go back to sleep, and if Master Yi was right, there could be worse and more dangerous things coming my family's way. I could try to protect them, but nothing I did would solve the ancestor problem and my father wouldn't forgive me for that.

Was I ready to just give up? To disappoint my dad again and risk never proving to him that I had value in our family? If I could send the ancestors back to their rest, Dad would see it as their approval of me, their acceptance. If the ancestors trusted me and listened to me, then I couldn't possibly be the evil monster Dad thought I was. It didn't matter if that's how it really was. It didn't matter if I really fixed the problem by helping a baby dragon. What mattered was what my father *believed*.

Could I live forever knowing he believed I was a monster? Knowing I hadn't done every single thing in my power to convince him otherwise?

I stripped off my backpack and set it on the ground at Junu's feet. Then I hopped over the guardrail.

"Minnie—wait! What are you doing?" Junu called.

"I got this, Red. Just—meet me at the bottom."

"What? Are you crazy?"

Probably. But I was a *committed* kind of crazy.

I picked my way down the steep incline, carefully choosing each spot to set down my feet so I didn't twist my ankle or anything. There were so many tumbled rocks, exposed roots and all of it covered with layers of dead leaves from years past. Even with the extra care, there was no way Junu could have kept up with me and my vampire speed. A quick glance showed me he was tracking my progress, but from the safety of the path. *Good.*

I reached the tree and stopped to consider my options. I moved around to the side that clung to the rocks. The water roared past as it hurried to the bottom of the mountain, the cold water spraying me with a fine mist. It was refreshing and beautiful, and terrifying. There was so much power in that onslaught of water that I wasn't sure if even I would be safe from its punishing power should I fall in. I reached up and tested the branch holding the flower. It was young and far too flexible to hold my weight, just as I'd expected. The branch above it, however, might work.

I began to climb, careful not to jostle the young limb too much. I didn't want to take the chance of shaking the branch and having the blossom fall off on its own. I made the higher branch and lay down along its length. If I could just scoot forward, I should be able to reach down and pluck the flower. Closer and closer I crawled, but the flower was still out of my reach. It felt like one of those optical illusions, like that scene in *Jurassic Park* where the T-rex is barreling down on the Jeep and it looks really close in the side view mirror, but you have that ironic moment where the mirror says *Objects may be closer than they appear*. Except in this case, the flower was further away than it appeared.

The branch I clung to groaned. And then cracked.

Omo.

I stretched out for the flower. Why couldn't I reach it?

The branch cracked again and this time I dropped with it as the bark and outer layers broke away. I was out of time. I had to grab that flower and get back to the shore before my branch dumped me into the torrent of water. I stretched out as far as I could go. Why did I have to be so short?

The branch cracked again, but I could barely hear it over the rush of the water. I had to be hanging on by just a few stubborn bits of wood. It was now or never. As the branch broke, I leap-frogged forward, my hand outstretched for the flower. My trajectory was on target, and I hoped that I could use the flexible branch and my momentum to Tarzan it back to the rocky mountainside.

Yeah. I was so not Tarzan material.

My palm scraped across the branch as I grasped for the blossom, and I felt *something* come away in my hand, but I had no way of knowing if it was the *right* thing.

And my Tarzan plan? It was never meant to be.

I flailed like a maniac, as if kicking and screaming would bring me closer to the shore as I plunged in an awkward, belated cannonball into the cascading water. All I could do was clutch the maybe-flower between both my palms and hold it against my chest as I was crushed by the water and shoved back and forth, tumbled end over end.

I offered the ancestors my gratitude that I didn't need to breathe, held onto that maybe-flower, and prayed that I'd survive the longest and most terrifying fall of my life.

CHAPTER EIGHTEEN

THE THING IS, THE ANCESTORS WOULD HAVE HAUNTED my family whether or not I was a vampire. Hanjo lived on their roof, and the *yeouiju* had fallen onto it. That's what drew the ancestors. It was a series of events that had absolutely nothing to do with me.

But if I hadn't been a vampire, there's no possible way I could have survived that fall.

I lay in a sodden mess of leaves and foam, the water pushing me painfully against the rocks. I was alive. Well, sorta alive, anyway.

The question was—*Did I get the flower?*

I still clutched my hands to my chest, and I felt something between them, but I still had no idea what it was, or if it was undamaged. Right then, all I cared about was that I was breathing, and my body was gradually healing itself from the sprains and bruises it had suffered during its terrible mistreatment. At least I was no longer falling. At least I was somewhat out of the downpour, as I had washed up on the rocky shore near the hermitage.

I lifted my hands to my face and cracked open my clasped hands to see what lay inside.

"Yes!" I yelled into the deafening downpour. Cradled beneath my palms, in perfect form and beauty, lay the very last *sansuyu* flower of the season. I'd done it! Now to get out of here and back to Master Yi before our time ran out.

With clumsy care, I rose to my feet and only then realized I was in full view of everyone gathered along the guardrail. And people were shouting. And other people were hurrying across the rocky shore toward me. People who looked suspiciously like police.

Still clutching my palms to my chest, I faced the men and tried to smile and not look, well, like a crazy drowned rat but something . . . else.

"Excuse me! Excuse me!" Junu called from behind the police.

"What were you thinking?" the first officer who approached me asked. He took my arm and sort of shook it while he scanned me. I refused to budge my hold on my precious cargo and he frowned at my immovability. "Are you hurt? You must need to go to the hospital."

"I'm fine," I said. "Really."

"Excuse me, officers," Junu said, barging in between the trio who'd approached me. His hair was extra mussed and he'd rolled up his jacket sleeves. He draped his arm over my shoulders and sort of sagged against me.

"What are you doing?" I whispered.

"Just follow my lead."

Holy guacamole. This was not going to end well.

"Officers, officers," Junu said in a placating tone. "I'm Sehun, I'm sure you've heard of me? I'm part of EXO—the world-famous boy band? And this is my girlfriend, Jung-min. Isn't she beautiful?" He kissed me on my temple. "SM Entertainment sent us out to create some buzz for our upcoming single and I caught everything on video." He held up his phone. "The fans are gonna go crazy for this. Beautiful girl, beautiful scenery—and your heroic rescue." He nodded at the men as if he could compel them to believe his ridiculous story.

"You're in EXO?" one of the men asked.

Junu leaned forward. "Don't tell anyone you saw me, okay? The last thing I want is to get mobbed by all the tourists. We're just trying to lay low, ya know?" He started walking me past them and upward toward the pathway out of here. "Sorry for all the trouble. But no harm, no foul, right?"

And we just walked out of there.

"What the—How in the world?" I whirled on Junu as soon as we were out of sight of the falls. "How did that even work?"

He smirked at me and gave me his best impression of a boy band idol.

"Oh my gosh. You really do look like him!"

"Koreans love their idols. Even the adults, no matter what they say. Those guys'll be more excited to tell their wives and children that they saw Sehun today and pulled his girlfriend from the water, than reporting us for trespassing and reckless endangerment." He whirled on me, his expression stern. "And it was reckless. What were you thinking?"

I grinned and held out my hands, palms up, the shimmering little flower catching sunshine in its petals.

"You got it?" Awe filled his eyes as he gazed at first the flower, then me. "I can't believe you got it!"

"And we'd better hurry and get it to Master Yi before time runs out," I suggested and Junu and I jogged over to the scooter. As he unlocked it, I dug one-handed through my pack and pulled out the container. Just as I'd hoped, it was a perfect fit for the flower and the damp paper towels I'd put in there would hold the flower nice and secure and keep it fresh while we traveled.

When I climbed onto the bike behind Junu, he shivered. "Gah. You're all wet." He tried to squirm away from me but there wasn't anywhere to go on the tiny bike, so I wrapped my arms around him. "Oh man," he complained.

The ride back to the temple would have been unbearably cold if I hadn't been a vampire, so I felt a tiny bit bad for Junu who was shivering by the time we arrived.

"Time's almost up!" he said as soon as he shut off the engine. "We've gotta hurry."

We didn't bother to take off our helmets as we dashed for the stairs to take us up to the park where the temple sat. We ran toward it and nearly trampled right over the Zen garden in our haste to reach Master Yi. He sat on one of the benches where we'd met before, his hands resting quietly on his knees, his eyes closed. He didn't react at all as we rushed up to him.

"Master Yi," Junu said. No reaction.

"We did it, Master Yi," I said. "We got the last *sansuyu* flower of the season!" I dug into my pack and brought out the container. I held it out to him. Still no reaction. I took off the lid, so he could see the flower inside. "See?" I pushed the container practically under his nose. Nothing.

Junu and I sighed in unison as we slumped onto the bench facing the master. "Now what?" I whispered to Junu.

He shrugged. "I guess we wait."

Ugh. Patience was not my strong suit.

We sat there for a really long time. The sun moved across the sky and the shadows lengthened as we moved into late afternoon. My stomach rumbled. We hadn't eaten since our stop at the noodle shop early this morning. I had food in my pack, but it somehow seemed rude to eat in front of the monk while he meditated.

I watched another monk gently rake the sand over the Zen garden. His movements were so fluid, it was like watching water move the sands of time. When he left, I stood and picked up one of the long rakes.

My clothes were still damp, and my body felt stiff from my daredevil feat followed by sitting for hours, so my first strokes with the rake were awkward and frustrating. Not at all conducive to the meditative state it was supposed to inspire.

As my body limbered up, I began to push and pull the rake in broader strokes, and with the movement my mind began to relax. I let it wander, reliving everything that had happened today in reverse order. When I came to that Zen feeling I'd had that led me to the flower, I stopped. How had that happened? Was it a higher power that showed me where to find the flower? Or was it the universe? Or myself, my own need, that had manifested the vision?

Those thoughts were deep and intense, so I traveled back to my time with Philo the other night. He should be in Italy now, maybe he'd even met with the Master already. Maybe he'd even seen Hashiki. I wondered what she wanted with him and why the Master would allow her demands to be met. I knew there were questions of hierarchy and genealogy at play in the vampire world, but Philo had been created by an Ancient as well, so Hashiki should hold no sway over the Master—no more than Philo did.

Those thoughts made me jag the rake and created sharp angles in the sand that didn't represent the ebb and flow of life, so I took a deep breath and let go of the frustration as I breathed out.

Thinking of Philo, of just the two of us, eased my troubled mind and soon I was swaying with the motion of the rake.

"It is a truly beautiful thing to see a mind and body as one. It is not something one sees too often these days, particularly in one so young."

I glanced over my shoulder to see Master Yi standing behind me, his hands clasped behind his back. A quick glance at the benches showed me Junu had fallen asleep on one.

I turned back to the garden to examine my work and cringed when I noticed some jagged spots I hadn't smoothed out. Master Yi seemed to understand my concern because he placed a warm hand on my shoulder. "Our minds are powerful entities that have the ability to shape our experiences and our future, just as the ocean shapes the rocks and land. Sometimes storms arise that interrupt the natural ebb and flow of thought and reason—yet they do not destroy us. And we always have the ability to try again." He leaned forward and placed his hands over mine on the rake's handle. Together we created a spiral pattern in the sand over the spot where my rake had slipped.

"Now, tell me how you found the flower."

I stood the rake in the storage box and Master Yi and I began to stroll through the small maze-like garden that radiated outward from the Zen garden. I told him how all of the trees had leaves on them and none had any blossoms. Then I told him how we were about to give up when I'd seen the image in my mind of exactly where the last blossom lay.

He laughed when I told him about my plan to use the soft young branch to swing me back to the shore—and then at the description of me falling into the falls.

"I am pleased that you quieted your mind so you could receive what was there, waiting for you."

"Was it magic?" I asked. "I've never experienced anything like that before."

Master Yi chuckled and shook his head. "Each of us is made of magic. We hold that power within ourselves—there is no magic outside of ourselves, only that which we create here—" He pressed his palm to his chest. "Only we have the power to affect our future and our fate. You needed a blossom, and so your infinite mind showed you where to find one."

"But how did *you* know there even was a blossom still out there? How did you know we could find it?"

He laughed heartily and patted me on my back. When he finished, he grinned rather wickedly at me. "I didn't. But I am very glad you succeeded." He gave my shoulder a squeeze as he turned and made his way back to the Zen garden.

What the heck? I spun on my heel to follow him, not at all sure I liked that answer, but since everything worked out, I didn't feel like I could complain about it.

I caught up to Master Yi at the bench, where he was jostling Junu awake. "It is time for you to be returning home."

"Did we pass the test?" Junu asked a bit groggily.

"Indeed, you did. Congratulations. I had no doubt you would both succeed. "Now listen closely, because I cannot say this more than once. Your second quest—"

"Wait!" I hurried to sit beside Junu and leaned forward, anxious to hear and memorize every word.

Master Yi smiled, but barely paused to take a breath before continuing. "You must obtain dragon fruit without paying for it and make noodles for those who cannot feed themselves."

"Dragon fruit?" I asked. "Does dragon fruit grow here?"

"Oh, it does," Junu said with a snort. "But it doesn't grow wildly. Only a few farmers grow it." He focused on Master Yi. "I can't steal from another farmer, Master Yi. It would be like stealing from my own father. Losing any amount of our harvest would be devastating to us. I can't do that to someone else."

Master Yi only shrugged and smiled. "That is your quest. How you fulfill it is up to you."

Then he rose and left us pondering our instructions, trying to reason them out.

"We have to do all this tomorrow?" I was less concerned about the stealing part, though I certainly wasn't happy about that, than I was about the obtaining, cleaning, cooking, preparing and serving the fruit in such a way that would satisfy the quest. I'd never even had dragon fruit before, let alone cooked it into something. And this thing would, presumably, have to be edible, as well. "There's no way." I moaned.

"Tell me about it." Junu and I trudged toward the scooter, our hearts heavy with our impending failure.

Dragon Fruit Noodles & Korean BBQ Tofu

(I found this recipe on Google. It came from
PitayaPlus.com. We're only gonna use the noodles
part, but it looks good. Maybe I'll make it for Philo
when I get home. :))

Korean BBQ Sauce

2 Tbsp coconut sugar
4 Tbsp Tamari or soy sauce
2 Tbsp rice vinegar
2 teaspoons sesame oil
1/2 teaspoon cracked black pepper
2 teaspoons fresh grated ginger
4 cloves garlic, grated
2 tsp red pepper flakes
1 Tbsp corn starch
2/3 cup water water
3 Tbsp scallions

Noodles

1 block tofu, drained, cubed
2 cups glass noodles
Sesame seeds
2-3 Tbsp Dragon Fruit Smoothie Pack (defrosted)
2 Tbsp black sesame seeds

In a small saucepan over medium high heat add all the ingredients except for the corn starch and water.

Whisk everything together and bring to a boil.

In a small bowl, stir together the cornstarch and water until it dissolves.

Gradually pour the mixture into the boiling sauce, while continuously whisking for 1 minute.

Reduce heat to medium-low and allow to simmer for 3-5 minutes, until the sauce has become thickened. Remove from heat and cool before pouring into a jar.

Drain and cube the tofu. Cook in a skillet over medium heat with a little sesame oil. Once fully cooked, toss and coat in the sauce.

Prepare the noodles as directed. Toss and coat in the dragon fruit. Served with the tofu. Garnish with sesame seeds and scallions.

CHAPTER
NINETEEN

JUNU DIDN'T HAVE MICROPHONES IN HIS HELMETS, SO WE couldn't talk during the whole drive home. And since I had no clue about dragon fruits or noodle-making or anything like that, there was no point in stewing over it. Even though I did. Finally, in frustration, I forced all conscious thought out of my mind and tried to do a little mind work. I hadn't been practicing since we came to Korea—except for my visit with Philo the other night. Okay, I hadn't done a lot of practicing at all for the past couple months because there'd been school and end-of-year exams and, you know, a new boyfriend.

Even though Philo and I had sort of been together for a couple months before the Sweethearts dance, neither of us had really been sure of where the other stood. The dance changed all that and from that moment onward we were a legit couple. Stacey and Mack called us PhiloMin—I called them MacStacey. Philo, of course, called them Stacey and Mack. He'd loosened up a lot over the past months, but it was still like courting a Victorian gentleman—which might not have been Stacey's speed but was perfect for me.

I loved how Philo understood how important school was to me. I loved how, even though I'd been so worried about his limitless experience in the whole relationship department, he understood that we had all the time in the world and so we could take things slow. Sometimes I think he enjoyed the challenge of coming up with ways to draw out the courtship. Like the time he took me mini-golfing—which was a riot because he'd never even played golf before and his commentary on the little castles and drawbridges was hilarious—and half-way through the game he plucked up our balls and led me away. He took me to an ice cream parlor and when I asked him why we'd left the game before it was done, he said it was so we could draw out the anticipation. And the look in his eye when he said that? Ooh-wee. He was not talking about golf, that's for sure.

Every now and then he'd surprise me in some random way by kissing me senseless and *omo*, those moments were amazing. Stacey and Mack were hot and heavy and I knew it wouldn't be long before they did the deed. I wasn't a prude—I didn't think it was wrong for MacStacey. But personally, I thought Philo's way was much, much better.

Whenever I saw him, passed him in the hall, looked at him across the dinner table, or accidentally touched his hand while reaching for something, I thought of our last interlude. Every solitary moment made me wonder—would he do it again? It was like a game we played, a very exciting, very sensual game.

The last time, right before I left, Philo had wheeled out my bag and I'd just closed my bedroom door. In a flash, he took my pack from my hand, dropped it to the floor, and pinned me against the door with his body barely an inch from mine. He rarely put his body against me, but again, I was totally fine with that. He dug his hand into my hair and held the back of my neck, controlling the kiss with his mouth and with his hand. He kissed me deeply and when his other hand lightly skimmed down my side, pausing briefly at the side of my breast, my breath caught—and Philo answered with a soft moan.

He'd never touched me there before. But that touch? It was like a promise of what was to come. And I was ready for more. Maybe not *more*-more, but I trusted Philo would take the next stage just as slowly. I think we'd both silently agreed it was a lot of fun and we'd like to draw out the game for as long as possible. But a *little* more would be nice.

I had the whole thing worked out. Picture this: Senior Prom. Yeah, I know it's cliché, but hey, there's a reason for that. It's like the end of childhood and the beginning of adulthood. We'd have a fun party, celebrating the completion of our senior year and getting into our first-choice schools—then Philo would take me to a beautiful bed and breakfast or private cabin or something, and we'd finally make love. And it would be perfect. And then we'd get a little apartment near Yale and live there together while I got my first degree—because living forever meant I could study everything I wanted as much as I wanted, which was exactly what I was going to do.

I sighed with deep satisfaction. My life was good. Better than good.

With my thoughts on Philo, I reached out with my mind in hopes of finding him. I'd 1) never tried to do mind work from the back of a scooter speeding down a foreign highway, and 2) never tried to reach someone so far away without being in a full-on dream-like state. So I whooped, even punched my fist in the air, when I found Philo's familiar and welcoming mind.

The bike wobbled and Junu turned his head toward me, probably yelling something I couldn't hear, but I was too excited to pay him much attention. I let my consciousness weave into Philo's for just a moment before the strain became too great and I had to pull back. It was barely a second, and Philo may not have even noticed it—but I hoped he did. Mind work was weight training for your brain. The more I practiced, the more I'd be able to do, so I was beyond thrilled that I'd been able to do that much on my first real try. I was gonna have to practice a lot more.

"What the heck were you doing back there?" Junu yelled as soon as he whipped his helmet off. He hadn't even turned off the scooter yet. "You nearly got us killed."

I took off my helmet and gave him my best puppy-dog pout. "I'm sorry. I just did something super awesome that I didn't know I could do and I sorta forgot where I was for a second."

"How could you forget you were on the back of a bike?" He was still mad, every movement jerky and agitated. And whenever he looked at me, it was with dark frustration. He reminded me a lot of our dads when he did that. Creepy.

All I could do was shrug. "Sorry," I said again.

He didn't talk to me while we walked back to the apartment building, and he stomped up the stairs. Outside the door to his apartment he turned toward me and the glare had softened to something more like consternation.

"What did you do that you didn't think you could do?" He sorta spat out the words, like he was still mad, but I could tell he was mostly curious at this point.

I debated how much, or even what to tell him. But then I shrugged internally and decided he already knew about imugis and vampires and the "real" world as Master Yi called it; this was no big deal in the scheme of things. "Every vampire has at least one special gift. Some sort of ability that gives them an edge—"

"Like super speed and strength isn't enough?" Junu looked wary, like suddenly vampires were a lot more dangerous than he already thought. Like maybe *I* was more dangerous than he thought.

I smiled and tried to look as human and unthreatening as possible—which wasn't at all hard because I didn't exactly rock the vamp vibe. I laughed a little self-deprecatingly. "Right. Well, my gift is mind stuff. Like, I can talk to people in their minds sometimes. I've never tried to do it while fully awake and across such distance, but I was able to touch Philo's mind all the way in Italy!"

Junu gave me a disgusted look and I blanched. Was it really that bad? "You touched Philo's mind?" And a mischievous grin split his face while the wicked gleam in his eyes told me he was just being a turd. I punched his shoulder with a little more force than I intended and he rubbed the spot. "A little less vamp next time, 'kay?"

I offered him an *oops, sorry* shrug.

"And have you ever done that to me—talked to me in my mind?" He seemed both intrigued and offended by the idea.

"Have you been hearing voices?" I laughed at his annoyed expression. "No, dork. I wouldn't do that without your permission—or unless it was a super dire situation."

"You mean you could've told me you were okay when you fell into the freaking waterfall?"

"I didn't think of it. Sorry. It all happened so fast."

"I thought you were going to die, you know."

"I'm sorry. I didn't mean to fall in. I thought I was going to land back on the shore."

"Does being a vampire automatically make you a ninja?"

"Well no, but—"

"Then next time, just aim for Minnie-level moves, okay? One thing I've learned is whenever you try to do a skill that's harder than what you're qualified for, you're doomed to failure."

"What? Are *you* a ninja?

"No," he said with some indignation. "I'm a gamer."

I gave him a quick squeeze around his middle and apologized for scaring him. When he hugged me back, I knew we were okay.

Once again, the apartment was empty. I checked my phone, but my parents didn't text and there were no new voicemails. I'm not sure I'd set up the voicemail on this new phone, yet. "Where are they? I'm starving."

Junu held up a slip of paper he found on the kitchen counter. "They've gone out for dinner."

"Well, sheesh. Nice of them to wait for us." I thought I was here to have a vacation with my family, but it seemed all my parents wanted to do was hang out with my aunt and uncle.

The lights flickered, went off, then came back on. Junu looked up at the ceiling. "Maybe we should go out to eat, too."

"Mind if I change first?" I'd made a point not to complain, but the truth was I felt pretty spectacularly icky. My clothes were crusty and muddy and felt like they'd been dried with starch. Junu shrugged and dropped onto the couch where he turned on the TV and immediately cast League of Legends while it booted up. I went into my room to fetch some clothes but when I went back into the bathroom, thinking I'd just do a quick sponge bath, I heard him talking to someone. I peeked into the living room and found him lounging on the couch with his headphones on. Fine, then. If he was gonna get his game on, I was gonna get a shower and wash some of Buril Falls off of me.

My timing was perfect. When I was finally ready, Junu had just lost a game so he was ready to be done with League for a little while.

"I've got an idea," he said as we left the apartment and he locked up. "Noodles sound okay?"

"That's pretty wide open since noodles are like a staple in the Korean diet," I said.

He chuckled. "This is true. The place I want to take you makes dragon fruit noodles."

"Oh!" I wasn't sure if that prospect thrilled me, but we did have to talk about the next quest, so why not? "And when we get back, we should go give Hanjo an update."

"You think he cares?"

"Wouldn't you? If your future rested in the hands of a couple of kids?"

He patted me on the head. "Speak for yourself, kid. I'm a man."

I rolled my eyes. "Whatever."

Junu's street was pretty typical of Korean neighborhoods. The pavement was old and rutted, with cars parked all along both sides. There weren't any sidewalks, so people just walked in the street—and there were always a lot of people walking. Not everyone owned a car, so they either rode bicycles or walked. Junu's apartment was pretty new, compared to the one across the street which looked like a pile of shanty houses stacked on top of each other, while the house next to his building was a super modern house with a garage on the main level.

It wasn't like at home where you could tell the upper from the lower class. Or where you could avoid the poor by only going to rich places. Here, your neighbor might be super poor or rich. The person sitting next to you at the counter at the porridge house might be a millionaire. Or they might be eating their last won. It was weird and kinda awesome. Then again, it might have just been that way in Junu's neighborhood of Jongno-gu. Not like three days had made me a Korea expert.

The night was stifling hot and I was glad I hadn't brought a sweater. The humidity was just about killing me and I couldn't understand how so many Korean girls wore their hair down—the humidity made it nearly impossible for me to keep my hair straight. I might have to check out a salon and see if they had some magical serum for Asian hair here. As we walked, I pulled my damp hair up into a high topknot.

"So, I've been thinking about our next quest," Junu said. "I don't have a problem with the making of the noodles or the serving them to the poor. I think we just use glass noodles and infuse them with dragon fruit. We can Google it. The problem, is getting our hands on some dragon fruit without paying for it."

"Are you sure it doesn't grow anywhere wildly?"

Junu shook his head. "It's not indigenous to this continent. It grows well here, but only in cultivated gardens like ours or on farms."

"If only your family grew them instead of your snake squash."

"I know, right?" He shook his head again. "It just doesn't seem right to take a farmer's harvest to give to the poor."

"Like Robin Hood," I said.

"What?" He gave me a questioning look.

"Haven't you ever heard of Robin Hood?"

"I guess he sounds sort of familiar, but I don't know who he is."

I laughed. "I guess it's a *him*, but I was referring to the story of Robin Hood. Basically, this guy in Medieval England stole from the rich and gave to the poor."

"Was he a real person?"

"Some people say so, but I don't know for sure."

Junu was silent for a minute as we walked. "Thing is, most farmers are not rich. I still don't like it."

"Well, do we have to steal the fruit? I mean, maybe we could work for it, or trade for it."

Junu stopped and turned to me, a slow smile spreading across his face. "That's perfect! Yes!" He pumped his fist into the air and I laughed. "I can't believe I didn't think of that myself," he said as we fell into step again.

I shoulder-bumped him. "Hey. Don't try to steal my moment of brilliance."

He grinned down at me and tried to pat my head again but I blocked his hand and dodged out of the way. And felt a vampire nearby. I stopped and Junu took a couple steps before stopping and sending me a questioning look.

"What is it?"

I gave him a tight shake of my head and held my finger to my lips. He opened his mouth to say something but I glared at him and he shut it. I listened, but of course I couldn't hear anything beyond the usual noises of a populated city. I might have stellar hearing, but vampires could be utterly quiet when they wanted to be. I breathed in deeply and sent an inquiring tendril of my awareness outward from my mind, kind of like I'd done with Thor when he was teaching me how to find living things in the forest. I'd found some wild animals that time, and a stray dog who wanted to adopt me. This time, I found a vampire.

I had only a moment to touch her mind before she shut it tight against me, but what I'd sensed in that moment rocked me to my core. I couldn't be positive, but it had to be Ying Yue—the vampire was female, ancient and seething with rage.

And she wasn't alone. There was at least one other vampire out there.

I ran to Junu. "Come on, let's go." I grabbed his arm. "How far to this noodle house?"

He didn't resist as I drew him into a run. "It's just around the corner."

I threw a glance over my shoulder and across the buildings and rooftops. I still felt them, but couldn't see them, which was not good. It terrified me to wonder about when or how Ying Yue might decide to show herself.

Dear Philo,

I can't wait for you to come here. I know it wasn't in your plans, but I really appreciate it. Things are...weird here. I feel more distant from my parents than I did back in Utah.

But you would love Junu. I want to bring him home with me.

Today I was able to touch your mind - did you feel it? Could you sense me? It was so brief, I couldn't tell what you were doing, or say anything to you, but I was riding on the back of a scooter while zooming down the highway!

I can't wait to see you next week. I want to take you to the Saguksa Temple and introduce you to Master Yi. He knows all about the supernatural world. I finally feel ready to learn more about...everything.

I've had a bit of an epiphany while talking to Junu. I talk a lot about accepting vampires for who they are, but I realize I haven't exactly accepted myself for who I am, rather, what I am. I can't keep ignoring that part of me. Accepting what I am will allow me to truly embrace who I have become. Right?

Sorry for getting all deep and serious, but I think if I can talk to anyone about this stuff, it's you.

I can't wait to see you in a few days! (I'm thinking positively!)

CHAPTER TWENTY

WE HUDDLED TOGETHER JUST INSIDE THE DOOR TO THE small noodle shop as I watched people walk by outside.

"What happened?" Junu asked in a whisper. "What's going on?"

I shook my head. "I-I'm not sure," I lied. "I just thought I heard something."

"What kind of something?"

"I dunno. Just . . . something." I wasn't a very good liar, and Junu's narrowed eyes suggested I hadn't convinced him this time, either. But there was no way I could tell him the scariest vampire I'd ever met might be following us. A vampire who had it in for me and wanted nothing more than to skewer me and leave me for dead in some swamp somewhere. Or worse.

I forced a smile onto my face. "I'm starving." A trio of young people got up from their booth by the door and I wanted to snag it. "Mind ordering for me again?" I gestured toward the booth and Junu shrugged.

There were other tables available, but I wanted to be able to see out the window and watch the door, and this was the best one for that. Junu stood in line for the counter and in through the door came Sang-hyeok, dressed in his business suit and looking every inch the suave entertainment executive and nothing like his dark vampire alter ego. However, when he took the seat across from me, I caught a glimpse of his fangs so I knew this was no social call.

"Tell me about the vampires who are following you."

"What vampires?" I so did not want to have this conversation. Not in a crowded noodle shop, not anywhere.

Sang-hyeok narrowed his eyes at me and frowned. His eyes were very, very dark. Like, vampire dark, and it gave me the willies. I still wasn't sure if he was friend or foe. Or why the council lady had made it seem like it wasn't possible for me to have even met him. Or why he delivered my supply at all.

After a moment of him staring at him with his scary unreadable eyes, I caved. "How do you even know there're vamps following me, anyway?"

The darkness in his eyes didn't fade. "I was driving by and saw you stopped in the middle of the street. I stopped too, in case you needed assistance. When I rolled down the window, I felt their presence. I parked and followed them for a while, but I lost them. And I'm not exactly dressed for skulking across rooftops." He offered a sardonic smile and I rolled my eyes, not sure if I was ready to play along with his jokes. For all I knew, he was working for Ying Yue. He might be planning to take that prized spot at her side and all he had to do was bring me in.

"Oh." I checked over my shoulder to track Junu's progress. He was ordering at the counter and hadn't seemed to notice our guest. He'd freak when he found Sang-hyeok himself sitting at our table. I couldn't wait.

"So? Who is she? Her energy is strong."

"I don't know," I lied. I kept my gaze focused on my phone, my fingers tracing the design on my phone case. I didn't know what abilities Sang-hyeok had, but I didn't want him to be able to read the lie on my face.

"I'll tell you what I know, and why it concerns me. You are young in more ways than one and you are untried, unschooled and ill-prepared for the dangers that lie in wait in our world."

"Hey!" I glared at him. "You don't know anything about me. I might be young, but you have no idea what I've been through."

He smirked. "Ah. Perhaps there may yet be a little fire in you. Good. You're going to need it if what I suspect is true." He used his thumb to point out the window behind him. "There is an ancient one on your trail and she does not have good intent in her heart."

"What do you know about hearts? Do you even have one?"

He placed his be-ringed hand to his chest and pretended to be wounded by my words. Then he glanced over my shoulder, his face growing serious again. He leaned across the table. "Keep your wits about you and do not be so foolish as to think you can face such a one as her." Then he disappeared.

Well, okay. He didn't disappear as in *poof*, but he used his superspeed which was more like supersonic with how fast he must have been going. He'd been so slick about it, Junu slid into the seat the vampire had just vacated and didn't seem to have a clue anyone had been there, let alone Sang-hyeok.

"Okay," Junu said as he transferred the bowls from tray to table. "We've got dragon fruit noodles with Korean BBQ *kimchi* and *haemul pajeon*."

"Yum!" My eyes grew wide as I took in the delicious pancake-like *pajeon*. "My mom makes this all the time and it's my favorite!" I gushed. "Thank you!"

Junu grinned and seemed to enjoy watching me organizing the dishes in front of me. "You're weird."

"Don't I know it!"

"Try the noodles, first. I want to know what you think."

"They're beautiful." The noodles were bright pink and presented in a shallow bed of broth with seared cubes of tofu and even a little pink edible flower. I took a bite of the noodles and chewed thoughtfully. "They're good. I think I expected them to be way more flavorful than this, so I wasn't sure I'd like them."

Junu smiled and dug into his dinner. "Yeah. Sometimes they can be just a little sweet, but not so much that they don't go with anything. Mostly they're used because they add color to a dish, but they're really expensive so not a lot of places serve them."

"But this place does?" It didn't seem high end, by any means.

"That's because the family grows them out back."

"Seriously? They can do that?"

He shrugged. "We grow gourds on our roof."

"I guess." A lot of Utahns had gardens and grew vegetables in the summer, but for some reason I just didn't expect to see anything like that here where the population was so dense and most people lived in apartments.

"So, do you know the owners of the shop? Maybe we could do work for them in exchange for some of their noodles?"

"We've gotta make the noodles, remember? But yeah, we should ask them." He took a bite of his food and chewed, glancing casually around the room. "I sorta know them. Not personal or anything, but they've had this restaurant here my whole life and I've come in here a lot. We'll talk to them after we eat."

It was getting dark outside when we finally piled our dishes onto the tray and stood to return them to the counter. The shop was still busy, but we felt like we'd been there too long already and unless we ordered more food, we should probably get going. There were no customers waiting at the counter so we hurried forward with our tray.

"Hello, Mrs. Pong," Junu said as he approached. He smiled and she wiped her hands with a towel, a big smile on her face. "My name's Junu and I'm really hoping you can help me and my cousin."

She glanced at me, her warm smile putting me at ease. "I know you," she said. "You've been coming here since you were a little boy. Are your parents well?"

"Yes, thank you." Junu fidgeted with his keychain, flipping it around and around his finger.

"Are they still selling tromboncino?"

"Yes." Junu grinned. "Do you want to buy some?"

She laughed and looked down. "No. Thank you. We only make dragon fruit noodles here."

"That's what I thought," Junu said and the uncomfortable moment that might have been was gone. "That's actually kind of what we were hoping to talk to you about." Junu glanced at me and I smiled my encouragement.

"My cousin and I have been asked to do a little humanitarian project. We have to make dragon fruit noodles but we can't afford to buy the dragon fruit." A tiny lie, but pretty darn close to the truth. *Good for you*, I thought.

Mrs. Pong's expression had settled into a more business-like expression, but she hadn't cut him off at least. "It is very expensive," she said.

"Right. Well, we were wondering if you would be willing to let us do some work for you in exchange for some dragon fruit. Enough to make, um—" he glanced at me and I shrugged. Master Yi hadn't said how many homeless people we needed to feed. "Maybe four bowls of noodles?"

Mrs. Pong frowned as she thought. "The dragon fruit are not in season just now—soon, but not yet. Come back in a month and maybe we can help you, but I am not sure. We only have a small garden." She picked up her rag and began wiping her side of the counter and moving away from us.

"Wait," I said. We couldn't give up just like that. "I ate your dragon fruit noodles tonight and they were delicious." Mrs. Pong smiled and nodded her thanks. "If your fruit isn't in season, how did you make them? Do you make them ahead, and then freeze them? They tasted fresh to me." I had no idea if the noodles were fresh or not, but the comment seemed to please her. Her smile returned and she drew near again.

"We make a paste with our fruit when they are in season. We can freeze it and use it throughout the year to make our noodles."

Junu and I shared a look. "Do you think we have to get actual fruit? Or do you think something like that would work?" I asked him. We stared at each other for a long moment before Junu shrugged and turned back to Mrs. Pong.

"Would you be willing to let us work for some of those frozen packs? Enough to make four bowls of noodles?"

"You could just buy the noodles from me," she said.

Junu and I both shook our heads. "In order to teach us about community service, we need to do everything ourselves." Ha! That was quick thinking on Junu's part, I thought.

"Well," Mrs. Pong said. "Let me talk to my husband."

Junu bowed, and I followed suit. "Thank you, Mrs. Pong. Thank you."

We hurried over to a side table and sat down, each of us trying to casually watch the action behind the counter without appearing like we were staring at them. Mrs. and Mrs. Pong had a lively conversation, but it was impossible to tell if it was going our way. Then Mrs. Pong disappeared for about five minutes. When she returned, they resumed their conversation but it was much less animated. Mr. Pong shook his head and Mrs. Pong returned to the counter.

She opened her mouth as if to call out to us, but we jumped to our feet and went to her before she had the chance. I don't know about Junu, but I was pretty sure we were out of luck on this one. Maybe another restaurant would be willing to sell us their fruit. If only we could go to the market and buy some dragon fruit—though Junu said you couldn't always find them there.

"Can you come in the morning?" Mrs. Pong asked.

I gripped Junu's hand. "Yes!" we said in unison.

Mrs. Pong laughed. "Come at 10:00 a.m. You can clean out our delivery van. We will give you enough of the dragon fruit paste for your noodles."

"Awesome!" I said.

"Oh," Junu said, and I threw him a questioning glance. "Is there any way we could come earlier? We need to be done with our challenge by noon." I was about to correct him, saying we had until three in the afternoon, but then I remembered we had to get to the temple by then. Which meant we should be feeding the people lunch and then hightailing it back to Master Yi. Which wouldn't give us much time to make the noodles.

Mrs. Pong looked over her shoulder at her husband, slicing pork into thin strips. She sighed and returned her attention to us. "No earlier than 9:00 a.m. I am sorry, that is the best I can do. We have deliveries in the morning."

Junu smiled and reached out to take her hand in both of his. "Thank you so much," he said, bowing as best he could with the counter between them. "This is an amazing help. Thank you!"

"You are welcome," she said as she pulled her hands away.

"Thank you!" I called as we left the shop. "That is so awesome!" I cried when we were out in the street.

"Yeah," he said. "Let's just hope that getting the fruit this way will satisfy Master Yi and that we can make the noodles in time."

I had no idea how hard it was to make dragon fruit noodles, but I'd always been good at looking at the bright side. "Piece of cake, Red."

I miss school. Is that weird? And it's not my friends—though I do miss them, sure—it's school I miss. I miss the smell of the science lab. The thrill of learning new things and mastering new skills. I love the challenge of tests and labs—and especially the joy of seeing a (preferably perfect) score.

Sigh.

CHAPTER
TWENTY-ONE

ON OUR WAY BACK TO THE APARTMENT, I PAID attention to our surroundings, my vamp radar on high alert. I couldn't let anything happen to Junu—he was innocent in this. I'd like to think that Ying Yue would wait to get me alone, but knowing her, she'd be happy to pick a moment when all my family was at risk.

My parents had no idea about what had happened at the dance in February. For all they knew, I had a lovely time with my friends and that was that. It was hard enough for them to accept that I was a vampire and my lifestyle was different now—I couldn't imagine what they'd do if they found out the danger I'd been in. Or the danger I might be in now.

Okay, I could imagine it. It would have something to do with being locked in the basement for the rest of my life and finishing school through online school or something. Thinking about it, maybe that wasn't a bad idea.

There was no way I could face Ying Yue by myself.

Thinking that, realizing it, made my shoulders relax. Up until that moment, I think I hoped that the Ying Yue threat was something that probably wouldn't happen. I mean, revealing herself and taking me down wouldn't prove her to be any great warrior. She could defeat me with her little pinky if she wanted. I was a nobody. A complete noob. Why would she risk being found by the Master just to get some revenge on a little high school girl? Hey, *I* could call myself a little high school girl, it just wasn't cool when someone else did it.

I'd call David when I got home and tell him about Ying Yue. He probably already knew all about her skulking around Jongno-gu and already had people in place to take her down. I was probably surrounded by friendly vampires at this moment and had nothing at all to worry about.

Our parents were just getting ready for bed when we got home.

"It's only 8:30," I said. "Why are you going to bed so early?" I kissed my mom on the cheek and wrapped my arm around her middle.

"We're going to Mount Jirisan tomorrow," Auntie said. "We want to be well-rested."

Junu and I shared a look, then we both burst out laughing.

"What's so funny?" Mom asked, pulling away from me. Her expression said it was not nice to make fun of Auntie and I should apologize right away.

"I'm sorry, Auntie," I said. "We aren't laughing at you—it's just that we were there today. The falls are beautiful."

"And Minnie should know." Junu's eyes gleamed mischievously. "Minnie got an up close and personal look."

"What do you mean by that?" Dad asked in his stern voice.

"Nothing, *Appa*," I soothed.

"And what are you doing galivanting around when you should be working on our problem?" He folded his arms over his chest and just as he lowered his elbows, the lights went out and a low moan moved through the apartment, growing so loud the house rattled. "This is no time to make foolish decisions, daughter. You have a duty to your family."

Leave it to Dad to continue scolding me during a haunting.

Auntie and Uncle rushed to the shrine and a match flared to life. They lit the candles there, as well as the end of a stick of incense, muttering prayers under their breath. I could see Dad's expression now, and he flicked a glance between me and his brother and his wife, before dismissing me with a snort. He joined them at the altar.

Mom dragged me into the room we shared. "Your father is very serious about this. You can see his family cannot live like this."

I drew my hands down her arms, trying to soother her. "I know, Ma. I do. And Junu and I are working on it. Today we had to go to Mount Jirisan to get a *sansuyu* flower. That's why we were there."

She frowned. "A flower? Who sent you on such a silly errand?"

"Master Yi. He's the one helping us, remember?"

She continued to frown, but I saw the moment she accepted my explanation.

"Well?" she demanded. "Did you get it?"

"Yes."

"Good."

The lights came back on.

"Everything's gonna be okay, Ma. I promise."

She regarded me for a long moment, then nodded curtly and shooed me out the door. I nearly ran into Dad as he came in.

"Let her go," Mom said. "I have news to tell you."

Dad still frowned at me as I said goodnight, but at least he didn't grill me.

Out in the living room, I found Junu sitting on the floor with his laptop and headphones. Auntie and Uncle must have gone to bed already. So I left the apartment and headed up to the roof. I wanted to call David, and if Hanjo came out and asked for an update, I'd give him one. After that, an early bedtime seemed like a good idea for me, too.

"Minnie!" David's strong, commanding voice made me feel as if I'd just entered his study and not like I was calling from thousands of miles away. A rush of relief went through me and I sagged down onto the roof wall. "I'm so happy to hear from you. How are you? How is your trip?"

I smiled at his eager questions. It was mid-morning in Utah, so he was likely busy with work, yet he made me feel as if he had all the time in the world for me. "Hi, David. I'm good. Exhausted, but good. You're never gonna believe what's going on here."

I told him about the *imugi* and our first encounter, and he laughed heartily. He said that would be a fun story to hear told around the dinner table, but he'd let me tell it. In David's house, everyone was expected to sit down for dinner together. I suppose I should say in *Manuela's* house, since the dinner thing was her rule. It was kinda old fashioned, and maybe a little weird, since most members of the family were really old vampires, but it was also one of the main things that made me feel like I belonged.

I told him about Master Yi and how he wasn't surprised to hear about the *imugi* and that he knew I was a vampire right away. "He said the supernatural wasn't what was strange, but that it was what was *real*. He said humans have created a world for themselves where anything they can't understand doesn't exist or has been relegated to the world of fantasy."

"He sounds like a very wise man," David said. "And he's right. This world was home to supernatural creatures long before humans walked upon it."

"Then why are we called supernatural? Shouldn't they, I mean, we, be what's truly natural?"

David chuckled. "You're not wrong, but not quite right, either. Humans were born of this earth. We were not."

I had to think about that one for a minute. "Uh, whaddya mean by that?"

He was silent a moment. "I think that is a conversation best had in person. It's not one I'm eager to have with you, but I believe that you will be ready, past ready, to hear what I have to say when you return. Will you allow me that time?"

I trusted David implicitly, and I had enough on my mind at the moment not to worry about inviting more things to ruminate over. "Sure. I need to talk to you about something else, anyway."

"I understand. Give me one moment and then my attention will be all yours."

"Okay."

He must have put me on mute, because the line went utterly quiet. So I had nothing to do to distract me from the prickling at the back of my neck and that pressure against my ribs that told me vampires were nearby. I also had the impression that Hanjo stood on alert, watching over me in the garden. I couldn't see him, but I felt him.

"Minnie?" I sighed with relief when David's voice returned to the line.

"I'm here." I walked over to the garden and sat down with my back toward it, so I could watch the rooftops around me. "It's just—well, that's why I called you. It's about the vampires here."

"I'm listening."

"I think . . . well, I'm pretty sure that Ying Yue has found me. I think she's been following me. At least tonight, anyway. And she might be nearby right now."

"I see," David said after a moment. "You're growing stronger, and I'm glad to hear it, but I had hoped you'd remain as you were a little while longer."

I frowned. "What do you mean by that?" I didn't like being kept in the dark about things that concerned me, and his mysterious comment before about vampires not being natural to this earth—I hated thinking that David was meting out my education bit by bit and there were important things I didn't know. Even though that's how teachers teach, it still riled me.

David sighed quietly. I don't think he meant for me to hear it. "As you age, you grow stronger in your abilities. One of those abilities that all vampires possess, allows us to sense when another is near. How close to you was Ying Yue when you felt her presence?"

"Pretty close, I guess. But I can feel at least one other vampire out there now and I can't see anyone. So I don't know how close they are."

"As with most things, the more you exercise this gift, the greater your strength will become and your range will grow. You'll also be able to sense who the vampire is— is this how you came to know it was Ying Yue?"

I noticed how he hadn't seemed at all surprised that Ying Yue was here. "I dunno. Maybe . . . not? I think I reached out with my mind, using my mental gift, not my vamp radar or whatever."

"Your vamp radar?" David asked with laughter in his voice.

I shrugged. "That's what I've been calling it."

"It's pretty accurate. I like it."

"So?" I prompted.

"So, yes," he replied. "I am aware that Ying Yue is in South Korea and that she has located you."

"You knew, but you didn't tell me?" Frustration and the tingle of anger made my voice rise and I fought to keep it even. I didn't think any vampires were near enough to hear me, but if your gifts grew as you aged, who knew how long-range Ying Yue's hearing was?

"I saw no reason to disturb your vacation. I am handling it."

I took a moment to reign in my emotions. I was a champion debater, dangit. I could have a conversation without freaking out. "I appreciate that. But I think you should have told me."

"I agree." His ready agreement surprised and pleased me. That was another thing I liked about being a part of David's family. Everyone treated me like a kid but that didn't bug me so much because I *was* a kid, especially compared to them. But when it came time for conversations, David pretty much gave it to me straight. He expected me to be able to deal with my reality, even when it was hard.

"I have had two men on Ying Yue's trail since we lost her in February. Excuse me, I should say, I have had my intelligence team on her trail, but it was only a few weeks ago that we became aware of her location—when she showed up in Seoul. Your parents had booked their tickets, including yours with your name on it, only forty-eight hours prior. You're going to be in Seoul—Ying Yue goes there. Suspicious, don't you think?"

I nodded. "Yeah," I said on a gulp.

"So I contacted my team there and had them watch for her. She's remained elusive, but not to the degree that my people haven't been able to keep tabs on her.

"She was confirmed to be following you when she turned up at the Saguksa Temple at the same time you were there with your cousin."

"When?" I gasped, my heart leaping into my throat as I realized I hadn't felt a thing, then.

"On your first visit. Since then, she's been seen near or around you pretty regularly."

"Yikes," I said.

"You have nothing to worry about, Minnie. We won't let her get to you."

"Does that mean, if I feel her nearby, then your people are close, too?"

"Yes."

"What if I can't feel them, only her?"

"Is that what you sense now?"

"No. I feel like there are more vamps out there right now, but I can't tell how many. And with more than one out there, I can't tell if one's even her."

"That strength will grow the more you use it," he reassured. "I won't leave you unprotected, Minnie. I trust my people to keep you safe."

"Okay." I hated the way my voice sounded so small and childlike.

"But I'd also encourage you to stay indoors, or in well-lit, well-populated areas. Try to limit your activities to the daytime."

"Okay," I said again.

We were silent for a long moment, then David asked, "Would it help if I came out there?" His voice was so soft, so caring, that it brought tears to my eyes. I wish Philo could come.

"No." I swiped at the tears. Philo was busy, but he said as soon as he was done, he'd come to Seoul for a visit. So I had that to look forward to. "I'm okay."

"Good." And there was no reproach in his tone, just love. And belief in me. That made me feel so much better.

"Oh, David. I know you gotta go, but I met this weird vampire guy here and I was wondering if you knew him."

"Oh?" And I did not miss the note of tension in that simple one-syllable word.

"Yeah. He's the artistic or talent director of SM Entertainment here or something, but that wasn't the first time I met him—that was just the first time I met him in the real world. Or, the unreal world. Gah. My mind's all messed up now. Anyway . . .

"The first time I met him was my first night here and he was all wild and scary like a vampire out of the old movies." I laughed, remembering the way he'd been all dark and threatening. "At first I thought he might be a bad guy, but tonight he warned me about Ying Yue—he even followed her for a bit to make sure I got safely where I was going."

"Do you know his name?" David's voice was flat, completely devoid of intonation. I couldn't tell if he was angry or not.

"Yeah, it's Sang-hyeok."

No answer.

Not even any breathing on the line.

"David?"

Another pause, then, "Yes. I know him."

"Ohhkay . . . Well, is he friend or foe?"

"That . . . I cannot tell you. I suppose it remains to be seen. However, he is very protective of children, so I doubt he would harm you."

"Well that's reassuring."

"Don't let it trouble you," David said in a much more relaxed and normal tone. "But stay away from him, if you can."

"I'll try." But I hadn't been *trying* to be near him, he'd just been around. How could I stop the guy from showing up all over the place?

"I'm afraid I do have to go now, Minnie. It was so good to hear from you. Good luck on your noodle-making quest. I'm sure you'll do wonderfully."

I thanked him and we said goodbye, but I couldn't help but think that something had seriously spooked him—that or royally ticked him off. Either way, I didn't think that meant sunshine and rainbows for me.

Vampire Gifts I've Observed:
- ★ Strength (everyone)
- ★ Speed (everyone)
- ★ Vamp radar (everyone)
- ★ Mind gifts (Philo, Thor, Me, David?)
- ★ Calming (Siobhan)
- ★ Love (not sure what to call it) (Manuela)
- ★ Night vision (everyone)
- ★
- ★
- ★

CHAPTER
TWENTY-TWO

YOU ARE WORRIED, HISSED A VOICE IN MY MIND.

I whirled around to see two luminescent golden eyes just barely visible in the dark foliage. "I'm sorry I invaded your territory—I was kinda nervous sitting out there all exposed like that."

His gaze flicked around me and I wondered what he saw. *You were right to come to me. I will protect you.*

This time I realized it was weird to have a one-sided verbal discussion so I answered in my mind. *Thank you. I really appreciate that. I have to admit, I do feel kinda scared. I only wish you could come with me and protect me when I'm away from here.*

I didn't really know if Hanjo could protect me at all, and I didn't know why I suddenly felt like spilling my heart and soul out to him. There was just something about him that made me feel safe and secure. Maybe it had to do with performing the quests for him, but I felt close to him in a weird way.

Thanks to my night vision, I saw him cock his head. *Why do you not desire the power I possess? If you had it, you could defeat your enemies and you would no longer be frightened of anyone.*

I thought about that for a second. I honestly hadn't known his pearl could do anything for me, but I suppose it made sense if what he'd said was true—that it attracted all supernatural creatures. I shrugged. *It's not mine. I promised to help you protect it. I'm not gonna go against my word and just take it from you.*

Why?

Because that's not the kind of person I am.

What kind of person are you?

I laughed. *I'm not sure anyone's ever asked that before.*

Well? Hanjo prompted when I didn't answer his question. I'd kinda hoped he'd forget about it. Or that he really didn't want to know.

I sighed. *I dunno. I guess I'm smart. I want to go to university and get as many degrees as possible.*

That's the trappings of your life. Hanjo said impatiently. Tell me who you are. Inside your heart.

I glanced at him out of the corner of my eye. *I'm not sure how to answer that question.*

What is your greatest desire in life?

I didn't have to think about that one. *Prejudice really bugs me. I didn't notice it too much before I became a vampire—I mean, I knew it existed, but I lived in a pretty basic world with friends I'd grown up with, so no one really gave me any trouble for being Asian. But when I became a vampire? It was like I hadn't existed before. Like they didn't know me at all.*

They were suddenly afraid I'd bite them and drink them dry. They thought I was a monster. That I'd suddenly become super evil or something. But I hadn't!

I'd turned to face Hanjo fully now and he swayed gently amid the gourds which swayed with him. *My body chemistry had changed. That's it. Who I was inside hadn't changed at all. It drives me crazy that people can't see that.*

And I just learned that Junu is gay—that's um . . .

I know what homosexuality is, Hanjo assured me.

Oh, okay. Well, I just learned that Junu's gay and here in Korea it's totally frowned upon. So bad that Junu's lost all his friends and he thinks he can't even have a career as an entertainer because of it. It's just so wrong and . . . I hate to use the word unfair, but it is. Because everything that people thought about Junu is still true—he's still handsome, talented, funny and smart. He's still a good friend, and a kind person. But because what they perceive him to be has changed, they can't accept him anymore.

What I really want in my life, is to help people see that it's not what people are that matters, it's who they are. Until this week, I thought it was just vampires I wanted to help. I wanted to prove to people, maybe by proving there was a soul and that vampires still had theirs or something, I don't know, that while our bodies changed, who we were inside didn't.

I wanted to help families deal with the change of their loved one so they didn't have to lose them, like I lost mine. At some point I'd started crying, and I swiped carelessly at them, feeling stupid and alight with fiery passion at the same time.

But now, I don't know. Now I think people in general need to understand that people should be loved and cherished no matter what they are. I mean, not the bad people. I'm not saying that every single person gets a pass. But we should be a lot more concerned about who someone is than about what they are—be they gay or straight or trans or vampire.

Or imugi, Hanjo said and I could hear the smile in his voice.

Exactly. I laughed and felt the tension drain out of me.

You are a very passionate girl, he said.

I shrugged, embarrassed now that my diatribe was over. *Did that answer your question?*

It answered both of my questions. Your greatest desire stems from who you are, and you are a kind and gracious person who desires love and happiness not only for herself but for others—supernatural and human alike.

It took me a minute to let his words sink in. *Thank you, Hanjo. That's so kind of you to say.*

I do not intend to be kind nor unkind. I am simply stating what I see. And I see a young woman of great worth and ability.

I laughed self-consciously and fiddled with my fingers in my lap.

You wish your father would say such things to you.

Can you read my mind? I rocked back, a bit aghast that he could just pluck my thoughts from my mind.

No, no, he said with a chuckle. *But I have lived a very long time. While I have not spoken to many creatures during this time, I have had the opportunity to watch and observe. And my people are known for their quick intelligence and intuition. It is not hard to see what is in your heart when it is so plainly written on your face.*

And you're not a little bit self-conscious, are you?

Why should I be? I have only spoken the truth. Humanity's inability to admit their greatness—and their weakness—is among their many problems. If only you would embrace what is wonderful about you. Make it your truth, every day and in every way. You would be amazed at what you could achieve.

I guess— I thought about it a minute. *You're right. I need to take that advice myself.*

Yes, you do.

I smiled at Hanjo and felt as if he were smiling back.

There is something else that I can give you beyond my advice. Will you take it?

Oh, I don't want anything from you. You're gonna help me with my ancestors—that's enough.

His eyes closed briefly and I took it as acquiescence. *Still, I wish to give you something.*

I couldn't imagine what he could give me, so I shrugged. *Um, thanks. That would be nice.*

Come with me, he said and turned away. His sinewy form melted into the darkness and it was difficult to follow him. I had to focus intently to expand my senses.

Sometimes I forgot I was a vampire. I still felt so much like the same old me, that I forgot to use the gifts my new life gave me. Now I focused more on my hearing than my eyes, and found that I could follow Hanjo easily through the garden by listening to the very slight rustling sound his body made as it slithered over the rough rooftop. His body temperature didn't exactly make him stand out from everything else around us.

He led me behind a kind of narrow shed that looked an awful lot like an outhouse. He nudged aside something and a faint, pure white glow rose from the ground. *Come close, child,* he said.

I squeezed in behind the shed, but the brick half wall that surrounded the roof was gone here where another building had been cobbled together with this one. The next roof was about a foot higher, and a gutter had been attached to the new building. It was a half-hearted effort though—the end of the gutter was bent at an awkward angle. There wasn't much of a hole, and I probably wouldn't fall, but it still made me nervous.

A fall from this height would not hurt you, Hanjo said with a bit of snark.

I'd survive it, I countered. *But it wouldn't stop me from experiencing the excruciating pain of broken bones.*

Hanjo made a *tsking* sound. *The gap is very small. You will not fall. Come closer.*

I sighed and kneeled, cringing as the grit and gravel dug into my knees. I leaned forward onto my hands to get a closer look at the shining light. I felt the tug of power whispering to me. Hanjo had made it sound as if the pearl called to people, but I don't think I'd noticed it until that moment. Maybe it was because I was a baby vamp or something. Or maybe I just wasn't that sensitive to magic. Even now, this close to it, it only felt like a soft vibration, a pleasant hum inside my chest.

You may pick it up. Hanjo's voice in my mind held a tone of warm reverence.

Are you sure? I don't want—

Just . . . pick it up, child.

I wiped my hands on my thighs, then leaned forward and wrapped both hands around the ping-pong sized orb nestled into the crooked gutter. It seemed to roll into my palms under its own power, as if it wanted to be held by me. I rocked back onto my heels and cupped the pearl as Hanjo peered over my shoulder. *It really does look like a pearl,* I said. The light wasn't steady but swirled and moved around the orb while its surface reflected a milky, pearlescent texture with the hint of rainbow colors peeking through. It was stunning. Breathtaking. And, now that I held it close to me, unbelievably powerful.

How can such a small thing be so powerful?

You have only to look at yourself to answer that question.

I snorted and glanced at Hanjo, but he made no response.

And I was powerless to do anything other than stare at the glorious object in my hands.

When you made no attempt to take it from me, I feared you were immune to its call. Immune to its magic—though I haven't yet met a creature who was.

*Even humans are often drawn to its power and have gone
to war in an effort to possess it.*

This pearl?

Hanjo chuckled. *No. This one is new, and few have
ever known of it. But pearls have fallen to Earth before.
While dragons actively watch the sky for them, and hunt
them down the moment they fall, some have been found
by humans first—and no good ever comes of it.*

*Humans are not as strong as we dragons. They were
never meant to possess such greatness.*

A lot of things rose in my mind in response to that
statement, but I'd have to save my reproach for later.
Right then, all I could do was bask in the presence of
the pearl. A thought niggled at my awareness and
giddiness grew in my heart. Hanjo had said he wanted
to give me something. Was he giving me this? Was the
pearl mine now?

I drew it closer to my chest and Hanjo cleared
his voice.

*You are not ready to possess such power, child. I do
not judge you for wanting to claim it for your own but
remember who you are. Do you really wish to rob me?*

I looked up and over at him, startled by the
question. No. I gasped, trying to regain control. *No, I
don't want to take it from you.* Here—I pressed the
pearl toward him, suddenly wanting nothing more than

to be rid of it and the hungry way it made me feel. Hanjo made no move.

I knew you were a strong one. An honorable one. You will make a great warrior one day.

Warrior? I'm not a fighter.

Warriors come in many shapes and sizes and only a few are called upon to hold the sword. Now, Hanjo said, pressing near again. *Hold the pearl over your heart and close your eyes.*

But—

Just do as I say and trust me.

So I did.

Breathe in and let the power of the pearl flow into you.

I opened my eyes. *I don't want to take your power.* That moment a second ago, even though it had been brief, had scared me. I didn't want to be the kind of person who would take something precious that belonged to someone else.

Hanjo's kind, soothing voice seemed to fill my mind with comfort and peace. *The pearl's power is meant to be used and it is my gift to give. Using it will not deplete it but strengthen it. Just as using your own gifts do not weaken you but make room for your gifts to grow. Do you understand?*

I stared into his golden gaze and nodded.

Now. Close your eyes and imagine the pearl's light flowing into you as you breathe. His voice grew warm and deep in my mind. *Breathe deeply and let the light fill you until your whole body hums with its power.*

A distant part of my mind wondered if this was safe, but I'd already begun, and the power tasted sweet and made me feel alive—I couldn't stop now even if I'd wanted to.

When I could draw no more in, Hanjo's mind gently nudged me as if I'd been asleep. *Now ease the orb back into its hiding spot and cover it with the debris lying there.*

I opened my eyes and saw that the orb still glowed as brightly as it had before, maybe even brighter. It filled me with relief and gratitude that I could take from it, but not diminish it.

I wasn't happy about putting a precious treasure back into such a dirty spot, but I did as Hanjo asked, making sure every single bit of light was hidden beneath some damaged shingles, random bits of wood and plant debris. I sat back on my haunches.

Hanjo's presence in my mind felt like he rubbed my back or comforted me in some way. *Our connection will be greater, now,* he said as if he could read my mind. *Don't worry about where the pearl is hiding. It does not mind where it is kept, and it cannot be damaged or diminished by its location. Now. How do you feel?*

I moved to face him, sitting Indian style to give my knees a rest. Hanjo curled his serpentine body and faced me at eye level. I thought about his question and breathed in deeply. I smelled the bitter tang of tar, dirt, smog, green things growing and a myriad of other scents I had no name for. My night vision had been excellent since I became a vampire, but now everything popped as if I wore 3D glasses. Even in the dark, I could discern the shifting colors in Hanjo's scales and the flecks of purple and green in Hanjo's golden eyes.

I feel . . . I tried and failed to find the words. *I feel more. I don't know how else to explain it.*

Hanjo's eyes smiled and he bobbed his head. *And you are.*

Will this feeling go away?

I am afraid this exact feeling—the active power, the feeling of invincibility, will fade, yes. That is why the pearl is so coveted by all who seek it, and why it has been so dangerous in the hands of humans. Their natural insecurities demanded they take in more and more power until it became too much for them to contain. But you do not need to worry about that. And the power will never leave you. It is a part of you, now. You will feel it working on you, as you do now, as it fuses with your own magic, and then you will be as you are now, but better.

This is my gift to you, my way of giving thanks, for helping me grow and protect the yeouiju.

But I haven't completed the quests yet. What if I fail?

Hanjo's eyes were full of compassion and I wondered how I'd ever been frightened of him. I felt his presence in my mind as if he patted me on the shoulder. *You accepted the quest. You have already put your own life at risk for me. Even should you fail, though I do not think you will, I will have been grateful for your efforts. It has been a very long time since I have known a friend such as you.*

Guilt washed through me and even though it was quickly burned away by the power still warming me from the inside out, I still felt bad. *But I didn't just do this out of the goodness of my heart. I'm getting something out of this too.*

Because you benefit from something does not mean another benefits less. Isn't that what love is? Both parties are made better because of their love for one another. Why should friendship be any different? We are both benefitting—that does not belittle the good you are doing for me. Besides, as I understand it, you accepted my offer because you wished to put your ancestors to rest—a valiant desire—so your family could be at peace in their home. Is that not a selfless desire?

I sighed. *Except I want my dad to see me as his daughter again. Part of me thinks that if I can help with the ancestors, he'll love me again.*

Oh, dearest, Hanjo said. *The desire to be loved and accepted by one's parent is not selfish or greedy. Now. Let us not argue about this any longer. I am much, much older than you, and I have declared you to be a good person—a good person and a great creature. It would be rude of you to ignore me. So listen and remember what I have said to you this night. Yes?*

I smiled a watery smile and nodded. *Okay.*

Sleep now. Your body will need rest to finish absorbing the power. And good luck with your quest tomorrow—though I have a feeling you will enjoy great success.

I rose a bit unsteadily and walked beside Hanjo toward the garden. *Thank you for tonight, Hanjo,* I said as we reached the shadowy trellis he called home. *Not just for the power, but for the friendship and words of wisdom.*

He bowed his head. *It was my pleasure. And I too, thank you. Sleep well, child.* He slid into the green vines until I lost him to the darkness.

Tonight something amazing happened. I held Hanjo's yeouiju and its power filled me. Hanjo said it would seep into me and make me "more." I can already feel it.

I've never really explored my vampire side, other than doing some mind work. Maybe I wasn't ready to accept that I really was a vampire. That I had super speed and super strength. All I've done is run really fast. And that was to run away. I'm like a superhero now—or I could be.

I'm kinda like ... Mind. Blown.

CHAPTER
TWENTY-THREE

I WOKE THE NEXT MORNING, FEELING RESTED, ENERGETIC and ready to take on the day. No one else was awake, so I curled up on the couch and texted Philo.

I started to type:

Me: Hey. I know you said you might not have service, but I wanted to say hi and . . .

I paused. I'd been about to say that I was thinking of him, but Philo and I had never been too mushy or forward like that. But then I thought, *Ya know? Life is too short to go around worrying about what other people think*. Philo and I had been together for seven months— three of those officially, and I liked him. For the first time in a long time I felt confident and, well, like it was okay to just be me with Philo.

Me: . . . that I was thinking about you.

I pressed send and sat staring at the phone for a second as if he'd text me back immediately. *Pfft. Silly girl.*

I switched over to Stacey.

Me: Hey. Sorry I've been MIA. Things have been so crazy busy here. Hope you're having fun!

She didn't answer me either. Dang it.

I surfed around on social media for a while until I got bored, then I went over to Reddit to see what was what. An ad for their Korean dining Reddit appeared at the top of my feed and I immediately hopped over to Google and searched how to make noodles with dragon fruit puree and glass noodles.

By the time Junu stumbled into the kitchen looking for tea, I had already had some brewing and prepared with noodle instructions.

I beamed at Junu as I handed him his cup.

"Someone's awfully bright eyed and bushy tailed this morning. What happened? Did you turn into a *kimiho* last night?"

271

"Funny," I said, even though he wasn't altogether wrong. Not quite like the mischievous fox spirit he'd accused me of being, but I did feel . . . *more*, just like Hanjo said. Not as powerful as I had last night when I felt the power humming in me, but not like my old self, either. I felt bright inside. I couldn't describe it any other way.

I slugged his arm. "I'm gonna go get ready."

"Better wait," he said. "The parents are in a hurry to get going."

"Sheesh. When aren't they? They vacation like it's an Olympic sport."

Junu barked out a laugh. "Right?" He took his tea over to the table and opened up his laptop. I looked around, wondering what to do next.

"I wish we could go over and clean the van now, so we can make the noodles," I said. Except he'd already slipped his headphones over his head so I don't think he heard me. I glanced at the clock.

So I made breakfast. Now, my mother taught me how to be a good daughter. She taught me how to cook, how to clean, how to press clothes—everything a good Korean wife should do.

But I did not like to cook.

As in, I hated it with a passion.

That's why I wanted to be a scientist when I grew up. A very successful famous scientist. So I could have people do the domestic work for me and I could eat out or order in every night. I loved to eat but cooking just seemed so tedious. All that work just to consume it as soon as you were done. No thank you.

And so it was with the most priceless expression on my parents' faces that they found me just finishing up on the breakfast preparation. Those looks made it all worth it.

"Just go ahead and sit down, Mom and Dad. I'll bring your breakfast right out. Do you know if Auntie and Uncle are ready to eat?"

"Coming!" I heard Auntie call from the bathroom.

I set bowls of egg drop soup, *kimchi* and rice, along with teacups and a fresh pot of tea on the table. Junu pushed away his laptop and looked first at the food and then up to me. "This looks great. I didn't know you could cook."

"Neither did I," Mom said, and we all laughed.

"Neither did I," I admitted. "Let's hope I don't poison everyone!"

Auntie laughed. "It smells delicious and I am sure it will do us all good."

For the first time in days we sat as a family and enjoyed a meal together. Dad didn't even ask one thing about the ancestors or when I was going to fix the problem. It was wonderful.

I hugged all four of them when they left on their next adventure, then turned to Junu expectantly. He hadn't gotten ready for the day yet, and his hair stuck up every which way. And he had glasses on. Weird.

He must have read the question on my face because he pushed his glasses higher on his nose. "I wear contacts."

I shrugged. "I'm not judging."

My phone dinged and my heart leapt in response—but it was only a text from Stacey.

Stace: Heyyy stranger! Having a super time - hope you are too!

Me: It's good. So many stories to tell you when I get home.

Stace: ME TOO. Also, I'm thinking of . . . you know. I think I'm ready!

I stared at the phone for a second.

Me: Are you talking about what I think you're talking about?

Stace: *blushing emoji*

Me: Ok, that's not just something you can tell me in a text. CALL ME

Stace: Can't now but I will soon! Promise!

Me: BEFORE

Stace: ☺

Omo.

I looked up, but Junu had gone into the bathroom. How could I be standing all alone when my best friend basically told me she was gonna have sex for the first time? I know it was her life and not mine, and she'd always been more into that stuff than me, but it still felt super weird. The news left me feeling really lonely and alone. Everyone I loved was really far away in more ways than one.

I collapsed onto the couch, suddenly feeling so tired and lonely. With Junu in the shower, I had nothing to do but lie around and wait. When I opened my eyes next, it seemed like no time at all had passed, but when I looked at my phone, there was a sticky note stuck to the back of it.

Gone to clean the van, it said.

I clicked over to Philo's texts—still nothing.

With a sigh that carried the weight of all teenage angst everywhere, I got to my feet and stretched. I left my phone on the counter and went to get ready for my day.

When I emerged from the bathroom a while later, I found Junu rinsing a colander of glass noodles in the sink. "Did you get them?"

"Yup." Junu winked at me. "But Mrs. Pong didn't have time to tell me much about how to prepare them."

"Step aside, amateur." I nudged him with my hip and picked up a packet of puree. "All you have to do is add some water to the puree, cook the glass noodles, then stir the noodles into the puree. Let them soak a while until they're infused with the flavor and color of the dragon fruit and ta da! Done."

I worked while I talked, and pretty soon had the noodles resting in a soupy, deep purple mess. "Back in a bit. Gotta dry my hair."

I hurried through getting dressed, excited to be on the verge of finishing up our second quest. But when I stepped back into the kitchen, I caught Junu slurping up a noodle. "Hey!" I rushed toward him, but he just held up a hand to stop me.

"Don't panic," he said after he'd swallowed. "I was just checking to make sure they tasted okay."

I glanced around and saw that he'd drained the noodles and they were a beautiful, bright shade of magenta. *Perfect.* "And?"

He glanced at the clock. It was 10:30. "I think today turned out to be a piece of cake."

I slugged him on the arm.

"Ow! You do that a lot, you know."

Oops. "Sorry. But don't jinx us."

"You're not superstitious, are you?"

I cocked my hip and gave him a *are you kidding me?* look. "Let's see. I'm a vampire, you have an *imugi* living in your garden with a magic pearl, and your own Zen master thinks it's all totally normal. I'm not counting anything out."

He scrubbed his knuckles over my head. "Point taken."

"So." I turned toward the sink where the noodles waited in a colander. "You said you knew where to find some homeless people?"

"Yup." He began digging through the cupboards. "We need something we can take the food in."

"Do you have any Tupperware?"

He threw me a questioning glance. "Any what?"

"You know, plastic containers?"

"That's what I'm looking for. Mom will kill me if I use her good stuff, though."

"Wait," I said. "We can't just give them noodles, can we?"

"That's all Master Yi said."

"I know, but maybe we should add some eggs or fish?" I opened the small refrigerator and peered inside. "There's some leftover *kimchi*."

"Found them!" He pulled out a handful of green plastic things that looked like they were a hundred years old.

I wrinkled my nose. "What are those?"

"These, little cousin, used to be what Mom sent lunch in when I went to elementary school. I'm actually surprised she still has them, but I was hoping."

"Are they big enough?" I asked.

"Oh yeah. And she won't miss them. She probably doesn't even remember they were up there. I'll wash these, you get out the *kimchi* and we'll get this show on the road."

I grinned and pulled out the leftovers. "I'm kinda excited for this one—is that weird?"

Junu threw me a shy smile. "It's barely anything, but I'm happy to be doing it, too. Homelessness is a huge problem here."

"It is back home, too."

We worked in silence, dividing the noodles between the four containers and arranging *kimchi* in the leftover space. "Well, it doesn't look the most appetizing, but it should all taste good together," I said as I finished with the last container.

"Hang on, let me grab a pic for Master Yi." Junu held up his phone and I posed with the container tipped so the photo would capture the pink noodles.

"We should get one with the people, too," I said.

"Good idea. You ready to go? 'Cause if you are, we might as well leave now."

I nodded and grabbed my phone from the counter. I caught a glimpse of the face and saw I'd missed three calls—all from an unknown number. "Did you hear my phone ringing?" I asked Junu. I'd be ticked if he just let it ring and didn't tell me. He shrugged and shook his head no.

I held the phone to my ear and listened to the first message.

"Minnie—"

That was Philo's voice. Why was Philo calling me from an unknown number? What happened to his phone? My heart sank through my stomach to my toes and dread took its place in my chest.

"Okay, I'm going to call back and hope you answer."

I fumbled as I switched to the next message.

All it contained was something that sounded like an angry Greek word.

My heart beat hard and painfully in my chest as I played the last message.

"Minnie. I'm so sorry I missed you. I needed to tell you—I . . ." His voice sounded so strange. Like he was sick and hiding under a blanket, whispering so no one would hear him. *What is going on?* "I didn't want to tell you like this, but I have to let you know before—" I stopped and took a breath. "I love you, Minnie Kim. From the moment you called me out from drinking from the blood bag after I'd chided you for being uncouth, I loved you. If—No. Just remember, no matter what happens, that you are a brilliant star. A true gift to the world. Be you and please don't ever change. And please, please be careful. There are forces at work that—" he cursed again and there was a noise like he was moving or something. "I have to go. Be safe. Be bold. You are everything you need to be, and I—Remember I love you."

I love you.

"Minnie? Min?" Junu's warm voice near my ear startled me.

"What—?" I was sitting on the floor, my knuckles white from the death grip I had on my phone.

"You were listening to a message I think and then just sort of sunk to the floor. You were kinda out of it there for a minute. You okay?"

I stared at the phone and nodded slowly.

I love you.

Be safe.

No matter what happens.

There are forces at work.

The meaningless words chased each other around in my mind and I couldn't grasp hold of them, couldn't make sense of any of it.

"Min?"

I took a deep breath. "I'm okay. I'll . . . I'll be okay. Just, can I have like five minutes before we leave?"

Junu stood and held his hand out for me, helping me to my feet. "Sure." He stepped back and I walked past him and into my bedroom.

I sat on my mom's bed and stared at nothing. Then I closed my eyes and opened my mind, seeking for Philo, wherever he might be.

I found him almost immediately and a small sob escaped my throat. He was alive. He was okay.

Philo? I tried.

Minnie? His mind-voice was so quiet, so distant I could hardly make it out. But it was there. Now I did cry, but I tried to keep that from him. I didn't want to upset him.

Are you okay? I just got your messages—you scared me to—

Minnie, he interrupted, a little stronger this time. *Hashiki—she's dead. She . . .* His mind struggled and concern rolled through me again. *She made Ying Yue promise . . .* He drifted away.

Minnie! he called out loudly.

I'm here, Philo. I'm here.

You need to get out of Korea. Now.

What? No, I—

Now, Minnie. Please. Go home. David will protect you. I wish I could protect you, love. I wish I could . . . his mind-voice dissolved into nothingness.

Philo? Philo!

I waited, pushed, tried everything in me to regain the connection, but while I still felt him, his mind was utterly silent. Finally, I swiped at the tears that fell fast from my eyes, ruining the cuffs of my favorite Hello Kitty sweatshirt. *I love you*, I sent into the dark void that was Philo's mind.

I want to go home. I don't
want to be here anymore. I
don't care what Dad thinks - I
need to find Philo. I'll finish the
quests - that's just one more
day and I promised I'd do it. But
then I'm going to go to Italy
and find Philo.

It's my turn to take care of
him. Just one more day.

CHAPTER
TWENTY-FOUR

I TRIED CALLING DAVID. TEXTED HIM. CALLED AND texted Fearghus and Siobhan, members of my vampire family—and reached no one. Where could they all be? What was going on?

A soft knock sounded at the door, and Junu pushed it open. "Min? I'm sorry to bug you, but we've gotta go."

I stared at him for a second, taken aback that he was even there. I'd completely forgotten about him. In a rush, time caught up with me and I realized what we'd been doing before I got Philo's messages. I jumped to my feet. "What time is it?" I nearly screamed. This was something I could do. Something I had to do. I couldn't fail at this.

"It's okay, but we do need to go. But . . ." he peered at my face, into my eyes. "Are you sure you're okay?"

I shook my head. "I don't know what I am, but I know we have to keep working on this. We can't just give up, now." I glanced at my phone and saw it was almost noon. "Oh my gosh! Are we gonna be able to get it done in time?" Panic made me grip Junu's arm and for some reason that prompted him to hug me.

He held me tightly. The kind of hug that's meant to reach past your barriers, sink deep into your soul, and heal what hurts. It wasn't possible for all my fears to be erased, but the hug definitely helped and when he stepped back, I offered him a shaky smile. "Thanks. I needed that."

He gave me a half-smile. "Why don't you wash up." He gestured at my face and blood-stained clothes, empathy softening his features. "Then we'll go."

사랑해

We drove to the subway, where Junu parked illegally, and we ran down the stairs and inside the terminal. "I have no idea if we'll find anyone, but this is the only real place I know homeless people sometimes hang out." We didn't see anyone in the main area. It wasn't very busy, but it was well-lit—definitely no homeless or even people who seemed down on their luck.

"Maybe if we go that way, we'll find someone." I pointed toward the far end of the terminal, just past where the main part ended. There was a narrow sidewalk of sorts that I figured connected one terminal to the next in case workers had to get down there. I couldn't imagine anyone living there—it would be terrifying every time a train sped past—but I had a strong feeling we should check.

Junu shrugged. "Might as well. If we don't find anyone we'll have to, um . . . I don't know. Go to the poorer part of town I guess, or out to the country—we don't have much time, though."

Guilt gnawed at my stomach. I must have sat in my room for over an hour. Longer, maybe. I didn't even remember it. I know I'd tried to connect with anyone who would hear me, both over telephone and through my mind, but the only people I'd successfully done that with were Philo and Thor and it didn't even occur to me to reach out to him. I was still ticked at him for the things he'd said when he hijacked my time with Philo the other night. Plus, he wouldn't know what was going on with Philo.

"We'll find someone," I said with more confidence than I felt. And then . . . I felt sure. I moved forward more quickly now, passing Junu and hurrying to the end of the terminal.

"Minnie, wait. I don't know if it's safe."

"It's okay." I reached the edge of the walkway and peered into the near darkness. There might have been one light affixed high on the wall between here and the next terminal, but its light didn't reach the walkway beneath. I turned on the flashlight on my cellphone. When I flashed it on the walkway, my heart soared. We were in the right place. I knew it as surely as I'd known where to find the *sansuyu* flower.

"Excuse me?" I called. No one answered. "Hello?"

Junu reached me and looked over my head. "Anything?"

"I can't see them, but there are people out there." I lifted my light, but it didn't reach far enough. "I need to go see."

Junu turned his phone on, too, and it added a bit of light. "I don't know . . ."

I stepped out onto the walkway. "We brought food," I called out to the strangers. "We don't want anything in return. We just thought you might be hungry."

I turned to Junu. "Hand me the food," I whispered. "Maybe they'll believe us if we show them."

"Good idea." Junu dug in his pack and brought out the four cups of noodles.

I put away my phone and took the containers.

"What if a train comes? You could leave the containers right there on the floor."

"Then we won't know for sure that four people got the food. I'm going. I'll be fine. Unkillable, remember?"

He cursed and then I heard him say, "I bet a train running over you would do some serious damage."

I ignored him and moved forward into the darkness. Except it wasn't dark anymore—I saw better now than I ever had without light before.

"Hey," I said softly as I drew nearer. "My name's Minnie and a monk told me where to find you." Not exactly, but I thought maybe if they thought a religious person had sent me, they'd be a bit more inclined to trust me. "I don't have much, just a little noodles and *kimchi*. I'm sorry it's not more."

I reached them, and went down onto my knees, offering the containers with a bowed head.

I waited, but no one moved. *Please*, I thought.

I heard shuffling, and someone quickly took the containers. I remained as I was for a beat longer, then sat back on my heels. Before me, sat a grandmother and grandfather, a young woman who looked like she could be their granddaughter, and a very young child. *Four people.*

"Thank you for letting me serve you." I bowed my head respectfully. Then I stood and quickly walked back to Junu.

We grinned widely at each other but didn't say anything until we were outside on the street again.

"You gave them everything—were there four people?"

"Yup!" I answered brightly.

"Awesome!" Junu high-fived me and a couple girls nearby giggled.

We jumped onto the scooter and made our way through traffic. We'd have to hurry if we were gonna make it to Master Yi in time.

We made it with five minutes to spare.

As soon as Junu turned off the bike, I felt her. Ying Yue. And she was close. I didn't sense any other vampires. Maybe she was just better at tracking me, and David's men were on their way. It didn't matter. It was broad daylight at a public place and we had a deadline to meet.

We rushed into the garden area where Master Yi usually met us, but it was completely empty. We sat on our bench and waited. The appointed time came and went. Not even one monk came out to the garden, and a rake had been carelessly tossed to the ground. That was not normal.

Junu and I came to the same realization at the same time. "There's something wrong," Junu said.

"I know."

We both stood and took a few steps forward. I felt Junu's trepidation radiating off of him and my own nerves sang in response. I picked up the rake and set it inside its storage box. The pattern the last person had been making had been a gentle wave pattern, but it had been interrupted by a sharp slash. *Was it where the rake had been dropped?* I wish I'd paid attention.

"You stay here in case Master Yi shows up," I said over my shoulder. The feeling of wrongness, of evil, grew exponentially with every passing moment. Ying Yue was not only nearby, she was *here*. Like, just ahead of me.

Heat rushed into my limbs, making them tingle. I paused, unsure of what I was feeling, but after considering it, I decided I felt good. Besides, if Master Yi was in trouble inside, then I had no choice but to go in.

The temple appeared to be empty. I couldn't exactly shout in a sacred place, but I dearly wanted to call out. From what I'd seen on our previous visits, there were usually two or three monks here at a time. Why couldn't I find them? A dark corner beckoned me and I found stone steps leading downward. The smell of blood wafted up the cool steps and I practically flew downward. Maybe I actually did fly. I don't know how it happened, but one minute I was up there and the next I was downstairs—faster than I'd ever moved before.

An ancient, heavy door blocked my way. It moved easily on greased hinges as I pushed it open and stepped inside a brightly lit and completely unexpected room. An electric light bulb glowed brightly on the ceiling and there was a table with an open laptop on it, and a couple chairs. A tea tray held an old microwave oven and a tiny fridge filled one corner.

The bodies of two monks lay on the earthen ground, their blood still seeping from the wounds at their necks. They hadn't been killed for their blood. They'd been bitten, torn into, and discarded like rag dolls. I knew they were dead, but I knelt first at the side of one man, and then the other to check for a pulse. I closed their eyes when I found none.

That's all I had time for because Master Yi was still unaccounted for, and now that I knew Ying Yue had just seriously raised the stakes, I had to get back to Junu. Now.

Calling on the new energy that infused me, I raced up the stairs and back out to the garden. At first glance, it appeared that Master Yi stood talking to Junu, and a wave of relief hit me—overturned by horror when I caught a glimpse of Ying Yue's smiling face in the trees. She tipped her head toward Master Yi in some meaningful way, then disappeared.

At first, I took it as a threat. *He's next*, I thought she meant. But as I approached the master and Junu, my gut told me that was not Master Yi standing there. Junu caught sight of me and smiled—but his smile faltered when he caught the grim expression on my face.

"Junu," I said softly. "I need to talk to Master Yi for a sec. Could you maybe meet me at the bike?"

"Why? I wanna hear the next quest."

Master Yi slowly turned to face me then, and I saw right through him to the demon huddling inside. I couldn't be sure what Junu saw, but I had to assume he only saw his old friend and mentor. I, however, saw the maniacal *dokkaebi* demon staring through the master's eyes.

"Just do it. Please?" I flicked a glance at Junu, but I was unwilling to take my eyes off of the monk for long. Dokkaebi demons, if I remembered what little Korean mythology I knew, were mischievous demons who could be good or evil. By the malicious grin on this one's face, he wasn't interested in sharing tea with us.

Junu folded his arms. "No. I have as much a right to be here as you do. Besides," he continued as the monk and I stared each other down. I'd never heard of a *dokkaebi* possessing someone, but that didn't mean it wasn't possible. What I didn't know was if Master Yi was alive in there or not. "I've already told him about how we finished the last quest. He said we passed! We were just waiting for you to get back before he told us the last quest." Junu's grin was wide and infectious, but it had no effect on me this time.

"And did he tell you what happened to his brothers who normally work here?"

Junu flicked a curious glance at the monk, and then back to me. "No. Should he have?"

"No." I shouldn't have even brought it up. "Okay then," I said to the monk. "What's our next quest?"

Junu sidled up next to me and whispered in my ear. "You're being super rude, cousin. Cut it out." I didn't respond.

The monk smiled and the creepiness exuding from him made me squirm. "Your third and final mission," it said in Master Yi's voice, "is to defeat the demon and trap it."

A smile finally curved my lips. "Happy to."

"Wait. What demon? Can you give us any clues as to where we can find one? Minnie—do you know anything about finding demons?" He turned to me. "What the heck, Minnie? What are you doing?" Guess he wasn't impressed with my fighting stance.

"I'm about to kick some demon butt," I said. "And I'm gonna enjoy every minute of it." My only regret was that I'd be damaging Master Yi's body. If he was alive in there, and there was a way for him to survive this, he was not gonna feel good when he woke up.

"Min, you're freaking me out. That's Master Yi, and he is not a demon."

"Are you sure about that?" I asked Junu, but my eyes never left the monk's. "Look into his eyes and tell

293

me you're one hundred percent positive that's Master Yi in there."

The monk laughed.

"Why don't you just tell him?" I said to the demon monk.

"Where would be the fun in that?"

Junu cursed and stepped out of my peripheral vision. But he wasn't fast enough.

The demon snatched him, twisted Junu's arm behind his back, and held him before him like a shield.

I moved to the right, trying to size up the demon, the monk, having no clue what to do. I was no warrior. But what choice did I have but to fight?

The demon laughed and tightened his grip on Junu's arm, making him cringe and cry out in pain. Then the demon shoved Junu forward so he stumbled into me. We fell together, but I was quick to jump to my feet. The demon pounced on my back.

"Watch out! He's a master in Hapkido!" Junu called. I didn't know if that meant he believed me, or just that Master Yi could kick my butt. Either way, it didn't matter. I'd had a little fight training but nothing anywhere close to a master's league. The only thing I had going for me was my vampire speed and strength. And right then, there wasn't time for anything else.

I managed to throw the monk off me and lunged for a rake, but the monk grabbed my wrist, twisting and turning it, driving me to my knees. It laughed, and there was nothing human in that sound.

I relied on the demon's grasp to keep me steady as I leaned forward and kicked out with my right foot, catching it hard in the shin. It howled and its right leg crumpled beneath it. A spurt of blood streaked across the pale sand and I caught a glimpse of bone protruding from the back of the monk's leg before it straightened its robe. I might have only imagined the flash of pain on its face before it was replaced with that terrible almost-grin. Then I was rewarded with a kick to my stomach that sent me flying across the distance and slamming against the temple wall. Golden shingles rained down on me.

"Junu," I gasped. I couldn't see him, but I knew he was near. I hoped he stayed safe. "Get a—" I struggled to breathe. "A container."

The monk stood over me and I thought it would finish me, but it lifted me with both hands around my neck. Maybe it wouldn't matter if Junu got the container. Maybe I wouldn't defeat the demon, after all.

At first I kicked and fought, but then I remembered a lesson Philo had taught me. I went slack. Then I placed my hands together as if in prayer and thrust them upward, so hard and so fast that not only did I jam my fingers into the underside of the monk's chin, but I broke its hold on me.

I didn't have time to catch my breath, or to enjoy my momentary victory. Junu yelled, "Watch out!" and I spun to find the demon, rake raised high in his hands.

"The container!" I shouted to Junu.

"I don't have anything!" His voice sounded hoarse, like he'd been screaming, which frightened me. I hoped Ying Yue hadn't hurt him while I'd been busy.

"Find something! Hurry!" *What I wouldn't give for one of those ugly green containers right about now.*

I lost track of the fight then. Our movements were too fast for even me to track. All I know is that I fought to survive. It wasn't fancy, it didn't follow any special fighting forms. I used everything I could—from throwing sand into the monster's face to kicking, biting, and clawing.

I don't know how much time passed. It had probably been no more than minutes, but when I finally held the jagged, broken end of a rake against the demon's throat as it lay beneath me, I felt like I'd been fighting it my whole life.

"Here!" Junu shoved a stinky plastic container under my nose. It smelled of rotten fish and—

The demon suddenly bucked me and jumped to its feet. I braced for it to come at me, but it whirled and, in a movement so fast, so mind-blowing, it reached for Junu.

"No!" I yelled. "It's me you want. Fight me!"

With unbelievable ease, the demon monk lifted Junu high over its head. Junu bucked and fought at first, but I think when he got so high, it must have frightened him, because he lay still.

"Minnie?" he asked.

"I'm here," I said. "It'll be okay."

The demon laughed. "It'll be okay," it mimicked. "I didn't know vampires were psychics. Can you guarantee his safety, little one?"

"You're a *dokkaebi* demon, right?" I asked. It didn't answer. "This is a bit dark for your kind, isn't it? I thought you guys were more into mischief, not full on evil."

"You don't know anything about me."

"I don't. But I could, if you told me."

The demon scoffed. "No one talks to me."

"I would. I talked to an *imugi*—that's why I'm on these quests."

The demon monk tossed Junu to the side, just like that. Junu cried out and I heard him hit the ground hard. But the demon stood in front of me; I couldn't turn away.

I held out my hands in an effort to calm it, to appeal to it, praying that Junu would be okay.

"No one talks to *imugis*, either," the demon monk said.

"I do. His name is Hanjo. We came today to finish our last quest so Hanjo can level up and become a real dragon." I didn't dare tell him about the pearl—that would be like putting a target on my family's apartment. *Dokkaebi* were trickster demons and it would be right up this guy's alley to steal the pearl right out from under Hanjo's nose.

"You just want to kill me," the demon said.

"No, I don't!" I swore. "You're inside my friend. I'd have to kill him to kill you. I can't do that."

I felt the demon falter, like I'd said the wrong thing, so I hurried to make it right. "I've never had to kill anybody. I don't wanna start now. Please don't make me."

The demon scoffed. "You're a vampire. You're all about death."

I shrugged. "Maybe in the old days, but not so much anymore. We use donors now. And blood banks." Master Yi's face held a blank expression. Guess the demon didn't know what blood banks were.

"So, I'm gonna assume the quest I was given today was a real one. All I had to do was defeat a demon—check—and trap it—we can take care of that in a second. Nothing was said about killing. I don't have to kill you, see?"

"Maybe it wasn't really a quest," it said. "After all, maybe Master Yi isn't alive in here and the quest won't count since he didn't give it."

"If that was true, then there'd be no reason to trap you. I might as well just kill you. But I have a feeling that's not the case." I picked up the container Junu had dropped.

"Blech! What is this? It smells disgusting!" Even the monk made a look of distress. I held it at arm's length. "Look," I said, taking a chance. "I don't want to kill you, okay? I know you're not inherently evil." At least I hoped that was the case. "If there's a chance to save you and Master Yi, then that's what I want to do."

The demon moved behind Master Yi's eyes then, and for a moment I saw a flash of the master's spirit. "Truly?" the monk asked.

"Yup!" I grinned. I'd picked up Junu's heartbeat, so I knew he was alive, but I was anxious to finish this up so I could check on him. "Look, I know this is super gross, but if you go in, I'll take you where you want to go. Somewhere not too far, since we only have a scooter."

"A street market?"

I narrowed my eyes. "What will you do there?"

The monk folded its arms and smiled innocently. "I'm hungry."

I sighed, suddenly weary beyond words. "Deal."

I waited. He waited. All the while Junu was hurt somewhere nearby and who knew where Ying Yue was.

"So, how do we do this?"

299

"Oh, right." The demon-monk got down on the ground and for the first time I caught a glimpse of Junu sprawled on the grass to the right. His eyes were open, watching us.

He whispered, "I'm okay," just loud enough for me to hear. And oh, it was the best thing I'd heard all day.

"Just hold your vessel beneath my face, I'll do the rest." He sat on the ground and gestured for me to hold the bowl under him as if he was getting a steam treatment or something.

Turned out to be more like some gross vomiting action as black sludge bled from Master Yi's eyes and nose. I lurched backward, then tightened my hold on the container, forcing myself to endure it.

"Gross," Junu hissed.

"Sorry," I said to the demon, just in case it could hear. I didn't want to offend it. But my eyes watered from the horrible smell—like sulphur and tar and wet dogs. Mixed with the already incredibly stinky spoiled food container, I could barely breathe the stench was so bad.

Just as I thought I might faint, the last drop dripped into the container and I slapped the lid on tight. I fell backward and to the side, cool grass cushioning me.

I lay there, just breathing, just being alive for a minute before I sat up straight, eyes wide with worry. Then I dashed to Junu's side.

"Oh my gosh, are you okay?"

Junu lay on the grass, one arm flung wide, the other tucked against his side with what looked like an extra elbow. "Um, your arm is broken."

He groaned. "Kinda figured that out. How's Master Yi?"

I glanced over to the monk who still lay prone on the ground a few feet away. "I don't know."

"Go," he said.

"His heart's beating slow and steady. I don't know if his mind's intact, but his body is." For whatever that was worth. "I'm sure he'll be okay," I reassured Junu even though I only had hope.

I carried Master Yi to the shade where I laid him on the grass. Junu and I sat on either side of him, waiting in silence for him to wake.

The afternoon grew long, but Junu and I kept saying we would wait a little longer for Master Yi to wake. We didn't know how to handle the police on our own if they were to find out what happened here.

Instead, I worried about the bodies in the temple's basement, I worried about Ying Yue hiding out nearby because yes, I could still feel her near, and I worried about Master Yi and whether he would ever wake.

I called for an ambulance, but we'd have to wait a while before one could make it to us. Junu wouldn't be able to drive the scooter so we had no choice but to wait.

301

Finally, as the first wails of a siren came to my ears from a distance, Master Yi groaned and his eyes fluttered open.

I still haven't been able to reach anyone in the family.

Where is everyone?

What's going on?

I can barely think of anything else.

CHAPTER
TWENTY-FIVE

I NEVER HAD TO TELL MY DAD I'D BECOME A VAMPIRE. The high school sent him a letter. I often thought that if I'd had a chance to tell him myself, then maybe things would have been different between us.

I don't think that anymore.

I called Mom's cellphone, but it was Dad who answered. "Dad?" I was a little taken aback to hear his voice instead of Mom's.

"Yes?"

How did I tell him this? He'd hate me forever, if he didn't already. *Well, might as well just dive in.* I took a fortifying breath. "Dad, Junu's been hurt. I don't think it's serious, but he's being taken to Seoul National."

I waited, but there was no response. "Dad?"

"We will be there."

Was it my imagination that he sounded angry? Like he could barely stand to talk to me?

I waited in the hospital waiting room while the doctors examined Junu. I'd ridden along in the ambulance since I couldn't drive his scooter, but once at the hospital, I'd been pushed aside and told to wait. I didn't think Junu's injuries were life-threatening, but what did I know?

Right then I was thinking I didn't know much of anything. I didn't know anything at all.

Half an hour later, I spied my aunt and uncle bustle in, followed by my parents. They went straight to the desk but were told to wait with me. All four of them seemed to turn at once and look in my direction. But it was only my dad's gaze I noticed. It crossed the distance, past the others in the waiting room, and drove daggers into my heart.

My father strode purposefully toward me. He bore down on me and I cowered in my seat like a little guilty child preparing for a scolding. "What happened?" he demanded.

"It was probably that scooter of his," Auntie said as she joined us. She wrung her hands. "We should have let him borrow the car."

Dad cut her a dismissive glance. "Tell me."

I so wanted to tell him it had been an accident. That it couldn't possibly be my fault. But it wasn't the truth and lying just didn't come naturally to me. I'd be found out for sure.

"There was a fight—" I started.

Somehow Dad seemed to grow even more intimidating. "Did you get him into this? Is this your fault?"

I bristled under his glare. "We were trying to help the family. We were with Master Yi." I had no idea how to answer any of these questions without telling more about the supernatural world which would probably freak him out all the more.

Dad scanned the waiting room. "And where is this *Master Yi?*"

"He had some business to take care of at the temple, but then he said he would come." The master had been surprisingly good when he woke up, and didn't seem to be suffering from any residual mental issues as a result of being possessed by the *dokkaebi* demon. He had to have some fractured bones, but he said it was nothing he couldn't endure long enough to see to his brethren. He promised to get checked out after that, but he seemed more concerned about visiting Junu and me, than about coming to the hospital for his own care.

Dad harrumphed and sat on a chair far away from me, his arms folded. Mom didn't seem to know where to sit, but in the end, she chose him, as she always did. Auntie and Uncle didn't seem to be angry with me, but they huddled together near the entrance to the waiting room, anxiously waiting for news.

A doctor came in wearing turquoise scrubs and a friendly, warm demeanor. "Kim? Kim Jung-woo?"

My parents jumped up and I hurried to follow my family through the double doors and into a treatment room. Junu lay propped in bed, one arm in a sling, an ankle wrapped and propped on a pillow. He wore a few butterfly bandages over his left eyebrow, and a wide grin.

The doctor gave the parents a rundown on his injuries, but I knew he'd be okay. I seemed to have a sense about these things now—I could sense a person's wellness. Plus, the goofy grin on Junu's face relieved most of my worries. When he winked at me, the last dregs of guilt fled.

The doctor left and the parents drilled him for answers. I wondered what Junu would tell them, but I didn't expect him to tell the truth.

The parents hadn't known about Hanjo—but now they did. They hadn't known about the quests—but now they did. They hadn't known there was a terrible vampire stalking me, who tore out the throats of two innocent monks—but now they did.

"She's amazing, Uncle Jung-il. You should be so proud of her. She's smart and brave and everything she's done has been to help and protect our family.

And help the *imugi*! She's like one of those heroes from our old myths."

I appreciated Junu's words. I did. I'd been really afraid that he'd be mad at me, or afraid of me or something. But his words weren't enough to convince the adults of my innocence or goodness. As they slowly turned to face me, all I saw were four pairs of accusing eyes glaring at me.

Dad stepped forward. He poked his finger at me. "You did this. You and your evil ways. I should have never let you back into our lives. I knew from the beginning what you were. Nothing but a *gangshi*." He spit on the floor at my feet. "Nothing but the walking dead. You care for nothing but yourself."

"Uncle—" Junu tried, but no one was listening to him. I couldn't even see him past the wall of bodies facing me.

"I tried to accept you for your mother's sake, but you are a disgrace to this family and to our ancestors." He stepped forward again, his pointed finger now burning a hole into my heart as it pressed against my breastbone. "You will not speak to your mother ever again—"

Mom put a hand on his arm. "Father, no."

He whirled on her, spittle flying from his mouth as he shouted. "She is no longer your daughter!" He turned back to me. "Our daughter is dead."

He pushed me forward until I stumbled out of Junu's room.

"Uncle—Minnie, wait!" Junu's voice was lost to me as the door closed in front of my face and the parents all turned their backs on me.

So that was it. My family was gone. After everything I'd tried to do, everything Junu and I had done, to help— it still wasn't enough.

I wasn't enough.

My father was never going to accept me. He'd only been looking for a reason to reject me. And I'd just given him one.

I took several steps backwards as the shock worked its way through me. Once it reached my feet, I turned and ran.

I burst from the hospital and onto the street. People gasped and scattered away from me—bloody tears streaked down my face and neck and soaked into the collar of my T-shirt. I swiped at them with my hands, but soon my hands were a mess too and there was nothing to be done. I walked aimlessly, angling for the shadows, the alleyways—anything to get out of sight. Why did this city have to be so busy? Why were there so many people? I needed to disappear.

I stumbled upon a market packed with people shopping for their dinner. I kept my eyes on the ground and pushed through, desperate to get away. My eagerness made me clumsy of course, and I zigged when the woman in front of me zagged—and I ended up on my butt. It wasn't until that moment that I remembered the dobbaeki demon in my backpack. How could I have forgotten it? It probably thought I'd abandoned it. Even a demon deserved better than that. At least I was in the perfect place.

I edged my way to the fringes and found a stall selling deep fried crickets on skewers. Yum. At the back of the stall, I fished out the stinky container, opened it, set it on the ground, and ever-so-subtly used my toe to push it under one of the stall's tables. There were enough strong smells here that I didn't think the container would turn anyone away from the seller's cuisine. Because deep fried crickets.

I spied a dark and narrow dead-end alley where I was finally, blissfully alone. Spying a raggedy piece of cloth sticking out of the garbage can next to me and, not caring what it was or what it had been used for, I scrubbed at the blood on my face. It's not like I could catch a disease from it or anything.

Because I wasn't human.

And I should remember that, just like Dad said.

I thought of Philo. He wasn't human either, but he loved me—because no matter what Dad said, vampires weren't evil. They were capable of love. And Philo loved me and I loved him.

I needed to go to him. To find him. Help him.

With renewed purpose, I stood from where I'd slouched against the wall and turned to leave the alley.

And came face to face with Sang-hyeok.

"What are you doing here?" I didn't mean to bite his head off, but I hadn't even felt him approach. What if he had been Ying Yue? Fear felt like a living thing, flapping away in my chest.

"You are not safe here," he said. He grabbed my arm and tried to pull me after him.

"Maybe I'm not safe from you," I countered, pulling my arm away. "Maybe you're not safe from me."

He raised an eyebrow. "You think you could defeat me?"

I slumped. "No. I—"

He took my arm again. "Go. Go back to your family."

"No," I said. I resisted his push forward.

"What is wrong with you?" he asked, exasperation clear in his voice.

I whirled to face him. "Yeah—that's a very good question. What is wrong with me?" I stalked toward him. "Tell me, because I can't figure it out."

For the first time the stern, powerful Sang-hyeok appeared flustered, lost for words, and I grinned cruelly at him. "Just ask my father. He could tell you all the things."

"You're not safe out here." His tone was almost pleading, but I was unmoved. "Just go back to them."

"I can't! Can't you see that? Can't you guess it? You seem like a smart guy—figure it out! I'm out here all alone with blood on my face. You think I went hunting before I came to hang out in a dark alley who the heck knows where?

"I've been crying, you idiot. Because I'm a teenage girl and that's what teenage girls do when their families reject them."

He took a step toward me, a hand outstretched, but I backed away. "Forget it. I'm fine. But I'm not going back there."

Anger hardened his expression and it was actually an improvement. I didn't like seeing care in his eyes.

"Well you cannot stay here. Danger follows you." Once again, he grabbed my arm and started dragging me from the alley. No matter how I tried, his grip did not loosen.

"Hey, let me go!" I struggled and resisted, but he kept stalking forward.

"I think the girl said no. Doesn't no mean no, these days?" a woman said. A very familiar woman.

I slowly turned. Ying Yue stood before us.

My first thought was to run, but there was nowhere to run to. I might be able to scale the building—the new power Hanjo's pearl had given me hummed in my muscles and I knew I could do it. But could I do it before Ying Yue caught me?

"At last I find you alone. And in a nice, quiet spot where we can chat."

I whirled around, but Sang-hyeok was nowhere to be seen. What the heck? Nice of him to just leave me like that. Well, I'd just have to do this on my own. I'd never been a quitter before and I wouldn't start now.

I took a deep breath to calm my nerves and tried to pull it together. "What do you want, Ying Yue?"

She sauntered toward me, her movement lithe and precise. She wore her long black hair in a ponytail, with black pants and a long sleeved, collared shirt that stretched and moved with her. Perfect for skulking around in the dark. She didn't seem to have any makeup or jewelry on, yet she was still beautiful. Her eyes sparkled with a dark menace as she looked at me.

"Now. Is that any way to speak to your elder?" Her voice was honey sweet, disguising her wickedness.

"I have no respect for you. I will never honor you." Oh, those were brave words and secretly I high-fived myself, but really? I was about to pee my pants. I was gonna die there, in that dirty, lonely alley. That didn't bother me half so much as not knowing what happened to Philo. What if he needed me? The thought made my stomach lurch.

Ying Yue didn't seem fazed by my words. She continued to move toward me, her intent plain in her eyes. I backed up a step.

"You're a pitiful little thing," she said. "How is it you have managed to cause me such heartache?"

"I'm sorry," I said truthfully. "I honestly didn't mean to."

"Didn't mean to? Of course that's what you'd say. Those words define you. You're nothing but a careless child. A toddler thoughtlessly destroying the treasures of hundreds of lifetimes."

"I'm not the cause of your downfall," I protested. I was going to die anyway, I might as well tell it like it was. She couldn't kill me twice. "You didn't follow the rules. You ignored direct commands from the Master. That was you. I didn't do any of that."

She reached me then and I stood very still as she ran a cool finger down the side of my face. "So sad you've been crying. Did you get the news about your ill-fated lover?"

I stiffened. "What news?"

But Ying Yue didn't answer. She attacked.

Brutal and efficient, we exchanged no words, only blows. I fought her, but only because it was reflex to do so. We both knew what the outcome would be.

She would win.

I would die.

It might seem melodramatic, but I was okay with dying. At least right then, I was. My heart was so smashed and broken, death seemed like a welcome escape. The only thing that kept me going was thinking about how Philo needed me. I had to get to Italy and see for myself what was going on.

So I fought. If it hadn't been for the added strength Hanjo's pearl had given me, I wouldn't have lasted as long as I did, but after only a couple minutes, my strength faltered. Ying Yue was faster, stronger and infinitely more skilled than me.

As my efforts waned, sorrow ate away at my soul. *You're all alone*, it said. Even Sang-hyeok hadn't stuck around. *There's no one to help you. No one who cares.*

I wondered if Hanjo leveled up and got his pearl.

I wondered if the ancestors had found their rest.

Because *I* cared. And that voice in my head could just shut up because while my father might have rejected me, my vampire family had not. I had to follow Hanjo's wisdom and advice. I had to have more faith in myself.

I lay on the ground, grit and debris digging into my back as Ying Yue stood over me. "You are nothing," she growled. Victory shone in her eyes.

But she hadn't won yet.

I raised my knee as hard as I could and caught Ying Yue in the upper thigh which caused her to scramble back, giving me enough room to jump to my feet. Instead of falling to the ground, someone caught Ying Yue around the waist. Sudden fear gripped me. Had some vampire come to claim his place by her side?

Ying Yue broke the person's grip and whirled—revealing Sang-hyeok behind her.

They fought like two wild creatures, and it was only my own vampire abilities that let me track the action. They were fairly evenly met, but every time Ying Yue spun out of his grip, I was there to deliver my own kicks and blows.

Moments later she scaled the wall as I'd thought of doing only minutes earlier, and ran across the rooftop, disappearing into the night. I bent over, my hands on my knees, and looked up at Sang-hyeok, who stood straight as an arrow, staring down at me.

"What?" Was he gonna attack me now? Was he mad Ying Yue got away? Or that he'd felt compelled to help me? "I'm sorry you had to fight for me. But thank you. If it weren't for you, I'd be dead."

I straightened and took a couple steps toward him, but he made no move to leave.

"Why were you going to let her kill you?" His voice was gruff, almost angry.

I lifted the hem of my T-shirt and bent low so I could wipe my face with it. I was so sweaty and bloody. Gross. "I wasn't going to *let* her. But I didn't stand a chance against her." I straightened to face him.

"You could have tried harder."

I shrugged and looked away.

He took a step toward me and I stiffened. He stopped his approach. "You are such a foolish girl."

"So everyone keeps telling me." I flicked a glance at him, but I still couldn't read the dark expression on his face.

"Why are you even out here by yourself? Where's your cousin?"

I snorted. "Oh, he's in the hospital because I nearly got him killed."

He gestured toward the open end of the alley. "Did she attack you earlier?"

"No." I shook my head. "We were on a quest for an *imugi* and I had to vanquish a demon and the demon almost killed Junu." I said it like I didn't expect him to believe me, but he didn't seem surprised at all.

"That is not your fault. Did you force him to be there with you?"

"No."

Now Sang-hyeok shrugged. "Then it is not your fault." He said it so simply, as if there was no other option but for that to be true. He glanced around the dark alley. "And you are leaving? Running away?"

I bristled a little at that. "He's safe with family. The *imugi's* probably leveled up by now and the ancestors are resting. It's happily ever after for the Kim family."

317

"But you are here. It is not happily ever after for you. Aren't you also part of the Kim family?"

This time I looked him square in the eye. "No. My father told me so tonight in no uncertain terms."

He rocked back on his heels, either from the hard tone in my voice or the impact of my truth, I'm not sure which. "I see."

"I'm part of the Aristos family. And right now, someone needs me." I pushed past him, aiming for the street beyond the alley. "See ya."

Sang-hyeok grabbed my wrist as I passed him. I looked at him expectantly, but after a moment he let me pull away without a word.

I'm not human, I'm a vampire.
I'm proud to be a part of the
Aristos family.

They're all the family I have now.

New Skill:

★ Sensing the state of someone's
health—broken bones, internal
injuries. I think that's it. (me)

CHAPTER
TWENTY-SIX

I PRACTICALLY THREW MYSELF INTO THE STREET AND hailed a cab. "Incheon Airport!" I shouted at the surprised driver. He was about Junu's age, with platinum blonde hair, and for some reason I thought Junu would really like him. Without thinking, I snapped a pic of his driver info on the back of the seat.

"You okay?" the driver asked.

"Fine, thanks." I slumped against the door and stuck my earbuds in. I wasn't in the mood for chit chat or concerned strangers. I just needed away. I needed Philo.

I didn't turn on any music but used the muted quiet to try again to reach Philo with my mind. Still nothing. Where could he be?

It had been hours since I'd checked my phone, but there was absolutely nothing on it. Nothing from David. Nothing from the family. Nothing from Philo.

Even Stacey hadn't texted.

I'd never felt so alone in my entire life.

The traffic was heavy, and soon the steady rumble of the engine and gentle stop and go lulled me into an exhausted sleep. I dreamt I was a greyhound chasing a mechanical rabbit around a track. Except I wasn't a greyhound, I was me. Rich people were betting on me, cheering for me, but no matter how hard I tried, I could not catch the darn rabbit.

Somehow, in the way of dreams, the rabbit morphed from rabbit, to Dad, to Philo.

Finally, at the end of the race, the rabbit disappeared into its hidey-hole, but in this case, the hole gaped like a hungry monster and it chomped down on the poor rabbit.

People screamed and booed at my failure, saying I should kill myself. That I was nothing. No one. The world would be better off without me. And all I could do was crumple to the ground, crushed by the weight of their unmet expectations.

I jolted awake when the car rocked forward suddenly. The driver had braked hard at the toll booth into the airport. "We're here, Miss," he called over his shoulder.

"Okay," I said, just to let him know I was alive back there. I opened my app and scanned his code on the back of the seat, paying him before he even pulled to the curb.

"Do you need me to wait?" he asked when he'd put the car in park.

"What? No—I'm leaving."

"But you don't have any bags. I thought maybe you were picking someone up."

"Oh," I looked around dumbly. "Yeah, I travel light." I laughed, but we both knew it wasn't funny. This guy was gonna be telling all his friends about the crazy chick who went on an international flight without any bags. At least I had my backpack, wallet and the credit card David had given me. I never had found out what the limit on it was, but this trip might just answer the question.

"Look," said the driver. "Are you all right?"

I gave his question some thought. Was I all right? "You know," I said as I realized the truth. "I'm okay. I thought maybe I wasn't, but I think maybe I actually am." He stared at me like I was insane, but that didn't matter. I smiled when I opened the door and got out.

Despite the dream, I actually felt like I had a little perspective on everything. I hadn't failed—not the way Dad thought I had. With Junu's help I'd completed the quests, so I chose to believe that not only was Hanjo free, but so were the ancestors. I'd done exactly as my father wanted me to do.

I thought of the fragile *sansuyu* flower, and even though I'd crashed through who knew how many tons of water, I'd managed to keep the flower safe and hadn't lost a single petal. My body was eternal, but I could still be gentle and kind.

I thought of the look on the homeless family's faces when I handed them the food and they realized I really, truly didn't want anything from them. Many humans had rejected me for being different, but I could still love them and serve them.

And I thought of Junu and his goofy grin as he bragged about me in the hospital. That demon could have killed both him and Master Yi, but it hadn't. Both Junu and Master Yi could hate me—but they didn't. I might not be human anymore, but I had love. Wasn't that what life was about?

A lot of bad things could have happened, but they didn't—because I'd been there. I realized now that Hanjo had been right—I thought I was doing it so my dad would love me, but that wasn't it. I did it to help my family. To help Hanjo. To help the people sleeping in the subway terminal. To save Master Yi.

I was beyond sad that Dad couldn't love and accept me for who I was, and Mom was too weak to stand up to him—and stand up for me. But I wasn't alone. Not in the ways that really mattered. I had David, Fearghus, Siobhan, Manuela, Jack and even Mrs. Hamburg. I had

Junu and Stacey. And I had Philo. They would be my family now. They were all I needed. More than I needed.

As I walked through the automatic doors to the airport, a wide, authentic grin spread over my face. Because I knew, really *knew*, that they were lucky to have me, too. And even though we were all different, that we were as unique from each other as a family could get, it only strengthened our bonds. I couldn't wait to tell my vampire family about my little revelation over dinner, and see their reactions.

Fearghus would make a joke and Siobhan would scoff. Mrs. Hamburg would probably give some cautionary advice about never letting your guard down and Manuela would probably cry and hug me. David and Jack would understand and give me their nods of approval. They'd be thinking something along the lines of *took you long enough*.

And Philo would smile and tell me he loved me.

He loved me.

I hadn't had a chance to really process that, and as I let it become reality in my mind, I made my way over to the ticket counter, renewed hope adding bounce to my step.

"Minnie?"

I turned, still in a daze of thought, and came face to face with David, Fearghus and Jack.

"What?" I took a stunned step back, my brain spazzing out. "What are you guys doing here?" I threw myself at them, pulling all three into an awkward hug—especially since I was five foot nothin' and they weren't. When I pulled back, I caught a flicker of sadness in their eyes—but it was soon replaced with half-baked smiles.

I crossed my arms. "What's going on?" Even David shifted his feet and didn't meet my gaze.

"Maybe we can go outside?" he said.

"I'm just about to get a ticket to Italy." I looked up at the departure board and started to edge my way toward the counter. "I'm gonna go see Philo, so I've gotta go buy a ticket."

David stepped forward and put his arm around my shoulders. "Just come with me for a moment."

"Ohhkay." I went with him but my good mood soon morphed into dread. There couldn't be any good reason for him to want to talk to me in private. "You're kinda freakin' me out here," I said on a laugh.

David tightened his arm around me and once we'd gone through the doors, he pulled me over to a stone bench near the taxi line-up. We sat and faced each other.

He'd just opened his mouth when a whoosh of air moved past me, and Jack grunted. I turned to see what was up—and found Ying Yue with Jack standing before her, poised as if she might snap his neck.

"I tell her, or I snap his neck," she said.

I looked at David. "Tell me what?"

David stood. "No. That is beyond cruel, even for you."

She glared at David. Jack struggled, but he was no match against an ancient like Ying Yue.

Peace settled over my heart and I experienced another moment of clarity. I knew what she wanted to tell me. "Let her tell me," I said to David, though my gaze never left Ying Yue's. "Let him go."

She nodded at David. "Send your minions away. I wish to speak in private."

David glanced at Fearghus, who grunted and turned, though he fumed as if leaving might kill him; and Jack, who picked his cowboy hat off the ground and tipped it to us as he sauntered past. No one would ever know his life had just been in the balance.

"It's just the three of us," David said, his hands outspread. To me, he said, "Minnie, I'm sorry—"

Quick as shadow, Ying Yue jabbed David in the throat, rendering him speechless as he staggered back several feet.

"This isn't for him to tell," she crooned, a slow smile curling her full lips. She peered at me closely, as if waiting for some sign from me, but all I could do was watch her with grim acceptance.

I balled my fists at my side. "What news?"

She wrapped her arms around my neck, standing so close we might have been lovers. She rested her forehead on mine. "You took Hashiki from me," she whispered, eyes closed, breath cool on my cheek.

"I—"

"Had it not been for you, she would have had Philo as she always wished, and she would not have broken so many of the Master's rules." She twirled my ponytail around her fingers. "Did you know she was my only child? My last surviving child?"

I frowned. Could that be possible? Ying Yue was ancient.

As if reading my mind, she said, "The Master was careful and selective, choosing only the very best of humans to become his children. He created only three. David was the first." She rolled her eyes, as if David was the first in other ways that displeased her. "And *he* couldn't stop making children. He couldn't stop himself from saving poor suffering humans and granting them the gift of eternal life. Such a waste." She shook her head. "Isn't that right, David?"

Out of my peripheral vision, I saw David standing with his arms crossed, a look of thunder on his face. He didn't take his gaze off Ying Yue.

"Ki was no better—he nearly ruined his civilization. He couldn't control the monsters he created.

"I, however, minded my time. I took care to be sure the person I chose was ready for such a gift. That they were worthy. I chose only a handful—in all the world, in all my time, only a handful were worthy of my gift."

She suddenly jerked on my ponytail so hard it revealed my throat, and I gasped.

David flashed in between us and shoved her away from me. "You will not harm her."

I glanced around us and saw we were drawing a crowd. Could we compel all these people to forget? There were probably a hundred phones streaming us right this second.

"Of course I won't hurt her," Ying Yue said. "I only want to talk." That's what she said. And her words sounded true. But the look in her eye screamed violence.

"Where was I?" she asked. "Ah yes. I was telling you the sad tale of my offspring. Even my well-chosen have not survived. I have outlived them all. Hashiki—now she was truly special. I knew she would finally be the creation worthy of her creator. But you took her from me. All her potential, her remarkable gifts. All gone. Because of a little girl accidentally reMade.

"So I have a gift for you, Minnie Kim." She said my name as if it were a curse—and maybe to her, it was. "A trade, if you will, for taking Hashiki from me." She bowed with a flourish. "I have taken Philo from you."

It took a second for me to process her words. I stepped forward. "What do you mean—took him?"

She smiled then, a wild full-on crazy smile that was more terrifying than anything I'd yet seen. She shrugged. "I took him from you. From your family. From this world."

My toes touched hers as I leaned into her, fury burning slowly through my body. "You did not kill him," I challenged. Wouldn't I know if he were gone? Wouldn't I have sensed it?

She cupped my cheek in her palm and I flinched but didn't retreat. "You're right." My eyes fell shut and I let out a pent-up breath. "I didn't kill him."

I sagged and took a step back. "I knew it." She'd just been messing with my mind.

David took my hands in his. "Minnie, I—"

"Hashiki killed him with her last breath." Ying Yue jumped up onto the bench and spread her arms wide. "They're together now, as they were meant to be. Together at last in death.

"And so, I will purge my own demons as well. I just wanted you to know before I ended you. You have lost, Minnie Kim. You have lost everything."

David streaked past me—the next thing I knew they were fighting, their movements so fast I couldn't track them at all.

Jack and Fearghus joined us, but neither made a move to stop them. Stone crumbled as someone hit the side of the building. The bench was smashed in half.

"What can we do?" I shouted to Fearghus. "We have to stop this!"

"There's nothin' we can do, lass. We're as like ta get ourselves killed if we try ta intervene."

"But—" I turned to Jack, but he put his hand on my back, a look of sadness and regret on his face. And it's then I realized the truth in his eyes. His sorrow and regret weren't only for the fight that raged before us, but for the *truth*.

Philo really was gone.

Hashiki really had killed him.

He must have seen the realization in my face because he gathered me to his chest and wrapped his arms tightly around me.

"You bloody—" Fearghus' words had Jack and I whirling, only to see David on the ground and Ying Yue standing over him with blue electricity shooting out of her hand and into David's chest. "The devil break yer bones, ya wagon!" Fearghus yelled as he dove for her.

"What's going on? What is she doing?"

But Jack left me too, rushing in to help our brother. I didn't know what to do, how to help. I couldn't just stand here, helpless, while Ying Yue killed off my family. And they didn't stand a chance against her if even David had fallen.

While my brothers fought, I rushed to David's side. "Are you all right? David? Please be okay!" He took my hand in his but didn't open his eyes. "I'll be all right. It'll . . ." he struggled for a second, "take a lot more than that to take me down."

"What did she do to you?"

"She . . . harnesses the electricity in her body and . . . stores it . . ."

Okay, I could guess the rest. "Can Jack or Fearghus take her?"

His eyes opened then and homed in on mine. "You have to run, Minnie. Run as fast and far as you can." He gripped my hand so hard the bones rubbed together. "We'll be okay. I'll be okay. It's you she's after and you're not ready to face her." David rolled to his feet and shoved me away. "Run!" he roared at me as a blast of blue light sent Jack flying out into the road where cars honked.

David turned, threw himself into the air and came down with a whip kick to Ying Yue's head that sent her tumbling to the side. Fearghus took a part of that blow and stumbled for a second.

I did not run.

How could I have forgotten what
Hashiki could do?

Other gifts vampires can have:

★ The ability to manipulate
another person's/vampire's
nervous system (Hashiki)

★ Harnessing their own body's
electricity and using it as a
weapon (Ying Yue)

Hashiki's dead.
She killed Philo.

CHAPTER
TWENTY-SEVEN

I'D ALREADY LOST ONE FAMILY TODAY. I WOULD NOT lose another. But what could I do? I glanced around, embarrassed to see that the crowd of humans had backed away from us, afraid to be too close, I guess. Most watched the fighting, but others stared at me. What could I do?

And then a person near me shifted, and I saw the dragon emblazoned on the back of his sweatshirt.

Hanjo had said that I would forever be part of his family. That he saw into my heart and knew it to be true. Did he mean that? Would he trust my need if I asked for his help now?

Ying Yue stood on a pile of crumbled rock and held both hands out, sending streams of electricity into Jack's and Fearghus's chests at the same time. The threads of lightning were weakening, but so were my family.

Hanjo! I called in my mind. I balled my fists at my sides and squeezed my eyes shut. *Hanjo!* I used all my might, every bit of mental power I possessed, pushing all my energy into my need. *Please, if you can hear me—I need you!* I strained to hear a response but heard nothing, instead.

David was back on his feet, and he came around Ying Yue from behind. He bent and lifted the rock on which Ying Yue stood and raised it high, bunching his muscles as if to throw it *and* her away. It stopped the onslaught of power, but she merely whirled and kicked him in the head with her stiletto boot. Blood spurted across the wall and the crowd screamed. I screamed, too.

And I heard nothing from Hanjo.

Maybe the quests hadn't worked, and he was still trapped on the rooftop garden. Maybe he'd leveled up and disappeared. He was a dragon—who knew what they thought of people, or vampires, or anybody for that matter.

You served me well, Hanjo's smooth voice said in my mind. My knees wobbled and I nearly fell from relief, but someone bolstered me from behind. I glanced over my shoulder and found myself looking up into the dark eyes of a grouchy vampire. Sang-hyeok.

May I serve you, now?

"What?" I said aloud. Sang-hyeok shot me a curious look. *Please. Anything you can do—we're at Incheon—*

Screams erupted all around me and people scattered everywhere. They dropped their phones, their purses, and ran. Sang-hyeok looked behind me and up and up and up.

I turned and saw a glorious golden-eyed dragon descending from above, a bright orb pulsing in the center of its chest. *Hanjo?*

He was the size of a jumbo jet, and as he descended, his wings crushed the edge of the building and the overpass to the left. The purple frills at his neck fluttered prettily in the wind, but there was nothing pretty about him. He was fierce and terrifying and he reached down and plucked Ying Yue off the ground.

In one chomp, half of her lifeless body fell to the ground. I didn't want to think about what happened to the other half.

Motionless, with Sang-hyeok supporting me, I stared at Hanjo while pandemonium raged around us. People screamed, both out of fear and pain. There were injured, and I prayed none were dead. But Ying Yue was gone. Well and truly gone.

Thank you, I told Hanjo.

He bowed his head and rose to the sky with a great upswell of his wings. *We are family, little sister. I will always come when you call.*

The night was dark, with only a sliver of moon in the sky, but Hanjo's shadow was darker than night and I watched him fly inland until I couldn't see him anymore.

"You are a very strange girl," Sang-hyeok said.

"You don't know the half of it." I forced my feet forward. "Come on. I want you to meet my family."

I walked at first, then broke into a run until I was in David's arms. He held me so tightly. "I'm so glad you're okay," he said into my hair.

"Me too. I was so afraid."

David chuckled. "So was I."

"I nearly shite my pants," Fearghus said loudly. "Come 'ere lass. Give us a hug." He lifted me off my feet into a bear hug and whirled me around. "Nice 'o you to bring yer little friend to the party," he said. "But next time, ya might warn a man when a legendary dragon's about ta eat a person right in front o' his face."

"I really hope there's never a next time." I patted his chest in a *let me down you big oaf* sort of way.

"Well, I for one am glad ya have friends in high places, Miss Minnie," Jack said. He smiled shyly, his trademark cowboy hat lost somewhere in the scuffle.

"Come get a hug, Jack." I opened my arms.

"Whatever you say, Miss."

We hugged briefly before I noticed the cries and shouts around us had quieted. I pushed away from Jack. "What's going on?"

People all around us were helping each other pick up their things and trying to bring order to the chaos. No one paid us any attention.

"Hey," I turned to David. "Did you see my friend?"

David chuckled. "Your dragon friend? Yes, Minnie. I think everyone saw your friend."

"No, a man. He was right behind me. I wanted you to meet him—I told you about him on the phone. Sang-hyeok?"

My family went still.

"What?" David asked.

"You met Sang?" Fearghus asked, as if I hadn't just said that very thing.

"Yeah. He's gotta be here somewhere."

"Well, that'll explain the easin' concerns of the people," Jack said. "Someone's compelled 'em."

I scoffed. "He's one person. He couldn't have compelled all these people that fast."

"No," Jack agreed. "But he coulda made a mighty fine start."

"That's—" I turned to face them. "So you guys know him?"

"Not me," Jack said. "Not personally, at any rate."

"Yeah, I know the gobshite." Fearghus spat on the ground. I suppose that told me all I needed to know about that.

"David?"

But David was looking past me, and didn't hear my question. He moved forward and when I watched to see where he went, found Sang-hyeok standing some distance away.

"What's goin' on?" I asked Jack and Fearghus.

They came to stand beside me and Fearghus put his giant hand on top of my head, giving my head a little wobble. "Why, a family reunion, I'd say."

"Yup." Jack bobbed his head.

Relief workers showed up and draped blankets over our shoulders. They said an earthquake had struck the peninsula, and we were all very lucky to be alive. They encouraged us to sit down, so we propped ourselves against the wall of the airport and watched Sang-hyeok and David talk.

It wasn't long before the body shakes started. Despite my protests, Fearghus pulled me onto his lap and soon, I fell asleep.

사랑해
♥

Muted men's voices rumbled but I couldn't make out the words. I opened my eyes and found I was lying in a hotel room, the lights of Seoul shining outside the large window. I felt hollow inside. Numb. Like someone had taken an ice cream scoop and scooped out all my

feelings. All my worries and fears. I still knew stuff—
we'd fought Ying Yue and Hanjo had saved us.

Philo was dead.

I just couldn't feel anything.

I shuffled out of the room and into a common area
where David, Fearghus and Jack sat at a small round
table. A quick glance showed Sang-hyeok standing in
the corner like a brooding shadow. I frowned at him.
He was odd.

The men stopped talking and all turned to watch me
walk into the room.

"What's wrong with me?" I asked.

David flicked a glance at Fearghus, but it was him
who stood and took my hands. He led me to the couch
and sat down, pulling me down beside him. The others
kept their gazes downcast. Silent.

"Philo's dead." I didn't mean to say it so harshly, but
David flinched.

"Yes."

"How?"

"Minnie, I don't—" I could tell his tone was kind,
caring, but it didn't reach me.

"It's okay. I want to know."

David sighed and ran a hand through his dark hair.
Flecks of silver peppered it, and it was mostly silver at
his temples. Still, no one would ever know he'd been
alive since before the time of Christ.

He shook his head—not in denial of me, but with regret. "I don't really know. The news of his death came while we were on the plane coming to you. We learned that Ying Yue had taken out our protection team here and though I mobilized more, I knew I needed to come myself. To ensure your safety myself. Even by private jet, the journey is long. I'm guessing that since I've seen no sign of the second team, she must have discovered them as well."

I hadn't taken my eyes off of David's face, and after a glance at me he seemed to guess that I needed more. "From what I understand, the Master wished to use Philo to draw information out of Hashiki. She said she would speak to no one but him. However, no one truly understood the magnitude of her power." He stared at me with open wonder. "That you resisted her at all is astounding."

"Are you telling me Philo could not?" I should have felt something. I shouldn't have been able to say those words like they were nothing. Like Philo meant nothing.

David hesitated, then nodded.

"She can cause terrible pain," I said.

"Yes."

So Philo, my first sweetheart, my first real kiss, my first dance, my first everything, had died at the hands of the most cruel and sadistic person in the world. She'd probably lit all his nerve endings on fire until they devoured themselves and his brain shut down. It would have been a horrible, excruciating death.

And I felt nothing.

"He loved me," I said out loud, hoping the words would stir feelings in me. They didn't.

I wanted to cry. To scream. To deny the truth until his absence was so infinite that I couldn't deny it any longer.

Instead, I sat beside David on a couch in a plain hotel room and felt nothing at all.

CHAPTER
TWENTY-EIGHT

"FIX HER," SANG-HYEOK SAID FROM HIS DARK CORNER. David looked over the back of the couch at him, then at Fearghus.

I lifted my gaze to meet my big friend and brother. He was normally so jovial, but not today. No, not today. "Can you fix me?"

"Aye," he said. He shifted in his chair, but it wasn't the chair that made him uncomfortable.

"Why don't you want to?" I asked.

"Because you'll cry."

"And you don't want me to get blood everywhere?"

He snorted. "I don't care about the blood. I care about you, ya wee lass. As soon as I lift the blocker, you'll feel it all. Every last scrap o' it and it'll crush ya. I cannae bare to see ya in such pain." His eyes grew red-rimmed as tears rose in his own eyes.

"This is your gift?" I asked, unmoved by his emotions.

"Aye," he spat. "Bloody useless thing that it is."

Fearghus used a gift he hated to keep me safe from remembering my pain. I wasn't angry with him. I understood he did it because he cared about me. Because we were family. Without the blur of emotions, I could see now that I had stopped being a part of my father's family the night Tim drank me dry and tried to fix me by feeding me his own blood. For my father, I died that night.

But I hadn't. I was only transformed. It was only a chemical state change.

My father would never see it that way, though. And despite bringing me here, he never intended to see me as anything other than a *gangshi*. To him, I was dead, so who better to speak to the dead? He'd said as much on the plane, but I'd been too hungry for his love and acceptance to see the truth when it was right in front of my face.

"Thank you for caring enough to want to protect me," I told Fearghus. And even though I couldn't feel my gratitude, I knew I was thankful. "But, can you take it away, now? I'm tired of pretending that my life is still the same as it was before. It isn't—because I'm not the same."

"Minnie, you—" Jack started, half-rising from his seat, but I wasn't finished.

"I still believe that we vampires have our souls—whatever that might be. And that we're still the same people we were before. But I was foolish for thinking nothing would have to change." David patted my leg, but I couldn't even find it in me to force a smile. Whatever Fearghus had done had blocked me off from every single thing inside me that would show or feel emotion.

"I was trying to live a lie," I continued. "But I'm done with that now. Junu saw all of me—the girl me and the vampire me, and he still loved me. You guys love me—"

"Aye," Fearghus said. I hadn't noticed that he'd pulled out a black handkerchief at some point and was using it to wipe his eyes frequently.

"And Philo—a crotchety old vampire who never became a man, liked me and loved me for all that I was."

"Amen," Jack said.

"I want truth in my life and I want to start now. I promise to try not to freak out. I'll do my best to hold it together until we get home, but then I'm gonna need some serious time to cry my eyes out for a while, okay? But I'll do it in my room so you don't have to listen to me."

David laughed softly and pulled me against him. "You are loved, Minnie Kim."

And that—those two words, *Minnie Kim*—nearly had the power to break through Fearghus's block. Nearly, but not quite.

Fearghus came to kneel in front of me. "Are ya sure about this, lass?"

I nodded and he sighed loudly.

"Fine, then." He cupped my face in his hands and leaned forward. "Close yer eyes." I did as he said, and he blew softly on my face.

A wave of sleepiness swept over me and I sank into darkness.

사랑해
💜

I woke with my head in David's lap. He was gently stroking the hair back from my forehead, and it felt so nice that I lay there for a moment before telling anyone I was awake. The television was on, and they were watching one of my favorite game shows—a show I'd often enjoyed watching with my parents. Grief dug its jagged claws into my heart and I gasped.

They were gone from me. I didn't have parents anymore.

"Shh," David said. He tightened his arm around me. "I've got you."

"I'm okay," I said in a hoarse, shaky breath.

"If it gets ta be too much for ya, let me know," Fearghus said.

I didn't answer. I didn't trust myself to speak. I didn't want to rely on the crutch of Fearghus' gift—I needed to feel the feelings of life. Out of the corner of my eye, I saw Sang-hyeok sitting on a chair positioned at the end of the couch. He was still apart, but he was still here. And for some reason that felt good. It felt right.

I knew I needed to think about Philo, but I kept that part of my mind locked away. There'd be time for that. I didn't want to mourn him surrounded by these guys, no matter how much I loved them.

I struggled to sit upright and David helped me. When I was situated, Sang-hyeok handed me a bottle of water. "Thanks." I gave him a quizzical look. "You don't seem like the type to deliver water. What gives?"

He returned to his seat. "I assumed you'd be thirsty after your ordeal."

"Well," I said. I took a long pull from the bottle. "You weren't wrong."

We watched the show, Jack and Fearghus laughing out loud now and then.

I kept my eyes on the show, but asked, "How come you're still here?" No one misunderstood me. Out of the corner of my eye, I saw Sang-hyeok shrug.

So he was gonna play hardball, eh? Did they all think I was stupid or something?

I jumped to my feet and leaned past Sang-hyeok, who cringed away from me as if I had cooties and it might be catching. I flicked on the light switch on the wall behind his head. Then I placed myself in front of the television and faced the room. "Look. I get that you're all men, most of you born at a time when ladies were wilting violets and you're used to coddling us and taking care of us.

"And I appreciate it, I do. You gave me time, my body time, to get used to the pain of my grief. I love you guys so much for that. But I'm awake now and I feel like myself again, and there's stuff going on that everyone's ignoring—" I gestured with both hands toward Sang-hyeok. "I think it's time we all stop feeling sorry for ourselves and have a real conversation."

I folded my arms and glared at them. No one spoke.

Eventually I threw up my hands. "What is wrong with you people? David, you're what? 2500 years old or something? Fearghus? A thousand?"

"1200, give or take," he muttered.

"Jack, you've got a couple hundred on you, right?"

He shrugged and nodded. Waved his hand in a so-so gesture.

"And I have no idea about you—" I jabbed a finger at Sang-hyeok, "but I'm guessing from your superspeed and general jerky aloofness that you're pretty darn old.

"So here I am surrounded by men who should be older and wiser than me, and yet the kid is the one willing to have a real conversation and talk about the truth." I put my hands on my hips and stared down at them. "What's wrong with this picture?"

Fearghus and Jack had the good sense to look abashed, David smiled ruefully, and Sang-hyeok had his arms crossed and his chin on his chest.

"Well?" I demanded.

I waited so long I thought for sure my whole speech had been wasted. I sighed. Maybe I'd go have a bath.

David stretched out his long legs. "Sang-hyeok is my child. He is very old, but very stubborn."

Sang-hyeok snorted and David cut him a glare.

"Many years ago, long before Jack's time, Sang decided he was better off alone than with a family. He has disgraced this family by hunting instead of using the banks and refusing to register with the council. I suspect he pays off the local officials since he's hardly keeping a low profile. Why he came to your aid, or why he is here, is beyond me. He refuses, as always, to speak to me."

"Oh," I said, rather brilliantly. I quirked my head at Sang-hyeok. "You're my brother?"

He lifted an eyebrow.

"So, wow." I collapsed onto the couch.

"Yep," Fearghus agreed.

"Well, I guess that explains why you're such a jerk," I said. Everyone laughed. Even Sang-hyeok. "But what I don't understand, is why you even bothered with me. You were watching over me. You saved me from Ying Yue—"

"You were holding your own," he said.

I snorted. "I don't think so. And then you showed up at the airport. What's the deal?"

I faced him. Everyone, I think, was facing him. Watching him. This terribly dangerous warrior vampire squirmed in his seat.

"As I said," he finally said. "You are a very strange girl. At first I took notice of you because you were a strange vampire in my territory."

I sat up straight and held my hand out to him, palm flat. "Wait a second. David said you hunt—are you hunting for humans, in Jungno-gu?"

Sang-hyeok flicked an annoyed glance at David. "I do not hunt. Not anymore. I know a few people who are willing donors. It is perfectly legal."

"Okay," I said. "Carry on." Thor preferred his food that way. So did a lot of vampires. I didn't like it, but strictly speaking it was no different than how my donors went to the blood bank to donate blood. It's still voluntary—if not altogether sanitary.

Sang-hyeok gave a mock bow of his head. Smart alec. "So when I observed a strange new vampire in my midst, I naturally took it upon myself to see what you were about. That is how I observed you and the *imugi*."

"So you were spying."

His jaw clenched, but he didn't reply. Definitely spying.

"I hadn't seen an *imugi* in a very long time," he continued, "so I drew closer. Close enough that I could surmise what the situation was, and where it would go from there. I knew nothing of your problem with the ancestors until I entered your home—but when you went to see the Zen master, it all made sense.

"When you live for a great many years, life can become stale. Boring. You were a bright ray of sunshine, so to speak. A very unusual creature doing unusual things—"

One of the other men snorted, but I couldn't tell which.

"It was entertaining."

"Oh yeah," I said, a harder edge to my voice. "It must've been so entertaining to see me fighting a monk while he tried to kill my cousin. Why didn't you help? Maybe Junu wouldn't have gotten hurt."

That muscle in his jaw jumped again. "Do not judge others on what you cannot see, little one." We stared at each other for a long moment. I probed gently at his mind, but it was locked tight. Just as I was about to withdraw my presence, he shone a tiny pinprick of light onto a singular memory. It only came in flashes, as he worked hard to protect the rest of his thoughts from me, but I understood that he had probably fought with Ying Yue while Junu and I tried to deal with the demon monk. That would explain where she disappeared to. I had wondered about that.

I quickly withdrew from his mind and gave a short nod. *Thank you*, I meant to say. His lips quirked slightly, which I'm pretty sure meant *you're welcome.*

When a vampire dies, only ashes remain. David said he would arrange for Philo's ashes to be sent home to Utah. I've already begun thinking about the memorial service.

Oh and Fearghus can take away people's feelings. Can he take away their physical pain, too?

CHAPTER
TWENTY-NINE

WE STAYED AT THE HOTEL FOR TWO MORE DAYS WHILE Incheon National Airport was under construction. Sanghyeok left the night we'd spoken and hadn't returned.

Not once had my parents tried to call me.

Junu had texted me, though. He'd been released the same night he'd been injured—he said Korean hospitals didn't believe in keeping patients overnight. Considering Korean hospitals were some of the most famous in the world, I found that funny. Maybe they treated foreign patients who came in for luxury treatment different than their local patients.

He said the ancestors had been quiet and the home felt right again—though he said you could cut the tension in the house with a knife. Auntie and Uncle weren't pleased with the way Dad had treated me in the hospital. They were embarrassed that they'd let me leave without standing up to him. Maybe I'd go back and see them again. Someday.

I was finished packing but check-out wasn't for another hour, so everyone was just hanging around. I was looking forward to going home, even though it also terrified me. Philo wouldn't be there. And he'd never be coming back.

At home, I'd let myself grieve and I wasn't sure how much that would hurt. The pain pressed against me from the inside like a monster chewing its way out. I was strong. I could hold onto it until we got home. After that? No promises. But at least I'd be safe, with the only family that really mattered. My phone buzzed and I reached for it.

Junu: I looked for your friend last night

Me: Hanjo?

Junu: Yup. Either he just doesn't like me and wouldn't come out or he's really gone.

Me: I coulda told ya he wasn't there

Junu: Why didn't you? I feel like an idiot now. I sat up there for like two hours talking to the gourds.

Me: LOL sorry

Me: you know the earthquake at Incheon?

Junu: yeah?

Me: HANJO

Junu: Seriously???

Me: 🐱🐱🐱

I stared at the phone, but no more texts came. For the umpteenth time I thought about texting Stacey, but I didn't. I knew I'd cry and that was reserved for home. Lucky home. As it was, I'd cried all over my sheets that first night. I had to leave the largest won I had as a tip and hope the cleaning staff would just think I'd had a terrible nosebleed.

Plus, MacStacey was maybe formalizing their love pact and I didn't want to ruin it for them. Thinking about love made me think about Philo again and that just wouldn't do, so I texted Junu again.

Me: I've faced a lot of problems in my short time in Korea. I think it might be a while before I dare to come back

Junu: Haha I get it. I've been thinking of coming your way

Me: I know I'm your younger cousin, but would you consider taking some advice from me? Don't let distance come between you and your parents. Don't lie to them. Stop pretending to be someone other than you are. You deserve to be happy.

Me: I hope your parents will love you for who you are. I believe they will. I just . . .

I didn't know how to say what I wanted to say. And then I did.

Me: . . . don't want you going through life trying to please your parents. Your life is yours. It's the only one you've got.
Junu: Hang on

I heard voices out in the main room so I picked up my bag and went out to join the others.

"Oh, hey!" I said brightly to Sang-hyeok who stood in the door, neither inside nor outside the room. "What's up?" I looked from him to David and back again. "Sheesh, you guys. Talk already."

Sang-hyeok took a deep breath. "Father, if I may, I would like to come home with you." They were pretty words, but Sang-hyeok made them sound as if he were spitting nails.

Someone dropped their bag to the floor behind me. "Well, I'll be nickered," Fearghus said. "Never thought I'd see the day."

David though, true to form, stepped right up to Sang-hyeok, and wrapped him in a hug.

After a second or two, I could no longer keep in the giggles. It was the nuttiest thing I'd seen in a long time. There was David, in his long-sleeved dress shirt all prim and proper, with his arms wrapped tightly around a tall Asian man wearing a black trench coat, his arms hanging loosely at his sides. Just when I thought the hug had probably gone on too long and David ought to let poor Sang-hyeok go, his arms came up to encircle David and my giggles turned to sighs.

"I'm happy to have you, my son," David said as he welcomed him into the suite.

Sang-hyeok glared at everyone and stepped inside, dropping a duffel bag to the floor.

I threw my arms around him, trapping his arms at his sides. "I'm glad to have you, Sang-hyeok." I knew the hug would bug him. It was just fun to see him glower.

"Call me Sang," he growled.

"But what about your big fancy job at SM?"

For a guy who dealt with the entertainment industry, you'd think he'd be a lot more comfortable with being put on the spot but right then he looked like he could just turn around and leave and forget the whole thing.

"My fancy job requires much travel. It matters little where I live," he growled. I tried hard not to snicker.

Jack stepped forward and shook Sang's hand. "Howdy. I'm Jack. Guess that makes us brothers."

Sang pursed his lips, but he nodded.

"There are rules, ya know," Fearghus said from the table. He made no move to greet Sang, and I wondered what the story was between them. One thing about vampires—there was plenty of time for the stories to come out.

사랑해
♥

I was just buckling into my seat on David's private jet when my phone dinged. I slid it out and looked at the screen.

> **Junu**: I told them
> **Me**: Wait. What??
> **Junu**: Yup
> **Me**: Don't leave me hanging! What happened? What did they say?
> **Junu**: They said they've suspected for a while and they love me and are proud of me no matter what.

Dang tears again. I pressed the back of my head to the seat and looked up at the ceiling, trying to will away the tears. When I had them in control, I went back to my phone.

> **Junu**: I know it sucks for you, but I think seeing what happened between you and your parents really scared my folks.

I smiled.

Me: Scared them straight, ya mean?

Junu: Har har.

Me: Seriously though. I'm happy for you. Super, duper happy.

Junu: So what did you say was the name of that cute taxi driver guy?

사랑해
♥

As we flew across the Pacific, I felt home drawing me nearer as if my heart had been hooked and someone was winding up the line. The more time that passed, the closer we got, the more my heart hurt.

I wasn't sure I was ready to face what was to come.

But I would because . . . that's what people do, right?

사랑해
♥

The welcome at home was subdued, and I was grateful. Even though I'd only been gone a week, it would have totally been Manuela's style to have a major feast prepared with cake and everything. Okay, there was cake, but Manuela said she knew I was tired and would send the food up to my room when it was ready, along with a large slice of cake.

She hugged me tight and kissed me on both cheeks. "I am glad you are home where you belong, *mi bebé*." I stepped right into her embrace. It wasn't my mother's hug, but it was *a* mother's hug and she was mine, too. She was family.

My bags had already been brought up, but I didn't go straight to my room. I continued down the hall to the last door on the left. I stood facing it for a long moment, then quietly slipped inside. I wouldn't cry in there. I didn't want to mess up his things. But I took one of his soft sweaters he loved to wear out of the second drawer of his bureau and pressed it to my nose. I breathed deeply of the smell of him. The boy I would never get to love.

I dragged my feet as I moved toward my room. I resented the cute brightness of it. The happy stuffies on my bed. The BTS posters on the wall. Maybe I should have stayed in Philo's room where the dark colors suited me more right now.

I threw myself onto the bed and stared up at the dull twinkle lights on my ceiling. I didn't feel like turning them on. I pulled the edge of the comforter up and over me and rolled onto my side.

Something crinkled beneath me.

It was a bright white linen envelope. I hadn't noticed it because it was the same color as my duvet. I turned it over and saw *Minnie* scrawled on the front in Philo's elegant hand.

Omo.

Did I have it in me to open it? When had he left it here? Why had he written me a letter? He wouldn't have known he would die. The questions wouldn't stop, so I decided to put an end to them. I sat up and opened the envelope.

It was only one sheet of paper with a few paragraphs. I smoothed the sheet on my bed and pressed the heels of my palms against my eyes in an effort to compose myself.

Dearest Minnie,

This is just in case I'm not here when you get back. I've only been summoned by the Master once before, but he kept me in his court for over a year. I truly hope he doesn't ask that of me again! I will tell him all about you and I'm certain he wouldn't want to keep us apart.

I can't wait to see you. Already it's been too long.

I meant to tell you something before you left, but I lost my nerve.

I've fought in battles, seen all the best and worse the world has to offer. And yet I'm afraid of what you have done to me. No, that's not quite right. I'm not afraid of what I feel, I am only afraid you might not feel the same.

I've suffered through my existence because that was what was required of me. I had moments of peace—my years with the monks taught me the most about how to live, and I was happy with them. But I never knew joy until I met you.

You challenged me, bested me, befriended me. I know you fear our age difference and I can't explain it away or dismiss it—experience is a factor that lies in unequal parts between us. However what I do know, is that with you, I feel young again. In every way, I feel like a young man in your presence. Eager to please you. Desperate for a kind word from you. Hungry for your kiss.

Everything feels new to me, because of you.

You are my joy and my light, Minnie Kim.

I will tell you my secret as soon as I see you. But after I have held you and kissed you. Those must come first.

Until then—Philo

The paper crunched and crinkled between my fingers, and despite my best efforts, a couple drops of watery blood stained the pristine white. I read the letter again and again.

I knew what he wanted to tell me and I remembered how those words had sounded in his voice.

I lay back on my bed and closed my eyes. After a moment of deep breathing, I sent myself to the spot where we'd met before in the mind-space I'd created for us. I knew he wouldn't really be there, but I'd always had a vivid imagination. And in a weird way, I thought he might be there. In spirit. Master Yi would tell me the spirit is eternal—and he is much more wise than me.

I conjured Philo coming toward me. He wore that crooked half-smile I loved so much as he stalked toward me. There was something hungry in his gaze that made the butterflies flutter restlessly in my stomach.

"You weren't at the house to meet me." I made my voice sound accusing, like I was mad, but I couldn't keep from smiling.

His brilliant blue eyes captured mine and wouldn't let me go.

"I didn't want to greet you in front of the family," he said hoarsely. "I wanted you to myself."

"You did?" Gosh I sounded like such a little girl. He grinned, but didn't speak.

He approached me slowly, intentionally. As easily as if we had done this a hundred times before, one arm encircled my waist while he lifted my hair away from my neck with his free hand. He pulled me close and lowered his lips to mine.

The kiss was soft but there was no hesitation in it. No doubt. When he deepened the kiss, I made a little mewing sound that was embarrassing at first, but when he answered with a low growl it became part of a beautiful memory.

Philo pulled back, one thumb caressing my cheek. "I love you, Minnie Kim."

It was a beautiful dream that I chose to make into a memory. It didn't matter if it was really real or not. It was real to me, and I knew Philo would want me to remember him this way.

So I looked into his eyes that were as deep and clear as the Aegean Sea, and told him for the first and last time, "I love you too, my Philo."

Check out the next Minnie Kim book,
Blood Moon
available now!

Join Ali's newsletter for a
free book & never miss a new release!

https://alicross.kit.com/thiscreativelife

As always, your honest review
is immensely appreciated!

my friend, Hanjo♥

ALSO BY
ALI ARCHER

DESOLATION

Sacrifice (prequel)
Become (book 1)
Desolate (book 2)
Destined (book 3)
Desolation Diaries (v. 1-3)

MINNIE KIM: VAMPIRE GIRL

First Kisses Suck (book 1)
Deadly Sweethearts (book 2)
Seoul Demon (book 3)
Blood Moon (book 4)
Den of Death (book 5)

THE EDEN PROJECT

Dragon Protocol

ACKNOWLEDGMENTS

Minnie might be a great artist, but I'm sure as heck not! Thankfully, I know a fantastic artist, Adrian Ropp and he was willing to bail me out. Imagine me though, asking a professional artist to draw like an amateur teenage girl! Ha! Adrian was up for the challenge though, and Minnie and I are forever grateful! Check out Adrian's art at AdrianRopp.com.

I faced a lot of family and financial troubles during the production of this book and I am so very grateful to God for seeing me through, to Christine Weston Bryant for cheering me on, to Lorie Humpherys for editing on the cheap for me, and to my Support Group, er, Fan Club for the awesome everything. I love all these people.
L O V E.

And just so you know, my family faced our storm and made it through. Whew!

Love ya!
Ali <3

ABOUT THE AUTHOR

 **Ali Archer** is the USA Today bestselling author of young adult fantasy and science fiction, including the Desolation series and the Minnie Kim: Vampire Girl series.

Ali's always loved science fiction and fantasy, as the first books she read were by such greats as Isaac Asimov, Ray Bradbury, and Lloyd Alexander. But when she discovered *Dragonriders of Pern* by Anne McCaffrey—a perfect blend of fantasy and science fiction—her own imagination was set aflame.

At eleven, Ali met Ms. McCaffrey in one of the single most illuminating moments of her life. When she told the eminent writer she wanted to be an author when she grew up, Ms. McCaffrey said, "Never let anything stand in the way of your dreams." Ali's been following that advice ever since.

LET'S CONNECT!
www.aliarcher.com
www.Faccbook.com/aliarcherbooks
www.Facebook.com/groups/AliCats
www.Instagram.com/aliarcherbooks

SUBSCRIBE TO MY NEWSLETTER
https://alicross.kit.com/thiscreativelife